I0715647

SAVE THE QUEEN!

DESA Files #5

CHRISTIAN WARREN FREED

Copyright © 2024 by Christian Warren Freed

Cover design by BroseDesignz
Author Photograph by Anicie Freed

Warfighter Books
Holly Springs, North Carolina 27540
https://www.christianwfreed.com

First Edition: Oct 2024

Library of Congress Cataloging-in-Publication Data
Name: Freed, Christian Warren, 1973- author.
Title: Save the Queen!/ Christian Warren Freed
Description: First Edition | Holly Springs, NC: Warfighter Books, 2021. Identifiers: LCCN 2024913438| ISBN 9781957326481 (trade paperback) | ISBN 9781957326498 (Hardcover)
Subjects: Parnanormal Urban Fantasy | Epic Fantasy | Fantasy

Printed in the United States of America

10 9 8 7 6 5 4 3 2 1

DREAMS OF WINTER
The Fractured Universe #1

'Dreams of Winter is a strong introduction to a new fantasy series that follows slightly in the footsteps of George R.R. Martin in scope.' Entrada Publishing

"Steven Erickson meets George R.R. Martin!"

"THIS IS IT. If you like fantasy and sci-fi, you must read this series."

LAW OF THE HERETIC
Immortality Shattered Book I

'If you're looking for a fun and exciting fantasy adventure, spend a few hours in the Free Lands with the Law of the Heretic.'

WHERE HAVE ALL THE ELVES GONE?

'Sometimes funny and other times a little dark, Where Have The Elves Gone? brings something fresh and new to fantasy mysteries. Whether you want to curl up with a mystery or read more about elves this book has something for everyone. Spend a few hours solving a mystery with a human and a couple of dwarves - you'll be glad you did.'

Other Books by Christian Warren Freed

The Northern Crusade

Hammers in the Wind

Tides of Blood and Steel

A Whisper After Midnight

Empire of Bones

The Madness of Gods and Kings

Even Gods Must Fall

The Histories of Malweir

Armies of the Silver Mage

The Dragon Hunters

Beyond the Edge of Dawn

Fractured Universe

Dreams of Winter

The Madman on the Rocks

Anguish Once Possessed

Through Darkness Besieged

Under Tattered Banners

A Time for Tyrants

A Good Day For Crows

DESA Files

Where Have All the Elves Gone?

One of Our Elves is Missing

From Whence It Came

Of Elves and Men
Save the Queen!

Tomorrow's Demise: The Extinction Campaign
Tomorrow's Demise: Salvation
Coward's Truth

<u>The Lazarus Men Agenda</u>
The Lazarus Men
Repercussions: A Lazarus Men Agenda
Daedalus Unbound: A Lazarus Men Agenda*

A Long Way From Home+

<u>Immortality Shattered</u>
Law of the Heretic
The Bitter War of Always
Land of Wicked Shadows
Storm Upon the Dawn

<u>War Priests of Andrak Saga</u>
The Children of Never

SO, You Want to Write a Book? +
SO, You Wrote a Book. Now What? +

*Forthcoming   + Nonfiction

SAVE THE QUEEN!

ONE

The drone of engines sent ripples through the private plane as it coursed across the Atlantic Ocean at thirty-five thousand feet. Sparse clouds peppered the night sky, showing the moonlight in spots on the ocean far below. A handful of passengers slept, tossing and twisting in their seats to find an elusive sense of comfort. The cabin was dim, quiet save for the muted whispers of the pair of flight attendants chatting in the back.

Alone in the middle of the plane sat Yurgis Alores. He was one of eastern Europe's most prominent arms dealers and a ranking leader among the dark elves. He'd answered the queen's summons to North America with hesitation. Whispers and rumors of Morgen's intent circulated quickly. Ever the snake, she proved unpredictable in the wake of the high king's demise. Cold and calculating, Yurgis turned his focus on the newspaper in his hands instead of questioning Morgen's motives. He despised being torn from his work, especially with multiple wars flaring across the region. Armies needed bullets and the guns to fire them. He supplied them. A natural disdain for humanity spurred his greed, making him rich beyond measure since the invention of gunpowder weapons.

For Morgen to summon the heads of all the great families, against tradition and in the face of the now empty office of the prime minister, suggested the clans were entering a dire time. Yurgis frowned at the thought of his independent stature diminishing. It had happened before, during the worst examples of human history but never to the point where all the clans were involved. Having done everything in his power to grow his private empire, the elf sat smug at the head table.

His perpetual scowl returning, Yurgis turned the page. Too many headlines bespoke ill times approaching. Continued wars in the Middle East. A tightening of the global economy as radical ideas struggled to take root. Natural disasters upending countless lives. A cataclysm of unprecedented proportions. He did not know how to counter any of it but made efforts to consolidate his considerable assets in the event the queen lost all control. He had no personal feelings for or against Morgen. She was the queen and the sole ruler of the clans. But her proposal undermined his aspirations in unprecedented ways not seen since the great schism. Perhaps the time had come for a changing of the guard.

New blood was needed to guide the clans into the future. A future riddled with human interference and the possibility of endless war. Yurgis saw an opportunity to sidle through the cracks, whisper in Morgen's ear and, if done right, find himself in a position of power few of the ruling houses enjoyed. Folding the paper, he motioned to his preferred flight attendant for his nightly cocktail. She offered a tight smile before heading to the galley to prepare it.

Yurgis glanced out the window to his right, admiring the dark calm of the world. His gaze lingered on the slivers of moonlight dancing on the ocean far below. He often wondered what it was like to be so free. It was a dream. Stifling an unexpected yawn, the dark elf settled into his chair and waited for his drink so he could grab a few hours of sleep before reaching North America.

His first inkling of trouble came when the jet shuddered. The engines whined, increasing power. Yurgis frowned and hit the call button on the armrest of his chair. The jet exploded a moment later. Wreckage plummeted the five miles down in fiery streaks of melted metal and ruined dreams before plunging deep beneath the waves to a forever resting place.

Constance Burris watched her husband with a twinkle in her eye. He diligently finished packing her suitcase. That he did so in only a pair of red boxers did not go unnoticed. Married for centuries, the high elves found innovative ways to keep their love strong, inspired. Her golden hair cascaded halfway down her back, partially concealing the light pink jacket from behind. As ranking members of the high elf ruling committee, Constance and her husband forced high elf policy in the wake of the king's unfortunate assassination. Dim thoughts pushed into her mind, shifting her demeanor.

The stress of holding the clans together was wearing on them. Constance walked with a slower step despite the fires of her love. Her shoulders drooped a fraction lower than before. She felt thin. Almost gaunt. Once a friend of Morgen's, Constance looked down upon her contemporary. Much of the pain and heartache could have been avoided if the queen opened negotiations sooner. She tried. Lord knew Constance tried to make amends before it was too late Still, the word of Morgen's proposal came as a surprise to many considered 'in the know.'

"I don't like it. It's not like Morgen to be so direct," Darden said with crossed arms. Ever the loyal husband, he frowned upon any suggestions presented by the dark elves, queen or not.

Constance smiled, weaving the charming illusion of control and love she often used to get her way. Not that he protested much. True love softened the hardest mood she discovered. They'd been together almost longer than she remembered and felt their love strengthen with each passing year. As long as she let Darden believe he was in charge. She crossed the bedroom with fluid grace honed over centuries of practice and placed a hand on his forearm, squeezing just enough to show appreciation.

"Darden, this is what the clans need," she cooed. "We have been at war with each other for so long I forget what true peace is like. If Morgen is true to her word, this is our one opportunity to end the conflict and rebuild all we have lost."

"If," he grumbled. "Morgen has lacked honor for decades. Why should she change her colors now?"

"Perhaps she is just desperate, dear husband of mine." They'd held this conversation numerous times over the past few years. Her hand slipped up to cup his cheek. Constance ran her thumb through the short hairs on his cheek. "I have to believe we are all capable of change. Otherwise, what's the point to all this?"

"I would feel better if I were accompanying you," he replied, pausing to kiss her fingertips. "I don't like you heading into that viper nest without me."

"I won't be alone and we'll be together the following day," she replied. "The location is secure and in the middle of the city. Nothing bad is going to happen, Darden. Remember, she has the Old Guard for security. I'm sure we'll all be fine."

"Provided I can negotiate this deal," he snorted and watched her stroll to the door. "Love you."

She paused, looking over her shoulder. That familiar gleam that melted his heart every time twinkled in her crystalline eyes. Constance smiled and placed her hand on the door handle. "Love you more."

The explosion shattered the windows and doors in a hail of flame of melting glass.

Standish Opal woke up dour. Not that it was a change of character for the dwarf, but not how he wished to start his day. He much preferred easing into that surly nastiness he was known for. The dwarf lord longed to retire and put the triviality and political backstabbing of the clan leaders behind him. He'd come a long way since a child working the mines in South America, clawing and scraping his way to the top under the false impression doing so would eliminate much of the challenges and hardships in his life.

What a fool. When he finally took his seat at the table, he'd discovered leadership was far worse than any gang squabble down in the mines but at least now he held the power to affect the outcomes of his people. Standish brushed through his competition with the natural stalwart attitude many of his kin exhibited. He became a powerful force, often getting his way where others gave up and stepped aside. Respected and powerful, he failed to understand how Alvin and Morgen allowed the schism or why it continued.

Life was better before the unification. Before humans showed their true colors and dominated the planet. A firm believer in species remaining separate, Standish advocated for a return to the old ways, where dwarves seldom dealt with elves. A time when life was hard but fair. Nothing good had come from uniting under the elven banners. His assertions proved true when Alvin was killed. The clans fell into disarray since. He fully expected Morgen to either be removed from office or abdicate the throne and did his best to push the agenda.

Standish brushed off his negative thoughts, slipped into his favorite swim trunks and a robe and headed toward his backyard. He passed several staff and functionaries, ignoring them all on his way to alleviate the coming day's stress with a few laps in the pool. Dwarves and water seldom mixed, but he found himself enjoying the human luxury with unusual gusto. It helped there was little chance of him drowning in five feet of water and with an army of servants watching his every move.

His sandals flapped beneath his heavy step. Muscled, as all true dwarf warriors were, Standish made an imposing figure. The red of his beard faded to grey and wrinkles decorated the corners of his eyes, but he had never felt more alive. Well, except for those glory days of wielding his axe in battle. Nothing compared with that adrenalin rush. His mood darkened as visions of battlefield glory were slowly replaced by what was expected of him in the coming days.

The approaching summit in Raleigh with the clan leaders left him trapped in a strange place from which he could not figure his next step with clarity. Perhaps a dip underwater would inspire the insight he needed to handle endless days sequestered with his contemporaries. Standish doubted even the pleasant tranquility of a quick swim was enough to calm the warning in his heart.

He shed his robe, tossing it on the chair and rolled his shoulders, then cracked his neck to each side and plunged into the water. He made it halfway before his entire body was wracked with a burning sensation. From head to toe, he felt afire. Breaking the surface, sputtering and flailing, he caught a glimpse of the flesh melting off his right arm.

The dwarf tried to scream, to shout for help, but no words came.

He burst apart in a sweep of ash and dust.

Across the world, elves, dwarves, giants, and trolls, readied to travel to the United States at their queen's demand. Clan leaders and tribal elders were called from far and wide, for this was to be a moment long remembered in the annals of history. Anticipation ran high among the rank and file in the hopes of at last finding peace and moving forward.

Confusion and expectation clashed. Protests broke out in different countries. Official petitions filed with the high courts. Not everyone wanted a return to the old ways. After all, there was no money in peace. The last time the clans prepared for such change came at the dawn of the great schism and the sundering of the tribes.

No one in the clans could say what was to happen, though each harbored unique illusions they freely shared to any who would listen. Yet for all the grandeur and promise carried on the winds, something sinister lurked just out of sight. A shadow in the corner. A whisper in the back of the mind. A time of peace. The continued rise of violence. And end of all things. Supposition ever proved the demise of the mighty.

Prayers were muttered when no one was looking. Shamans and soothsayers went from house to house in the desperate attempt to ward off any approaching evil. The turbulence of the moment shifted the balance. One thing was certain: the clans were at the precipice of changing forever and the hour had already grown too late to turn back now.

A new dawn approached. One from which the foundations of eternity would cement and grow. And the one woman responsible heard every voice from the top of her tower.

T W O

Daniel stifled a yawn and attempted to stretch without opening his eyes—he couldn't move. Pinned beneath the sheets and hot, Daniel tried turning sideways with a grunt. Eyes opening, he saw the wet nose inches from his face before registering the whump-whump-whump of a tail slapping against the mattress. Otto had decided long ago that the bed was just as much his as his owners and had no qualms about pushing people out of the way so he could get comfortable. One missed opportunity and years later, theirs was a constant struggle for who got more leg room.

"Really, Otto?" Daniel was rewarded with a hearty sniff then lick. Chasing the fragment of sleep, he shifted only for one hundred plus pounds of fur and love to pounce on him with the energy of a toddler. Otto ensured there was no going back to sleep.

"Okay. Okay."

Snaking a hand free from the sheets, he ruffled Otto behind the ears in the hopes of placating the dog enough to slip out of bed and hit the bathroom before jumping into their day. He was rewarded with the increased thump of Otto's tail striking the comforter.

Daniel rolled over, unsurprised to find Sara's side already cool. She always liked getting up before him, even with the kids away at his mother's for their spring break. Daniel had no such qualms. All the stress and responsibility of figuring out dinner each night, helping with homework, ferrying the kids back and forth to their sporting events melted off his shoulders the instant the kids disappeared inside his mother's house and he peeled out the driveway. Free for two weeks!

The smell of coffee hit just as he started getting dressed.

With no kids and no looming deadlines, these were

the quiet days Daniel once hated. It took years to get accustomed to not being on the clock. Endless hours of uncertainty, lacking purpose or mission on the backside of his army time. He filled that void with writing, conventions, and signings up and down the east coast.

Coming out from the bathroom he was greeted by both dogs circling him like land sharks going in for the kill. Otto noticeably was directing him to the stairs. At his grunt and hand motion for them to go ahead, the dogs howled and dashed away. Daniel knew the dog was being his usual obstinate self. Bernese Mountain Dogs were smarter than average and just as stubborn until they got what they wanted. Daniel knew the dogs had already gone outside and been fed. Otto was just being Otto at this point, upset Daniel lingered in bed a full hour after the sun popped up.

The kitchen was empty, but he heard the clicking of the keyboard down the hallway. Sara was likely busy in their office, making her morning rounds of calls and checking email. Nothing ever slowed down in the life of a realtor. A man of few spoken words, he couldn't think of a single person he had that much to say to this early in the morning, if ever, yet Sara did it daily and enjoyed it. He snorted. She kept insisting he make new friends but, at his age and temperament, Daniel deferred to his standby line of already having enough friends and there just weren't any empty slots. Her glare at his response hadn't changed in the last five years. Nor did her comment of him growing up and finding more friends. It wasn't that he couldn't. It was that he didn't want to. Thank you, U.S. Army.

Daniel poured a cup of coffee from their old glass percolator and headed onto the porch to watch the dogs chase after each other with the sort of reckless abandon he almost longed to engage in. They reminded him of dwarves charging into untenable situations without any intelligence beforehand. Tulips and hyacinths bloomed in their garden beds, turning the fading winter drab into a kaleidoscope of orange, red, and purple. Leaves were just budding and with them the hated pollen spores on the tall pines lining his backyard.

A perennial nightmare for those with allergies, clouds of yellow would soon start blowing across the state, coating everything in their path. It was widely acknowledged as North Carolina's fifth season. Pollen never bothered him until recently when, much to his dismay, Daniel discovered one could develop allergies. Instead of jokes he now tried finding succor in bottles of antihistamines. He swore the pollen did its best to make up for lost years with him.

Hot coffee trailing down his throat, Daniel ignored the first of the yellow stains and checked their five-tiered planter. Seeds were already growing. Soon he could transfer them to the raised bed gardens they decided to build last year when rising costs at the grocery store started swallowing more of their paychecks than appreciated. Even if it was just a few cucumbers and tomatoes, a dollar was a dollar.

Finished with their business and remembering they were hungry, the dogs bounded up the stairs, bumping into him as they raced inside. Following them, Daniel went through the morning ritual of making sure they had their vitamins, both his and theirs. Once those duties were satisfied, he headed into the office to give his wife a kiss. His gaze fell on his laptop on his side of the desk, closed and untouched for days now, before planting a soft kiss atop her head. She smiled at him but kept talking on the phone.

Daniel stalked off to his favorite chair by the window to read, hoping this would be the day he found the inspiration to start writing again. He hadn't written a word in months, not since his rescue of Wally down in Charleston. Not for lack of want. He had plenty of stories left to tell, but the words just didn't want to cooperate. Sure, there'd been scribbles and notes, promises of grandiose tales ready to spring to life. But that's where it stopped.

In truth, Daniel had been unable to get beyond the

barrier of being considered a comedian in the elf world. He didn't know why it bothered him so much, but each jest, every little jab over the course of his adventures, especially from those obstinate Steiners, left him that much less inspired after he returned to his routine. He knew it wasn't writer's block. That was never an issue for him. He simply lacked the desire.

Exhaling, chest feeling heavy, Daniel settled into his chair, offered his neighbor—whom he was convinced was a troll— across the street his middle finger, just as he'd done daily for the past year after the man called the police on him, and picked up the book he was reading. He made it a handful of pages without paying much attention before Sara headed his way, or perhaps herded was the better term as both dogs guided her to his chair. Otto jumped on his lap before he could put the book down, oblivious to knocking both book and bookmark out of Daniel's hands in his quest for happiness.

"Morning sleepy head," Sara said, humor in her gaze as he squirmed beneath one hundred pounds of dog. "How did you sleep?"

"Well enough," he replied a little out of breath. "It would have been nice to get a little more, but you know who," he gave Otto a half shove, half pet, "decided I had had enough."

Otto tossed his head back, tongue hanging out the side of his mouth with a mischievous grin on his face. Daniel smiled back. At the start of his writing career, he decided to use Otto for one of the main characters in a children's book. The dog never let him forget it.

"They're as bad as kids," Sara laughed.

"I know. Here I was hoping I might get in a few more hours than normal now that the actual kids are gone for the week, but I suppose we all have our routines."

"Speaking of which, what does your day look like?" she asked, making him wince.

Sunlight framed her face, accented by her blonde

hair spilling over her shoulders. Dressed in her workout clothes, he knew Sara was about to head off to her yoga class before going into work. He also knew she worried about his inability to start writing again.

"I was thinking about starting my next book," he told her. "I can't keep putting it off. One of these days the words will flow again. Just like the spice."

"You're a dork, you know that, right?" she chided playfully. "I don't know what I saw in you."

He smiled. The scruff of several day's growth scraping over his cheeks. "Does it matter? You liked it and here we are."

"I mean, you could shave a little more." Sara nodded. "Way too late to turn back now. I guess I'm stuck with you."

"I mean, if you want to take your chances out there," he gestured to the street, "be my guest. I can almost guarantee you won't find any better."

She placed a hand on her hip, leveling a conspiratorial gaze at him. "Pretty confident in yourself, huh?"

"You haven't given me a reason not to be," he replied with as straight of a face as possible. Otto offered a bark in support. "See, even he agrees."

"He's just a dog, Daniel."

"And a better judge of character than most people. Then again, Ms. lady over there hasn't picked her head up since you two came over to interrupt my morning ritual." At her eye roll, he asked to change the subject, "What time is yoga?"

"In a few minutes. I'll probably be late tonight. I have a client meeting at five."

"Again? Why so late? Don't these people have any respect for time?"

They'd been through this a thousand times since she first got her real estate license. "You know I go where the clients need me. This couple doesn't get off work until four and it's a new listing. I need to jump on this before summer market hits."

"I know, I know. That doesn't mean I have to like it," he groaned. Otto placed his head on Daniel's leg, staring up at him.

"You do want to go on vacation this summer, don't you?" she asked. "Besides, you just don't want to cook tonight."

"Fair enough," he conceded with a grunt as Otto jumped down. "Pizza and beer?"

She reciprocated the kiss on his head from earlier and headed for the doorway. "Do better. Have fun writing. Love you."

"Love you too," he mumbled, mind already racing forward to what he might whip up for dinner. No slouch in the kitchen, and Sara knew that, he considered breaking out the smoker and testing out a new pork belly recipe he saw online.

The dogs raced from the room. He knew they would head to the front windows. Tails wagging and a few rehearsed barks they'd then track the car pulling out of the driveway before settling into their day. No matter how old they got, it was the same thing every single time and a welcome constant to their otherwise unstable lives.

Daniel finished his reading and another cup of coffee before taking them for their morning walk, hoping to find the seeds of inspiration somewhere along the way. Names and scenarios collided in his thoughts. Intriguing ideas without any foundation to build off. Frustration settled in and he focused on the dogs instead.

An hour later he found himself with third cup of coffee, much against his doctor's wishes, and sitting at his desk eyeing his laptop with apprehension. He slowly lifted the lid, pressed his fingerprint to activate the screen, and stared at the empty document that was already waiting for him. Every time a new idea for the continuing adventures of Tavis Halfhand sprang to life Daniel found himself reliving nightmares from the past few years. The explosions and chaos of New York. Watching Alvin disintegrate after his own daughter assassinated him. Hordes of goblins dying from the barrage of grenades he and Angus Schneider tossed into them. Critical jokes at his behest. Was this the source of his unwillingness to write? Not being taken seriously?

With that realization staring back at him, Daniel gingerly set his fingers to the keys and began to type. The words flowed for the first time in months. He was back.

Tavis Halfhand, now an old man, had fulfilled all the prophecies. King of the land, he sat upon a broken throne with a sword that had seen better days and a weary mind. He never dreamed reaching his goals would leave him alone, empty to the point of breaking. He longed to take up the sword one more time. Venture forth into the uncharted lands for a final adventure that, in all likelihood, determined the path of his legacy.

Tavis found himself at an unexpected crossroads from which he could not escape.

Time, it seemed, had finally caught up with him.

THREE

Sitting back in his chair, Daniel realized the sun was dropping over the houses. A glance at his watch confirmed the hour. He had been writing for hours. He hadn't pulled anything from the freezer, leaving him in a culinary bind when Sara returned home, soon. Cursing his lack of attention, he saved his document and closed the laptop, knowing she would be back at any moment.

Daniel worked his way to the kitchen, moving around circling dogs eager for attention. He paused to let them out before getting their dinner ready—at least someone in the house was going to get a good dinner. The thought of Sara admonishing him for forgetting to cook made him cringe.

Though the day got away from him, he rejoiced in having knocked out close to eight thousand words in one sitting. A feat he had not accomplished, or even thought to, in years. His fingers ached from the strain and his shoulders were sore, but he felt good. For too long, he languished under the lack of interest in writing. Daniel didn't know if what he wrote today was any good or going to survive the final editing cut when he saw too many of his carefully crafted words lying on the floor in red tatters, but they were words. And that was enough. *Angus and Fritz can kiss my ass! Joke of the clans. I'll show them.*

Another glance at his watch showed it was truly too late to start cooking. And he hated eating late the older he got. Resigned, he reached for his cellphone. Pizza it was. He just wished she liked the same kind as he did, but at this point anything was better than the wordless scowl of her disappointment. Daniel grabbed his keys as Sara strolled through the door.

"So, either you cooked and cleaned and left it warming in the oven or…"

He shrugged. "Pizza and beer?"

"Fine," she relented in that special way suggesting he knew she would. "You drive."

Daniel already had his keys in hand.

They headed for the front door and discovered a slender woman dressed impeccably with her hands folded before her when he opened it. Platinum blonde hair in a tight bun poked up from behind her head. The glasses accented the angles on her face, lending her a less severe librarian appeal. Both dogs started barking from the kitchen as the stranger's scent hit them. Daniel's stomach twinged but it was Sara who reacted first.

"Aislinn?" she asked. "What are you doing here?"

The first pang of danger echoed in Daniel's mind upon discovering the gargoyle was nowhere to be seen and Aislinn was looking at them without an ounce of her normal friendliness.

The dark elf handed an envelope to Sara, careful not to touch skin, and intoned, "Daniel and Sara Thomas, Queen Morgen requests your audience tomorrow."

The queen? I don't work for her. We've done enough for the elves. It's time I took care of us. Hell, we're supposed to be going on vacation in a few days! Daniel's concerns were compounded by the almost impossible tale of werewolves and giants hiding in Fayetteville awaiting him when he returned from New York. The thought of Sara in danger sparked concerns.

"You can tell her to fo—"

Sara laid the back of her hand on Daniel's chest stopping his words. "Certainly. Any particular time?"

Aislinn adjusted her glasses, showing a slip of uncomfortableness, prompting Daniel to stiffen further. "Before 1 p.m. The clans are approaching a tremendous moment, and the queen has need to speak with both of you as soon as possible."

"Why us? Haven't we done enough for your clans already?" Daniel snapped, ignoring Sara's withering glare.

He wanted to snatch that envelope from her and tear it to shreds.

Forcing a dangerous smile that looked completely out of place on her, Aislinn said, "That is for the queen to discuss, Daniel Thomas. I shall report you will attend." She nodded. "Good night."

She turned and left without another word.

The click of her heels striking pavement mocked him. The dogs fell silent, their job done. Simmering over the perceived implications of the future, Daniel stayed silent until her sedan was gone from sight: "What the hell was that about?"

"Daniel, you can't just talk to them anyway you like," Sara admonished. "She is a direct report to the queen."

Hurt twisted his stomach at her defense of the elves over him. "What? They're not even supposed to exist! I don't work for the queen, Sara, and neither do you. The less we have to do with them the better our lives are. Look what happened the last few times. You almost got killed by werewolves!"

Sara glanced around, ensuring none of their neighbors were lurking within earshot, before replying, "Will you keep your voice down? The last thing we need is a neighbor thinking we're nuts. You especially."

Any protest he had died in his throat. More than one of their friends knew about his PTSD from the wars. A few neighbors made sure to give him a wide berth, though Sara believed their concerns unwarranted. Daniel hadn't hurt a fly since retiring from the army. Well...

"Ok, fine. But you have to admit nothing good comes from dealing with the elves. I don't like being at their beck and call."

"But she does," Sara countered with more ease than he found comforting. "She knows both of us and, unless I'm wrong, trusts me after saving her life."

"I'm going to need more than beer," Daniel

muttered and motioned for her to head to the car.

For the better part of his military career, none of the higher ups in his chain of command knew his name, yet here he was retired and now a pawn for the queen to call at whim.

They pulled into their driveway a short time later, bellies full and sleep beckoning. Daniel and Sara were beyond the need to prove their youth, content with going to sleep at a reasonable hour and staying low key. That initial creative burst calmed in the wake of Aislinn's appearance, leaving him brooding over what the future held.

Daniel put the truck in park and hopped out, eager to get inside and undo his uncomfortably tight belt. "I think I ate too much," he said, rubbing his aching belly.

"You always do," Sara countered and shook her head. "I don't know how you do it. Twenty some years later and you take it personal when you can't eat a whole pie!"

"Hurtful," he joked. "You know me. I can't back away from a challenge. It's the restaurant's fault!"

"You'd only get a t-shirt out of it, silly," she replied.

Sara's eyebrow rose and he sighed. She had seen him do more than his share of foolish things since first agreeing to date him, but tonight was the worst. A local pizza joint, and one of their favorites, offered a unique challenge of eating an entire deep-dish pizza in less than an hour for a special they were having this week. Plenty attempted it. Most failed. Daniel decided this was his night... His name joined the ever-growing list of disappointments. He was going to pay for it, and soon, with how his stomach was clenching.

"I almost made it though."

"Have fun on the toilet tonight." Sara hurried inside and up to shower first. She had called dibs in the car, and he figured it was probably better for her to get in and out before he had to get in there.

Daniel groaned and headed for the kitchen and bottle of antacids in the cabinet. Both dogs sat before him, obedient pals looking for a handout. If he wasn't already feeling bad, he would have obliged. *Sorry guys. This is all about me right now.* They sauntered into the bedroom together just as Sara was finishing her hair. One look at her and all those bad thoughts disappeared.

"What?" she asked.

Daniel leaned against the doorframe, pausing to flex his legs. He ignored his stomach gurgling. "You know. The kids aren't here..."

"Uh huh."

He gave a conspiratorial wink. "Come on. Are you going to make me say it? It's been a while since we had the house to ourselves. Hell, I didn't plan on getting dressed tomorrow and…" A particular strong stomach cramp had him clutching his stomach and throwing a hand up over his mouth.

Sara wrinkled her nose and closed the door on him. "So romantic. Maybe we should wait until you're sure not to vomit. I don't know what you were thinking. Trying to eat a whole damned pizza like that. Does our insurance even cover random acts of foolishness if I have to rush you to the ER to get your stomach pumped?"

"I'm fine," he pleaded, knocking once on the closed door. "Just a little gas. I already took the Tums." After getting no response, he turned to the dogs, who were nestled in the middle of the bed and looking at him like they questioned where he planned on sleeping. "I don't think she's falling for it guys. I might have bit off more than I can chew tonight."

They whuffed in response.

"Yeah, me too." Another gurgle followed by a belch that he tasted had him going back to the door to say, "Sara, let me in! I think the bathroom is calling."

He wasn't sure if she was scolding him or laughing under the camouflage of the hair dryer, but the door didn't open. "Sara…"

The sing-song chime on his phone stole his attention. Frowning, Daniel snatched the phone off the dresser and headed for the kid's bathroom. "This is Daniel."

"Daniel Thomas, Agent Blackmere. I trust I did not catch you at a bad time?"

Daniel's night continued worsening. He suppressed a groan. "As a matter of fact, Blackmere, I was just about to drop the kids off at the pool."

"A little late for swimming, don't you think?" Blackmere replied. At Daniel's silence he added, "I trust you have already heard from the queen."

Shit. There it is. "How the hell did you know that?"

"We're the government. We know everything." Blackmere replied flatly. "What did the queen want?"

"Her flunky was waiting for us when we were walking out the door to head for dinner. All she said was Morgen needed to see us tomorrow." Daniel took a deep breath. "Look, Blackmere, what's going on? What major event do the elves have planned?"

He leaned against the bathroom doorframe, silently urging the conclusion to the conversation. A long pause had Daniel's stomach rumbling in a different way.

"I'm surprised you don't know already. Morgen is calling all clan leaders and family heads in for a meeting. We don't know for sure, but rumor has it she wants to reconcile the clans."

"End the war?" Daniel's mouth dropped open. "Does she have enough support to do that?"

"We'll find out soon enough," Blackmere replied. "The real question is what does she want with you."

"I'll let you know," Daniel told him, mind racing. "If this is true, why isn't DESA more involved?"

"A delegation is being sent to North Carolina," the agent explained. "I'll be there as well." "Listen there is something—"

"Daniel, I don't need to tell you this could be

momentous. It also has the potential to go sideways real fast. Keep your head on a swivel and take nothing for granted. I'll be in touch."

Confused and worried Daniel took care of his business with the bathroom and sauntered back into the bedroom.

"What was that all about?"

Still staring at the phone in his hand, Daniel groaned. "You're not going to believe this, but that was Blackmere. I think we're about to get sucked back into the world of the el— Hey, where are your clothes?"

A worried look darkened her face before she shook her head and she stepped to him. "The elves can wait until tomorrow. Come here. We have unfinished business to attend to."

"I love it when you talk dirty," he managed before she planted her lips on his.

FOUR

Daniel pressed the button for the top floor and stepped back into the elevator before glancing at Sara. He didn't know why he agreed to go along with Morgen's plans. He owed the elves nothing. In fact, it was quite the opposite. They managed to steal much of his time and energy while piling him with unnecessary stress. Just because the first adventure proved thrilling, a much-needed relapse to a world he almost forgot, didn't mean he wanted more encounters after that. Encounters that got even more dangerous and involved his family.

Age and responsibility conspired against him. Not that he considered himself old, but years of wear and tear in the army took their toll. He stayed in shape by going to the gym three times a week and taking long walks with the dogs, but he knew he was well short of being combat ready. The last harrowing event in Charleston proved that.

Daniel needed a vacation. One him and Sara were planning. Somewhere far from the intrigues of the elves and government overwatch. Somewhere neither could reach him without effort. The thought of settling on a quiet island in the middle of the Pacific enticed him, regardless of Sara's opinion of finding a quiet mountain home for the week.

"Will you relax," she chided as he shifted his weight back and forth. "Keep that up and you'll bring this thing down. I have other things to do than die in an elevator accident, Daniel."

"This is a bad idea."

She grinned, warm and knowing. "Of course it is, but it's far from a trap. Morgen owes me. She won't do anything."

Returning her grin and feeling relieved she was by his side, Daniel said, "Whatever you need to make you feel safe. The last time I was here didn't quite go the way I expected."

"We'll be fine," she soothed. "Norman won't let anything bad happen to me."

Daniel didn't know how wise it was to trust a gargoyle, even one seemingly dedicated to ensuring Sara remained safe. Norman Guilt was many things, but he belonged to the elf clans at the end of the day. He held up his hands in mock surrender as the elevator chimed. As the doors opened, he took a deep, steadying breath, smoothed down the front of his shirt. He almost stumbled into the waiting gargoyle.

"The queen is expecting you," Norman rumbled.

Daniel found the gargoyle's voice like grinding rocks together. Coarse and painful to hear. He wondered if it hurt Norman to speak. Sara slipped past him to give Norman a hug. The huge man stood there, arms hanging at his sides, before reciprocating as if only then remembering human customs of greeting. Daniel felt strange with the interaction. His mind knew Norman was a gargoyle protector, but his eyes only saw Sara hugging another man.

"Norman! So good to see you!"

He untangled himself and stepped back. "It is good to see you as well, Sara Thomas. If you please, follow me."

"I think we know the way by now, pal," Daniel said with feigned jealousy and made to step around him.

Norman blocked his path, bending down to whisper, "This is not a typical day, Daniel Thomas. You must be on your guard. Much has happened since last we met."

"What do you mean?" Sara asked, keeping her voice low.

The gargoyle stiffened, casting a wary look back down the short hallway. "It is not my place to say more. Be warned. Danger lurks within these walls."

He turned and strode off, expecting them to follow.

Daniel's senses heightened as Sara shifted closer to him. Rather than giving into temptation to remind her he told her so, the former soldier focused his mind on the likelihood of trouble. *Damn these elves and their games. Why can't they just get along and act like the rest of us? Or act like my characters?* The trouble was, he lamented, they were.

Norman led them through the crowded dining room, filled with recognizable CEOs, business leaders, and a scattering of state level politicians. Those with power flocked to others in the room, leaving the handful of normal people sitting adrift in a sea of money. Plenty of people joined the club in the hopes of establishing connections with the right people, knowing they didn't quite fit in. Others forced their way in. Daniel did his time at the club and moved on. They weren't his crowd.

He had his time in the sun: television interviews after deploying to Montana to fight forest fires and speaking before groups of people who sent support to his unit while he served in the Middle East. Those awkward encounters did little to prepare him for the journalistic hounds clamoring for interviews and buzz quotes after each new book release. Just the presence of a camera had his skin crawling.

"Ah, Mr. and Mrs. Thomas. Thank you for coming on such short notice," Aislinn's walked toward them. A pair of guards flanked the door to Morgen's office.

Norman bowed and ambled off. His assignment complete.

That's new. What kind of trouble are we getting into here? Daniel gave her a clipped nod. "Do we go on in?"

The elf bristled but maintained her composure. "Allow me a moment to announce you, *sir*."

Rebuked, he winced as Sara's elbow clipped his ribs. Daniel moved a step away and stood with his hands folded before him. His eyes never left the large elves guarding the door. Mean and imposing, they glared back. Elves or not, he knew he could take them in a fair fight. The gargoyle lingering in the hallway suggested otherwise.

Aislinn returned a moment later. "The queen will see you know."

"Thanks," he replied and squared his shoulders on the guards as he passed. He ensured Sara went ahead to avoid taking another shot to the ribs.

Morgen, queen of the dark elves and sole ruler of the clans, sat behind her mahogany desk. Long, dark hair flowed halfway down her back, tied in a tight tail that did not so much as tug on her impossibly perfect flesh. Her manicured nails clicked against each other as she watched them enter. Daniel never failed to be impressed by her regality, even while knowing she represented a darkness the world did not need. The door clicked shut behind him, trapping him with the originator of many of his problems.

"Thank you for coming."

She threw him off immediately with her words of welcome.

"I know we have not always seen eye to eye, as you humans say, but I have come to respect the two of you these last few years. It is not an easy admission for me."

"Thank you," Sara spoke, passing Daniel a side glance before continuing. "If you don't mind, could you tell us why you asked for us?"

"This is…difficult to say," the queen drawled. Morgen plucked a document from her desk and handed it to Sara. "Read this and I will answer any question I can."

A trio of vultures swooped by their dark wings casting shadows over the office. Daniel felt a chill, as if being warned. *Don't get involved. Only death awaits.*

She finished reading through the paper and knew she shouldn't have gotten out of bed this morning. "They are all dead?"

"And others," Morgen confirmed. "Almost twenty family and clan leaders, captains of our people. And all within a three-day span."

"But why?" Sara asked, the shock in her voice

reflecting in the horror on her face.

Reading over her shoulder, Daniel's face paled at the size of the list.

"I suspect it is in retaliation for my call to unify the clans," the queen explained. "We are being hunted and, while I have suspicions, lack the information to know the truth. What I do know is I cannot stop this chain of events. The time has come to rebuild what was lost, before it is too late."

Daniel cocked his head, spying the vultures soaring back. Logically, he knew they nested on the high rooftops, but nothing was ever face value when it came to the elves. "Too late for what?"

Clearing her throat, Morgen said, "For everything. We are at a crossroads. The rise of the goblin nest confirmed this. The only way for the elves to survive is by squashing old disputes and moving forward with one voice. We can longer withstand the pressures of light and dark clans while maintaining a balance with humans. Either we stand as one or fall."

"Who do you think killed these people?" Daniel ignored her campaign speech and asked what Sara was thinking. "Were they all on your side?"

"Some were. Others not. As I said, nothing is confirmed," she replied.

Daniel stiffened. "I thought we were friends."

Morgen's nostrils flared. "What if I told you there was an organization who has been influential since the dawn of civilization? Power brokers and arbiters of their brand of truth and justice?"

He snorted. "The Illuminati doesn't exist. They're a myth."

Her eyes narrowed to slivers. "They call themselves the Invisible Hand. No one living knows how they began or by whom. To date, my people have yet to infiltrate their ranks. Centuries of effort washed away. Everyone we have sent asking questions of seeking the truth have either gone missing or been killed."

"An impressive enemy," Daniel conceded, doubting the full truth in her admission. "Why are they after the elves?"

She shook her head. "Not all questions have answers. The Invisible Hand moves through the world unseen, unnoticed. Those who have the misfortune to encounter one of their agents find their lives irrevocably altered."

Daniel was never one to accept conspiracy theories or half-baked theories. "How does one identify these mystery agents? Seems to me you can't kill what you don't know."

"They are all marked with the same tattoo on the back of their hand. A multi-headed serpent inside a great circle," Morgen said. "It is their only tell. One seen too late."

"I don't get it. What is terrifying enough to bring us into the fold?" he asked. "You could have had Aislinn or Norman warn us if we were in danger. There's no need to haul us all the way to Raleigh for this news. What else are you after?"

Morgen leaned back in her chair, the red leather in stark contrast to her black dress. "Ever the perceptive one, aren't you Daniel? Very well. I appreciate not beating around the bush. I have summoned all elven leaders to conclave. We will either reconcile our differences and unite or not. That remains to be seen, but there are numerous competing factors. Your government has sent a delegation to watch over us, as if we were children threatening to ruin a planned vacation."

Daniel's glare echoed the rush of emotions flooding him.

"While I anticipate no initial threat to you and your wife, there is another factor I have in mind. Daniel Thomas, I would like you to be on hand as a silent observer for the conclave and a liaison with DESA when they arrive. You will be tied in with our security detail. Armed and given all actionable intelligence, without compromising our integrity. Naturally."

He felt his stomach drop through his shoes. "Naturally. Why me?"

"Because you are the one constant I have no doubts about," she replied. "You are precisely who and what you say you are. A man of his word, whether I like it or not. I need that, now more than ever. While I do not expect violence, the threat of the Invisible Hand frightens me. Do this for me and I will consider our interactions complete. What say you?"

There it is. Thrown to the wolves with total release dangling like a carrot. How do I keep getting myself into these situations? You'd think once or twice would be enough by now. Blackmere's offer to join DESA is looking better by the minute.

Puffing out his breath, he turned to Sara who nodded. Daniel told the queen, "You got yourself a deal. When and where do I need to be?"

"Aislinn will handle the details. Thank you," Morgen answered before shifting her focus to Sara. "And you, Sara Thomas, I have something special in mind for you as well."

FIVE

I was just starting to get back into my writing groove and I get drawn back into this messed up world. Why can't they just leave me alone? And I managed to get Sara dragged into it too. Or did I? Morgen didn't ask for me alone. Why do I feel like I'm not being told everything? Damned elves!

"Are you all right?" Morgen asked.

How could I possibly be all right with any of this? Since meeting you I have almost been killed a dozen times. I should be in therapy for this but no. Here I am, the gullible, happy soldier preparing to embark upon yet another suicidal mission. Why am I not an alcoholic already?

"Fine," Daniel answered with a slow bite of his bottom lip.

Morgen studied him for another moment, curious to see his thought processes play out in facial expressions. She found humans frustratingly amusing. Satisfied he was in hand, she decided to focus on Sara. The woman served her well in the past and provided an outsider's perspective.

"I would like you to be close to my side throughout the proceedings. This is a once in a lifetime opportunity and I need sharp eyes and ears who think differently than I."

"But I'm human," Sara protested.

"Precisely why I need you," Morgen replied. "Don't fret. You will not be the only human in attendance. Your government has ensured that much. DESA representatives will be scattered throughout the conference. You will not be in danger as I wish you to remain anonymous. Behind the scenes, as it were. Inconspicuous in every aspect. I want you to watch everything. Make notes of who shows support and who poses a problem. You not being an elf is invaluable. I also do not expect you to accept out of any obligation. This is a dangerous moment, for us all."

"My obligation is to my family, Morgen," Sara said. "You know that. With Daniel already here, why would I be anywhere else?"

The queen's shoulders slumped, just a fraction. Her eyes lost a bit of their hardness. "Good. Thank you. You earned my trust last year. Do this for me and I shall be in your debt."

"You could pay off our mortgage if you're feeling generous," Daniel suggested.

Sara's elbow caught him in the ribs. "Daniel!"

"What? I was just saying," he protested between strangled breaths.

"Any compensation will be discussed once the conference is finished," Morgen interjected with an eyeroll before the pair devolved into squabbling. "Now, if you please, see Aislinn for your assignments."

"When does all this happen?" Daniel asked. Sara paused in the door and looked back.

Morgen cocked her head. "Why, Daniel, immediately of course."

"Pay off our mortgage?" Sara fumed, her voice barely restrained.

Daniel shrugged, offering his best innocent look. "What? She said she owed us. It's the least she can do, considering."

"And you just had to chime in. I swear, you need to learn better timing with your comedic relief. She's the freaking queen."

"Who said I was joking? And she's not my queen," he snapped, his mood darkening as the reality of what was happening set in. "I didn't ask to be part of this. Didn't want us to be part of this."

"Neither did I but here we are," she countered, arms folded across her chest and feet planted firm in the tile. She couldn't help but feel a part of this tirade was for show. She knew those hidden truths he only whispered to himself when he thought no one was around. "Daniel, I think there's a real danger here."

"Yeah, this Invisible Hand act," he scoffed. "I don't like it. Why hasn't Blackmere mentioned them before?"

Blackmere. There was another problem altogether. It was like deploying to Iraq all over again.

"I'm sure Thaddeus has his reasons."

At her soft tone he had to hold back another scoff. He failed to understand what Sara saw in the government man.

"Uh huh," was all he managed. "We'll see, but I swear this is the last time of being involved with this mess. Here I was thinking our politics were bad."

She slipped an arm around his and rested her head on his chest. "You said that the last time. Relax, Daniel. We don't even know what to expect."

"That's what worries me. Here she comes."

He wanted to reach out and hug her for all he was worth. The conflict in his mind ramped up, as it usually did until clear orders of operation were in place. Daniel hated this feeling, trapped between wants and desires. It didn't dawn on him they were alone in a hallway until the click of Aislinn's heels on the faded tile broke their conversation. Mask slipping into place, Daniel sidle in front of Sara and the elf.

"If you would both please come with me. The queen has given specific instructions regarding your disposition," the elf began, head cocked at his mannerisms. "Mr. Thomas, I believe you are already acquainted with Goran the armorer?"

He squared his shoulders, back stiffening. "I am. I take you want me to head down there now?"

"Your escort will be here shortly. We are leaving nothing to chance," Aislinn said before he could protest. Her matter-of-fact tone left much to be desired, though Daniel suspected the facade on purpose. "Our head of security is on the way. You will report directly to him for the duration of the conference."

"Tell me it's not one of those damned dwarves," he said more forcefully than intended, and louder.

"What's that about dwarves?" a deep, gravelly voice barked from behind.

Daniel winced, recognizing the voice. Choosing to avoid making eye contact with his wife who tried pushing past him for a better view, he turned to see Max Schneider storming up the hall. The dwarf was dressed in a smart black suit reminding Daniel of a government spy. Complete with gold jewelry on his fingers and in his beard, the father of the Schneider brothers bore no friendship with Daniel. They had almost come to blows several times during the Charleston adventure, leaving Daniel hoping they never saw each other again.

"Well, well. If it isn't our little author boy," Max chided.

Daniel refused to take the bait, especially not in front of Sara. "Max. Matters must be bad for her to drag you back into the fold," he spoke slowly, dragging out each word in a false southern drawl. "Thought you were out of the game?"

The dwarf glowered. The sound of teeth grinding crawled down Daniel's spine. Any pretense of civility was forced as they squared off in the middle of the hall for any to witness. Until now, the dwarf patriarch was a passing memory that he ignored. Finding him here, dominating the hallway and being Daniel's direct supervisor, sent ripples of severity through him.

"What can I say? The queen heard my efforts to

rescue your precious human and decided I was more asset than liability," Max said after long moments of silence. "Looks like she thinks the same of you."

"Looks like it," Daniel agreed.

Sara's slimmer figure slipped between them. "Daniel, are you going to introduce me to your friend?"

He unclenched the fist he hadn't realized he held and mumbled a silent apology to her. "Of course. Sara, this is Max Schneider, father of—"

"Angus and Fritz!" she finished with a smile, holding out a hand. "I remember them well. It is a pleasure to meet you, Max."

The dwarf accepted her hand with a skeptical look. "You know my boys, eh? A pair of knuckleheads but they mean well. Good to meet you as well."

Sara beamed. "There. See? Now that we're all civil we can save the machismo for our enemies."

Daniel relented. He had a feeling enough bad things were barreling their way without making waves with the dwarf. "They're not here, are they?"

"Who? Angus and Fritz? Nah. They'll be around later." Max leaned closer to whisper, "Can't let them off the leash for too long, eh?"

"As amusing as this is, we must be about our work," Aislinn interrupted. "We are on a specific timeline. The first cars are already arriving."

"Elves and their damned timelines," Max grumbled. "Like they don't live for thousands of years, eh kid? Fine, let me get Daniel down to the armorer."

"Thank you, Max," the elf said. "Sara, if you will follow me. We must get you changed into more suitable clothes."

"What's wrong with what I have on?" she asked.

Aislinn tsked. "You are in the service of royalty now, not going to a buffet. The queen will not be seen with anyone appearing beneath her station. This weekend, you represent the throne, even if you are expected to be a shadow. You must dress the part."

Giving Sara a hug and a lingering kiss, he watched Sara walk away. They were now wholly immersed in the elf clans and whatever promises of danger or violence that came next.

"You're definitely paying off my house after this," Daniel mumbled.

Miles from the pinnacle heights of downtown Raleigh, in a secret dining hall deep underground, twelve men and women sat behind masks of anonymity. Enshrouded in black robes and hoods, they sat in silence. Dim lights cast shadows across the chamber. Those in Raleigh knew the room for what it was, the playground of those with money and power. One of two unique rooms beneath one of the city's most famous steakhouses, the walls clung to whispered secrets through the decades. This day, a fresh wave of sinister thoughts would be mentioned. Uttered to the whims of those seeking the same goal. The complete and total eradication of the elf hierarchy.

A short figure slipped into the room, stopping before the empty chair at the head of the table. He slammed the iron staff, capped with a winged dragon, on the floor three times. Those assembled rose—the rustle of robes mingling with chairs being shoved back. Heads turned to witness the towering man entering the room, their spoken leader. As one, they bowed their heads.

He swept his gaze over the assembled before gesturing them to sit. The man announcing him knocked the iron staff once more then departed the room. Still standing, the leader raised his arms to the ceiling. The others imitated him. The tattoos on the backs of their right hands winked in the flickering candlelight.

"As begun with the dawn, we continue with the night," the leader's voice rumbled through the hall.

The twelve repeated his words.

"Welcome friends and brethren," he said after

silence settled in. "It has been a long road, but fate has conspired to bring us together here, now, at our hour of resurgence. Today marks the beginning of the great fall. Empires will shatter and the children of the Invisible Hand shall rise to assume our rightful positions as stewards of the earth. Today, my friends, we begin our last assault on the halls of the elves. Today, their world falls and ours rises. Death to the elves!"

They rose in twos and threes, fists stabbing the sky.

"Death to the elves!"

SIX

"I thought the armory was underground?" Daniel commented after the elevator reached the ground floor and Max gestured for him to exit.

The dwarf grunted and took a left toward the Fayetteville Street exit. A security guard waved but said nothing as they passed through the rotating door and into the mid-morning sun.

Daniel hurried down the steps in an effort to match the dwarf's stride. A trio of businessmen shifted past, forcing him to bite back the litany of questions burning him up inside. Daniel caught a shirtless man bicycling toward him. The pair of American flags waving off the back of his bike made Daniel grin, even if he thought them out of place.

"Where are we going, Max?" Daniel asked and took a seat on one of the concrete barriers surrounding the base of a tree when the dwarf didn't respond.

At Max's silence, he tilted his head back, craning to see the top floors where Sara remained, locked in a den of creatures she did not understand yet somehow trusted. Every instinct screamed for him to head back inside and go to her. Elves were anything but subtle. Their underhanded ways threatened every aspect of civility, and she was trapped with the worst of them. Doubts over agreeing to Morgen's wild scheme surfaced, making him question his decisions.

Daniel's opinions devolved the longer he dwelled on it. Seeing the list of names of the deceased did little to ease his troubled mind. If many of the upper tiers among the elf clans could be eliminated so easily, what chance did he and Sara stand? He didn't know what this Invisible Hand was, or if to believe they even existed. More likely it was a rogue faction of elves hiding in plain sight. Running a hand through his hair, he blew out the now stale air from his lungs.

"What's on your mind, soldier boy?" Max gestured down the street after seeing the consternation grip Daniel. "Hope you're up for a walk. That's where we are heading."

"The concert hall? It was the middle of the day." No doubt the center was filled with staff and symphony musicians practicing for their next performance... Yet when Max nodded and began walking, Daniel followed.

"You gave Morgen your word," Max said without waiting for him to catch up. "Damned foolish that was, but a man is nothing without his word."

"How do you do it, Max?" he asked, choosing to ignore the quip.

"Do what?"

Daniel stepped aside as a group of young businesspeople crowded down the sidewalk, flocking toward one of Raleigh's coffee shops. "Stay hidden without losing your minds? I can't imagine its easy, not with your history."

"Doing research for your next book?"

Heat warmed his cheeks. "No. You know I don't write about the truth. My worlds are pure fantasy, or so I thought. How was I supposed to know all the races I wrote about were real and walking among us in plain sight?"

Max halted in midstride, jabbing a meaty finger at him. "Look, you proved your worth down in Charleston by keeping my boys alive. You have my gratitude for that, but no more. We are forced to work alongside each other for the duration of the conference. I'm not going to like you. Not having drinks after work. None of your hummie nonsense."

"I didn't expect anything less," Daniel replied. "Now, if you can just tell me more about what we're doing. I'd like to get back to my wife." He braced, expecting a storm.

Instead, the dwarf rocked back a half step. Winds whipping down the canyon of high rises tousled his hair, jangling the fetishes in his beard. A grin broke that granite façade. The whites of his teeth shined through the dark of his beard. "Good man. I don't like people who won't get down to business. Morgen is worried about all this falling apart. She knows this is her one shot at reuniting the clans and, with so many leaders assassinated enroute to the conference, isn't willing to leave anything to chance. Our job is to ensure this conference goes off uninterrupted by these Hand bastards."

They resumed walking, marching down the long street toward Raleigh's premier concert hall where the North Carolina Symphony called home. It was also one of the main graduation venues for the massive high schools in the county. The perfect place for a large gathering.

"How many personnel do you have?" Daniel asked.

"Five hundred. Mostly elves and dwarves. The two guarding Morgen were Old Guard. They don't fall under my command, but they'll be on site. DESA is sending an unknown sized contingent to supplement our efforts," Max explained. "Which is where you come in."

"Me? I don't have anything to do with DESA," Daniel protested.

"That's not what the birds whisper. You've been embedded with the feds for years now, whether you know it or not. Wasn't it your wife who made a call for help while we were down south?" Max explained. "Regardless, it's out of my hands. Morgen wants you interfaced with the top."

"What are you talking about? The top of what?"

The dwarf's grin widened, toothy and leering as they crossed the last street before hitting the sidewalk leading up to the hall's front doors. "Soldier boy, you're about to be a liaison between the clans and the government. Seems you've been a special request."

Stunned into silence, Daniel's thoughts swirled. The thought of serving two masters simultaneously never entered his mind... Working with one hadn't gone according to plan yet. He couldn't imagine the chaos of two conflicting entities demanding his focus. A quartet of men in casual suits flanked the main door. He had no doubts they worked for Max. One opened the door for them. He and Max headed inside.

"Mr. Schneider, can I have a word?" a slender elf asked as he strolled toward them from the main staircase leading down.

Daniel watched, growing suspicious. The elf's eyes flickered across the area, never settling on one person for longer than it took to blink. There was stiffness in his step, making his movements jerky. Stuttered. Daniel's gaze dropped to the elf's hands a split-second before the elf reached into his jacket.

"Gun!" he shouted.

The hall burst into action. Several elves and dwarves drew weapons and secured doors.

Daniel wrapped his arms around Max, tackling him out of the line of fire as a shot was fired. Guards rushed forward, grabbing the elf by the arms from behind. A punch to the gut knocked the wind from the elf and the gun from his hands.

Swearing, Max pushed Daniel off and rose. His knuckles cracked as he balled his fists. "Don't kill him. I want answers."

Locked in place, the assassin struggled and strained in a desperate attempt to break free.

Max stormed closer, the devil blazing in his eyes. Daniel felt a little sorry for the would-be assassin. Just when the dwarf was a step away, the elf broke into laughter. Guards looked around, failing to find the humor. Daniel's skin crawled.

Max's eyes widened. "Stop him! Don't let him bite down!"

The warning came too late. Daniel saw the elf bit down on the capsule now bulging in his cheek. His body rattled, shaking as white foam bubbled from his mouth. He burst into ash and smoke a moment later, disintegrating in the elves' hands. Daniel was unable to tear his gaze away from the obscenity of the dark ash on the red carpet. He spied the remains of a capsule in the detritus. "Cyanide."

Not replying to him, Max sifted through the ashes. Snatching the capsule, the dwarf stood. Daniel could see the dwarf's anger growing, recognizing the insult Max had just been given by having his security detail infiltrated with apparent ease. The elder dwarf made a show of crushing the capsule in his hand before casting it away.

"How did this happen? I want answers."

A red-haired elf clasped his hands before him, the grey of his suit brightening his jewel-like eyes. "Sir, everyone was vetted as per your instructions. This man had to have been turned after being assigned to the conference."

"Not good enough," he glowered. "I want another round of checks. Look for family problems, financial, anything we might have missed. This cannot happen a second time. The queen will be here this evening."

Security detail snapped to and hurried off to comply with his orders.

Max turned his glare to the lone dwarf remaining behind. "Get a broom and clean this up."

Daniel's eyes returned to the ash on the red carpet. He felt his already tepid grasp on the situation slipping away. He had come to expect certain levels of danger in dealing with the clans, but nothing prepared him for the daring assassination attempt in broad daylight. Morgen's fears were manifesting, threatening to drag everyone down with her.

Following Max down to the ground level, he rounded on the dwarf once they were alone. "I need a gun."

"I need a drink."

A grumble of hunger ran through Daniel's stomach, producing a chuckle. For reasons he could not explain, he found the idea of being hungry in the middle of a crisis amusing. Wiping his face with the palm of a hand, he slumped into one of the empty chairs around a small bar at the end of the hallway. "There's no telling how many other agents have been subverted. You said five hundred?" Daniel asked. "How are we supposed to sift through them in time?"

"We do the best we can. Too bad you're not going to be part of the solution."

This again. Daniel peeled his hand away, expecting to find a smug look on the dwarf's face. There wasn't.

Max stood, feet shoulder width apart and arms folded across his impossibly wide chest, gazing at him with a furrowed brow. Real concern lingered in the corners of his eyes, belaying the seriousness of the situation. He was responsible for the queen's life. Any failure in duty meant forfeiting his life. Or worse. Daniel was suddenly glad he wasn't in charge.

"Goran has set up a small armory in a truck out back. Go draw your weapons and report back. I'll hand you off to the feds when you return."

"I don't think that's what Mo—"

Max held up a hand. "This isn't negotiable, Daniel. We are out of time and, believe it or not, I can't trust anyone except you. Not my ideal scenario, but one I won't pass up. I need you to relay everything you see, even if it means turning in someone you thought you could trust."

Stunned by the admission, Daniel asked, "Any limits to what I can draw?"

"No heavy weapons. Exterior guards are stationed on the roof and at points surrounding the building. They have long rifles. If you can't conceal it, don't draw it. Goran also has standing orders in case you forget," Max replied.

"Fair enough."

Daniel wormed through the back corridors usually reserved for waiting performers and sets. Dark walls and low lighting put his hair on end. He couldn't stop flexing his firing hand. The incident in the lobby rattled him. The assassination attempt confirmed Morgen's fears. Her network was infiltrated. That lack of reliability set him almost alone on an island in a sea of roiling hostility. Sure, he had Sara and, by default, Norman Guilt, but they were away on another assignment. For now, it was him and Max.

Fighting back the fear, Daniel exited the back door and hurried down the small flight of stairs leading to the parking lot. Goran's truck sat by itself, nestled against the rear of the building. Daniel couldn't keep his grin from seeing the tie dye wearing giant again. Of all the creatures he had encountered since entering the world of the elves, he liked Goran the best. Unlike the others, the giant lacked judgment. Daniel wished more of the world demonstrated that trait. Perhaps then they wouldn't have half the problems they did.

"Goran, it's me Daniel," he called out. "Max says I need to grab a few weapons."

The back door swung open with an ear shattering groan of twisted, rusted metal. Daniel winced but climbed the steps.

"Daniel Thomas. Good to see you again, my man," Goran's deep voice rumbled through the truck. "Pick out the piece you like."

"Just piece? What if I need two?"

The giant shrugged. "Whatever you need, man. I'm just here."

Feeling a little better, Daniel began rummaging through the racks of pistols.

SEVEN

Armed, Daniel said his goodbyes to Goran and headed back inside to find Max. A glint of metal on the roof caught his attention. He spotted the barrel of a sniper rifle poking over the edge toward downtown Raleigh. Traffic was picking up, announcing the early stages of rush hour. Soon, the streets would be gridlocked with an endless stream of traffic and pedestrians. Ample opportunity for threats to converge on their position and cause havoc in the confusion.

Daniel took the angels on overwatch with a grain of salt, praying they remained loyal. The last thing he needed was a bullet in the back. Daniel reentered the hall. Foot traffic tripled in the time he had been with the armorer. Scores of elves, dwarves, trolls, and gnomes were filing in. He recognized none until a pair of dwarves sauntered into the middle of the lobby like they owned it all. Daniel rolled his eyes. He should have guessed. Where there was one Schneider the others wouldn't be far behind, no matter the circumstance.

Fritz spied him first and elbowed his brother in the ribs. The older brother stared at Daniel, a groan twisting his face. Fritz headed toward him. A grin displayed his impossibly white teeth.

"Angus, Fritz. It's been a while," Daniel greeted and shook Fritz's outstretched hand. "How have you been?"

"Good. Good. We've been keeping low since that day. Word is DESA was looking for us to answer a few questions thanks to Hayf's report," Fritz replied.

Angus halted beside his brother, ignoring Daniel's hand. "Bastard sold us out to his superiors. I knew I should have knocked a few of his teeth out."

"Great seeing you to, Angus," Daniel withdrew his

hand.

"You want to knock everyone's teeth out," Fritz countered. "Besides, we had other things to worry about. Morgen sent us back into the capital building to make sure none of Damon Pender's spores remained after the Old Guard cleaned it out."

Memories of the lich made Daniel shudder. Such creatures shouldn't exist in any world. His very being hinted at another world, of fae and fairies, lurking just beyond the border of reality and disbelief. The zombie-like monster that was Damon Pender threatened the entire planet and not a soul knew he existed. He'd make an excellent villain if Daniel could ever get back to writing.

"What happened to Pender?" Daniel asked, already having forgotten much of that weekend.

Angus confirmed his thoughts by jerking a thumb across his neck. "Got what he had coming to him, nothing more. Once the Old Guard is unleashed, they are unstoppable. Constantin Andros is as ruthless as he is professional. Not the sort you want to cross. How did you get roped into this?"

"Morgen called me in to help with security for her secret party," Daniel said. He thought he caught a glimpse of Max lingering in the crowd behind the dwarves. "Looks like I'm working for your father."

Angus started laughing. Deep, thunderous bellows turning more than one head. "Serves you right for all those stories you told. Well, looks like you'll have another soon enough. Old Max Schneider is twice as bad as either of us, and just as snarky. Have fun."

He left them to their amusements, ignoring Angus's murmuring to his brother about how his father was going to eat Daniel alive. Daniel noticed the tension that clung to the crowd. A miasma threatening to weaken resolve and rob strength. If he felt it than the others must too. Or did they? Daniel studied as many as he could as he passed. Most appeared engrossed in their conversations or watching entry points, not a one appeared worried beyond normal.

"Get your guns?" Max asked as he cut through the crowd to reach his side.

"I have a few, yes. What's next?"

Max thumped him in the chest with a knuckle, grinning when they both heard the satisfying thunk of Kevlar body armor beneath Daniel's shirt. "Good. You're going to need that before this shit show ends. Come on. It's time I turned you over to the feds."

"Lucky me," Daniel said and followed along, frowning and pushing his way through the crowds.

"Hey, cowboy."

Jerking to a halt, Daniel recognized the voice. He looked through the crowds before finding a man he never expected to see again. One with an eastern European accent and a piece of straw dangling from the corner of his mouth—Nevada Slim.

"What are you doing here?"

The crowds parted for Slim. The slender elf was dressed sharply in a tailored suit of darkest midnight with a pencil thin, crimson tie. "I could ask the same of you. Last I heard you didn't want anything to do with our world."

"I didn't, Slim. Lord knows I tried sneaking out, but it keeps drawing me back. What have you been up to since New York?" He ignored the whispers questioning whether he was 'the author' or not circulating through the crowds.

"It's Baron now, Daniel. My father getting killed left me with his holdings and titles. Not something I wanted but the queen wouldn't let me escape," Slim replied, an edge to his tone. "No more DESA strike team. No more free living. I've been bound to a desk for almost a year."

Daniel grinned, enjoying knowing he wasn't the only one locked in place. "How's that?"

Slim took the straw out and cast it on the carpet. "I hate every fucking minute of it."

They shook hands. Daniel taking the opportunity to pull his old friend in close, much to the angst of Slim's security detail that shifted closer. "Watch your back here."

The elf nodded, clapping Daniel on the shoulder before disappearing into the crowds. Personal security combined with Max's detail to form a defensive ring around Slim.

"What was that all about?" Max asked once Daniel caught up to him. "Rubbing hands with royalty?"

"He's an old friend."

Gaze lingering on the back of Slim's head, Max was unconvinced Daniel's explanation was straightforward. One assassination attempt already set him on edge. The big question being how did the killer know Max oversaw security and why was he being targeted? A man used to being in charge and a step ahead of his foes, the dwarf felt like he was barely treading water in the deep end of the pool without knowing how to swim. He'd already been a target once tonight, or had it been Daniel? That uncertainty gnawed on his confidence.

"This is getting out of control," he admitted aloud, the jewels in his beard jangling when he shook his head.

"What is?"

Max closed his eyes to recenter his thoughts. Ashamed to admit it, the assassination attempt rattled him on multiple levels. He knew he played a bigger role in this conference, often seeing himself as a roadblock meant to blunt knives seeking targets. As a dwarf, he had no issues with that. His people served as frontline troops and special details since the dawn of their society. Too many variables remained beyond his ability to control in this scenario, and time was running out to find answers.

"Daniel, we need to talk," he muttered. He felt like his resolve was breaking down. "I have a bad feeling about tonight. The storm is here. Hell, it's been threatening us for years and is bringing matters to a head. We're a step behind whoever is coming and that terrifies me." *The Mrs. told me not to come. Said this time was different than the others. And in true Max fashion I blew her off and sucked in both of our boys. How am I going to explain it to her if one of us dies?*

Daniel froze. For a dwarf to admit fear, at least in his experience, inspired foul thoughts. Any preconceived notions of the fabrication of the seriousness of this assignment went out the window as Daniel was confronted with a man facing real loss. "Max, you're just overthinking this," he attempted then. "An event this large, with so many high priority attendees is bound to draw the crazies. We survived the goblin nest. We will this as well."

"This is different," the dwarf countered before waving. "Bah! Listen to me, an old maid crying about the future. Don't mind me, lad. I think I've seen one too many battles." He paused to stroke his beard and scan the nearby area. "Come on, we don't want to keep the government waiting."

Worried over the exchange, Daniel followed Max through the still growing crowds. Security began rifling through the ranks. Others remained separated, guarding access points and main avenues of traffic flow. Every inch of the building was under now surveillance. Miniature drones, thanks to Goran's tinkering and wit, and the giant's inability to keep secrets around those he considered friend, lurked in the upper corners all but unseen by the attendees. Daniel didn't doubt assault and reaction teams were on standby nearby. He found it a remarkable operation.

Not that it did much to assuage his concerns over Max's temporary meltdown. He'd seen it before, and it never turned out well. Plenty of times in Iraq and Afghanistan he ran into leaders mired by doubts or filled with premonitions. After one too many IED strikes, Daniel ended up avoiding one of his leaders because of their anxiety. His strategy worked for a time, but casualties were always inevitable, and he had to report to that specific officer at the time. Max's sense of foreboding slowly filtered to Daniel and that was not what he needed right now.

Max pushed open the small service door to the rear of the stairwell, offering a crisp nod to the handful of dignitaries entering the nearby elevator, and gestured Daniel to go first. Drawing a deep breath, Daniel found himself in an access hall that according to a nearby map ran the length of the building, through all three venue spaces.

They hurried to the end and went up one flight to the second floor where Daniel found a room filled with computer monitoring tables and government agents scouring every detail.

"Daniel Thomas. It's been a while."

Daniel put on his best false smile and turned to face Thaddeus Blackmere. "Blackmere. How does it feel being back in Raleigh?"

Thaddeus Blackmere regarded him with veiled eyes. Daniel studied him in turn. Salt and pepper hair clung to his scalp, accenting the standard black suit Washington favored. From previous conversations, Daniel knew the man had spent a lifetime in service to his country, first in the Navy and then with DESA. Men like Daniel were a dime a dozen to men like Blackmere. The first time they met resulted in the zoo debacle and Alvin's death.

"Just thought I'd stop for some bar-be-que," the agent finally replied. "I assume you've been read in on the situation?"

"Enough. Max here didn't mention you by name though," Daniel remarked, casting a look at the dwarf. "I guess the government is worried too?"

A growl from Max's throat raised the hairs on his arms. Daniel saw Blackmere stiffen, casting his own look upon the dwarf. A few heads cocked in their direction, but none turned.

"This is a naturally tense situation, no different from any of the major nation leader's conferences,"

Blackmere explained. "We are here to monitor only. What happens today will have reverberations throughout the elf community for generations."

Daniel didn't doubt that. His sole question however remained: what happens when it all goes wrong? And how was Washington going to pick up the pieces if word gets out that elves were real? Panic would ensue, followed by anger and the instinctual human aggression that would eventually devolve into an open war of extermination. *I'll be damned if I let it come to that. Nothing is going to keep me from saving my family. Nothing.*

"I suppose I get to report to you for this," he said to break the awkwardness of the moment.

Blackmere nodded. "I want you running point between Mr. Schneider and myself until this wraps up and the dignitaries are back on their planes or convoys headed home. This is a high threat situation, and we need the best on the ground. That means you."

Daniel flushed. Human liaison indeed. He knew he was good, but this just confirmed he hadn't blown his chance and was still being courted by DESA… *So much for being left alone. What was my plan again?*

EIGHT

Sara felt like a secretary from a 1960s advertising agency. Not that she didn't look good. The shape and fit of the calf-length black dress seemed tailored specifically for her. Slender where it needed to be with just a hint of imagination, it fit like a second skin. As much as she found herself loving the look, she could not ignore the attached price. A thin layer of body armor lined the fabric. Weightless and capable of stopping a 7.62mm round, she was told it would save her life from potential snipers or assassins. Aislinn completed her outfit with sensible heels and a small handgun that fit in the briefcase at her feet.

"There," the elf declared with a beam. "No one will suspect you are as lethal as you are functional. I think this is a good look for you. I assume you know how to use this."

"You live with a vet and see how long before you can use a gun, but I'm not a fighter, regardless of what Morgen thinks, Aislinn," Sara protested. "That bit with the werewolves was an accident and a one-time event as far as I'm concerned."

Aislinn bristled at the mention of the lycans. Sara remembered then that the elf had nearly died when the pack leader made his assault on Morgen' inner sanctum. "Sorry," Sara offered.

"You are more than you think, Sara," she all but whispered. "These are difficult times and I fear much will change in the next day or so. Do not let your doubt or feelings of not belonging sway your judgement. The queen will have need of you soon enough, regardless of what she might say. I do not envy you for this."

"Neither do I," Sara said. *The one time I need Daniel he's nowhere around.* "What can I expect from this meeting?"

Aislinn glanced at the entry, as if fearful the queen

would storm in. "This must stay between us, but there is a movement growing in the clans. Many are not happy with her leadership, especially after they believe she played a role in the king's death. This is a dangerous time for the clans. Keep your wits about you. Trust no one."

"Why should I listen to you then?" Sara countered, sliding a step away from the elf. It dawned on her that she was alone, adrift in a sea of rising madness from a people determined to self-destruct. Perhaps she'd misjudged her initial opinions of Morgen. Sara started thinking this might be a mistake.

Aislinn's eyes hardened. "I mean trust no one you have not met before. I am as loyal to the queen as I was the first day I earned my position seven hundred years ago."

Damn. You look good for being that old. Sara shook her head to clear her thoughts. "What about Morgen? She's already professed no love for humans, especially Daniel and myself. What's to keep her from turning on me?"

The elf stiffened, pursing her lips in thought. It had been too long since any dared question the queen to her. The feeling was…uncomfortable.

"Morgen is the most honorable one of us all," Aislinn said stiffly. Color ran up her neck. "One does not question a queen. Now, if you are through with your foolish questions, there is much work to be done before we head to the conference."

She stalked off without further comment, clearly expecting Sara to follow. Much to her annoyance, Sara did. The click of their heels on the marble floor drove like daggers between her ears. Sara slowly began to concede she could get used to what she considered a spy's life, without danger of course.

Norman Guilt lurked in the hall of the upper floor waiting for Sara's return. When the elf and Sara appeared, he regarded them without speaking. He knew his taciturn nature was off putting to most. Of all the creatures he encountered since fleeing his decimated homeland, Norman found Sara the only one worthy of his conversation. Seeing her marching beside the elf inspired a frown, producing an echo of his darkest memories before entering servitude to the crown. He wished she wasn't here. Not now. Not for this. Norman withheld his sigh and adjusted his jacket.

The gargoyle suddenly felt foolish in the suit and tie Morgen insisted on. Once, he would have soared away, but his wings still did not work right after his battle with the lycan pack leader. Yet another sore spot in his relationship with the elves. He longed for freedom. The opportunity to stalk the ancient forests of his home in search of any survivors. Perhaps the queen might grant him this one request at the end of the conference. Norman doubted it. Elves were creatures of habit and once they sank their claws in, they almost never removed them.

Lamenting his station, Norman tipped his head to Sara as she stopped before him. "Sara Thomas, that dress suits you."

"Thank you, Norman," she said with a smile.

"It will stop most bullets and all arrows. A good choice," he admired the microfiber cut.

Her smile dropped. "Let's hope it doesn't come to any of that." She cleared her throat. "I take it Morgen is waiting on me?"

He nodded, having been waiting in place since Sara was first taken away. "The queen is most eager, and reluctant, to see this matter through. She does not say it, but I believe the threat of the Invisible Hand worries her greatly."

Sara's stomach clutched. Thoughts of a shadow organization of killers and manipulators lurking behind the scenes of power throughout history terrified her. She caught plenty of conspiracy theory documentaries and, while she seldom bought into any of them, knew each contained a kernel of truth. If this Invisible Hand did in fact exist, all signs pointed to a cleansing pogrom capable of bringing the elf clans to their knees for the decapitating strike. Aislinn's warning suddenly made a lot more sense.

"Best we don't keep her waiting," she said, laying a hand on his forearm. *I need to get back to Daniel's side. This is madness and nothing has happened yet!*

Norman stepped aside and opened the door for them. "A wise choice."

She and Aislinn entered the main lobby with Norman a respectable step behind, expecting to find the queen waiting. Instead, they caught a scattering of business professionals streaming in and out of the dual bars with cocktails in hand.

"That is the most I have heard him speak in a long time," Aislinn mused as they slipped through the streams to find the queen. "He must hold you in high regard."

"We got to know one another well last year. I trust him with my life," Sara replied. Though their quest had been rife with danger and traitors, Sara admired the gargoyle on a fundamental level many of her closest friends lacked. "I can't thank Norman enough for all he's done for me and my family." *Mostly him saving my life from that psychopath who tried to kill me in my own bathroom.*

Lost in thought, she stumbled into Morgen. The queen tilted her head down, watching Sara take a step back.

"It is time," Morgen announced.

If Sara thought the queen looked regal earlier, she had been mistaken. A smattering of self-control was the only factor keeping her mouth from dropping. Dressed in a crimson dress that shimmered with each movement, Morgen was the definition of regality. Her hair, luxurious and dark as the night, was pulled back in a tight bun that would have lent most women a severe look. On Morgen it only served to heighten her authority. No makeup, Morgen's face didn't have a crease or wrinkle on it. A raven broach decorated her left breast. The symbol of her house, before rising to become leader of the dark elves—or so Aislinn had explained when Sara declined having a raven pin herself.

Taking in Sara's silence, the queen glanced at herself. Seeing the pin, and noticing that is what Sara kept glancing at, had Morgen satisfied. The inclusion of the pin was a minor acquiescence of neutrality that she hoped would go far in others' eyes. She sought unity tonight, not further division. By showing her house sigil, Morgen hoped to avoid accusations of favoritism from those aligned against her. Tensions already high in the wake of so many deaths, the clans were ready to break. They also were making her a scapegoat. Should the worst happen, Morgen would go down in history as the ruler who allowed her kingdom to dissolve into ruin while the human world picked the bones clean.

It was the stuff of nightmares. She saw the end. Her end. The slow dissolution of all she worked so hard to avoid. Nothing she did stopped it. No hopes. No dreams. No sign of life after this conference. She prayed for strength during those long hours huddled with her knees drawn and tears streaming down her face. Pride was the downfall of many leaders and Morgen vowed to do all within her power to save the clans and keep the approaching storm at bay.

"Your majesty, Norman Guilt is awaiting to escort us to your vehicle," Aislinn announced.

Refusing to withdrawal further into her thoughts, Morgen gave both women an appraising glance. "I trust all is in order. Has Constantin deployed yet?"

"He has. The Old Guard is already in position in and around the hall," her secretary replied. "I have been assured of their escort as well. The Invisible Hand shall not interfere with your arrival."

"If only that was enough to soothe my concerns," Morgen murmured, concealing the depths of her true worry over the threat. "Very well, let us go. I do so hate keeping our vaunted attendees waiting."

The Martin Marietta Center for the Performing Arts was already filled by the time the sun began setting. To most of Raleigh, it was another night of entertainment and nothing to concern themselves with. Enough bars and restaurants filled downtown to keep the population occupied. No one made note of the crimson and blue lights decorating the Center, nor the odd menagerie surrounding the building. It was just another night in the state capital.

For elfkind, it represented the culmination of thousands of years' worth of dissent and hostility. Reservations were made, lines drawn, across the area in anticipation of the final truce that would see the clans reunited and solidified moving forward or the final break that would bring their downfall. None knew what the queen had planned. It was just made known that the elves were stepping out of the age of antiquity and into the new century. It was past time.

Morgen's armored SUV rolled down the street with Norman at the wheel, her arrival slow and calculated to make a statement. She studied her notes, memorizing those tricky bits of any speech difficult to nail down. She and Aislinn discussed everything from the moment she would leave the vehicle to the second she stepped back into it while Sara tried to catch as many details as she could. Nothing was left to chance.

A cursory look outside showed multiple squads of Old Guard. Stalwart defenders of the throne long before Morgen rose to power, they represented all that was right about the clans. Rigid with authority and sure of purpose, they were the best of the best from each race. Paragons of virtue she thanked the gods for. They represented the best of the clans, humbling as it was.

Norman rolled the SUV to a stop and killed the engine.

It's time.

Sara watched Norma move with impossible fluidity. The gargoyle had their door open before she realized he had gotten out of the truck.

Aislinn went first, as discussed while driving. Sara had felt a rush of anger when she realized the elf was a sacrifice. Yet, Aislinn did her job without comment. Certain acts were expected while serving the queen. In the event an enemy sniper had not been detected, Aislinn would not let the queen die.

Doing her best to ignore the rising fear threatening to rob her strength, Sara screwed her eyes shut and followed as the second to leave the SUV.

The expected shot did not come. No pain in her chest from a bullet's kiss.

Several heartbeats passed before Norman's subtle cough reminded her to open her eyes and move forward. Of the hundred or so men and women standing outside the building, not a one gave her more than a passing glance. Their eyes were glued to the car door and the elegance that was Queen Morgen stepping out. Captivated and enthralled, heads began bowing one by one. Sara found herself eager to get inside, if for no other reason than to get a glimpse into the innermost workings of elfkind.

While Sara marveled at their display, Morgen ignored them, as was expected, and took the lead, striding into the building and down the corridor the Old Guard cleared for her, for them. People bowed as they passed. Conversation faded until the small retinue swept past. Sara had been in this auditorium a few times for various events, nothing as serious as the elf conclave.

At their backs the crowd shifted in anticipation, though remained in place until Sara saw what had to be the Old Guard leader, Constantin Andros, nod his head in permission for them to follow. Fidgeting, Sara began counting guards lining the backstage area. Her heart skipped a beat, succumbing to the thrill of the moment.

Once inside the makeshift conference room, Sara watched the crowd flock to their seats, eager and terrified to hear the queen's words on this momentous occasion. There were no hushed conversations. No whispered criticisms or doubts as the queen stood watching them enter. To Sara it was clear the members of the clans knew this moment alone deserved silence.

The doors closed and Morgen, sole ruler of the elf clans and last of her house, took her place at the head of the table.

Sara held her breath.

NINE

His inner child was refusing to be put away as he saw this as a prime opportunity to shine. Decades of watching endless streams of shows, movies, and reading books left Daniel inspired by his sharp suit and holstered pistol nestled against his ribs. The only thing missing was a pair of sunglasses and an earpiece. He chuckled at the image, both amused and dismayed at how easily he slipped into this new persona. Perhaps it stemmed from a career writing fantasy, of constantly making up every nuanced detail for his stories, that provided him with a familiarity he hadn't known he held. Regardless, his presence as a security agent, labelling himself as a guard was too far beneath him for this affair, set him on edge. *Time to grow up and focus. It's game time.*

"So many people," he muttered. Daniel looked but failed to pick out Sara through the crowds. "How are we supposed to recognize a threat before they act?"

"Daniel, this detail is no different than providing security for a visiting dignitary. I assumed you had done this before," Blackmere replied, crossing his arms while keeping his gaze on the streams of people flowing into the main hall.

"I have, but never on this level. Most of my assignments were for things like the Army-Navy game or division commanders. Never for royalty." *Or elves.*

"Relax. We have every inch of this place covered. No one is getting in here," Blackmere insisted.

The gentle urgency in his tone did little to sooth Daniel's rising nerves. He fixed the older agent with a raised eyebrow. "You do realize someone says that right before it all goes south, right?"

"You watch too much television. We are fine. I expect this conference to go off without a hitch, at least from a security perspective."

The minute hitch in his speech, barely perceptible unless one was looking for it, sent ripples through Daniel's confidence. Thoughts of boogeymen souring his mood, he settled in for what he presumed to be a long night. Part of the problem stemmed from not being able to distinguish elf from dwarf or any of the other species in attendance. They all looked human. Curiously, he noticed there were no goblins present. Had the Charleston assault broken those relations permanently or was something more nefarious in play? He didn't want to know the answer.

Blackmere suddenly dropped his arms and stood a little straighter, his gaze fixed on a bald head worming through the crowd. Daniel followed his line of sight but found no reason for the behavior. Enough problems lurked among the gathering. What was the point in worrying over a single man? It was all he could not to think about Sara. Knowing she was out there, with the queen, and tangled in what he deemed an impossible mess with no easy way out put him on the defensive. All he needed was to see the back of her head. Anything to know she was safe.

"Heads up," Blackmere said. "I need you on your best behavior, at least for the next few minutes."

Frowning at the implication, Daniel asked, "What's up?"

"The boss is here."

So that's why you stiffened like a dead fish in the sun. I wonder if this guy is half the prick you are? Concealing his amusement by scratching the corner of his mouth, Daniel followed Blackmere's lead and straightened.

Their wait ended a moment later when the man emerged from the crowd. Everything about him screamed bureaucrat, from the cut of his suit to the way he strode through the assembly with impunity. Daniel's gaze fell to the man's right hand and the almost imperceptible patch covering much of it. Coincidence? He was experienced enough not to leave anything to chance, but Blackmere didn't seem taken off guard.

"Agent Blackmere, I will be assuming ground control for the duration of this assignment," the man said without a trace of emotion.

That answers my question.

He turned to Daniel and frowned. "Who is this?"

"Deputy Director Corman, this is Daniel Thomas. If you remember, he has worked with us on several occasions in the past," Blackmere supplied. "He has proven invaluable in our efforts to keep the elf civil war contained."

"Thomas, eh? I've heard good things. James Corman."

Daniel accepted the proffered hand, surprised by the firmness in the grip. It had been a long time since he shook a man's hand that had such confidence. The slight crunch of bones shifting was almost buried under the strong cologne wafting off Corman. Daniel did his best not to crinkle his nose or sneeze.

"Happy to help," Daniel lied.

Satisfied, Corman returned his attention to Blackmere. "I trust all is in order. No surprises or hiccups thus far?"

"None, sir," Blackmere reported. "This facility is sealed up from a security standpoint. I have coordinated all efforts with the elves. Max Schneider is head of security. He has things in hand, perhaps better than we managed."

"Has the queen arrived?"

"Not yet but she is enroute."

Corman pointed a thin finger at Blackmere, ignoring Daniel now completely. "I don't want any issues. Nothing goes wrong tonight. We can't afford it, Blackmere. Am I understood?"

To his credit, Thaddeus Blackmere stood his ground. "Crystal, sir."

"Good. Now, where is the opcenter?"

Max's voice thundered in their earpieces. "Head's up people. Her majesty is arriving. I want heads on a swivel.

No one so much as farts without me knowing. Clear?"

Max's deep voice reminded Daniel of a tiger trying to break free from a cage. Angry, impulsive. Every negative emotion he could think of without compromising his authority was shown in his delivered orders. Daniel caught the smoldering glower in Corman's eyes. *So, you haven't encountered our dwarven friends? Or maybe you don't like them either. They are a lot to handle on a good day. This should be fun.*

The dwarf halted before them, pausing to look at Corman. "Who's the string bean?"

"Deputy Director James Corman," Corman answered, dryly. "I assume you are Max Schneider?"

Daniel saw Max bristle but held his calm, as much as the dwarf could at least. "Mister, to you." He turned his glare on Blackmere. "What is this, Blackmere? I thought you had the ball?"

"I am a servant of the people, Max. The department does what it needs to. Please don't make this more difficult than it has to be."

Max sneered. "No promises." His gaze went back to Corman and Daniel swallowed a groan at the dwarf's look. "I need you to stay out of the way, Deputy Director. This is a dwarf matter."

"Don't mess up and you can forget I am here," Corman replied. Despite the tension, he remained calm. Almost too calm.

Max offered a noncommittal grunt and resumed barking at his staff.

Corman turned to Blackmere after Max left and said, "I like him. He's got character."

"He is a personality," Blackmere agreed with a hint of relief in his tone. "If you will follow me, sir. I trust you intend on greeting the queen when she arrives?"

"That's part of why I'm here. Your office should have been notified. Lead on, Blackmere."

Daniel settled in behind them, uncertain of this new

development. His gaze remained on James Corman's back. Something sat wrong with the man but what Daniel couldn't put his finger on.

Nestled in a secluded corner backstage, they stood a respectful distance apart. None spoke, though it was clear each sized up the other. Daniel stood off to the side with Blackmere and Max. The dwarf clenched and unclenched his fists nonstop. Sara and Aislinn waited across the room with a trio of Old Guards. All eyes were focused on the queen of the dark elves and the man from Washington.

"Your majesty, it is an honor to meet you," Corman said with a flourished bow. "I assure you all have been executed above standard. Your conference will go off without delay."

Morgen viewed the man with the natural distrust of one who had been subjugated for too long. They were not equals, though the human presented himself a step above her. That arrogance sat ill with her. Since the federal government decided to keep the clans down with the creation of DESA they often thought themselves superior. She longed to break those shackles and return her people to freedom. Compounding her insecurities was the fact no one notified her of such a high level official in attendance.

Wearing her best smile, Morgen expected nothing less. This is a momentous occasion for both of our peoples. It is time to put the past to rest. A new future is necessary, one where we will no longer require your overwatch. Perhaps usher in a new age of peace and prosperity as well."

He nodded. Rough and dismissive.

Morgen in turn dismissed him, sweeping her gaze over the small gathering and pausing on Daniel lurking a step behind Corman. Her tailors did a remarkable job of cleaning him up. Sara deserved a man like that. Clean. Proper. Elegant. Her gaze lingered on the human just long enough for him to notice. Appreciating her handiwork, Morgen slid in behind Max and continued on her way to the most important moment of her long life.

Sara wrung her hands. Nervous energy kept her bouncing from foot to foot, fidgeting. She hadn't been this nervous since their son's eighth grade graduation. At least then she had stakes involved. Regardless of the outcome today, Sara wasn't an elf. Never would be.

Aislinn frowned as she watched the human's hands. "You're giving yourself arthritis."

"Come again?" Sara asked.

Aislinn nodded at her hands. "That's not good for you."

The whisk of skirts and the clip of heels announced Morgen returning from her meeting with the DESA agents. A disconcerted look twisted her face. Aislinn bowed and asked, "Is everything in order, your Majesty?"

"I wonder," Morgen mused. "Best not keep our distinguished guests waiting. Go ahead and announce me."

"Yes, ma'am," Aislinn bowed again and gave Sara an unreadable look before slipping through the curtains.

"All rise for her majesty and regent of the clans, Queen Morgen!"

The rustle of over two thousand leaders, dignitaries, and heads of families rising filled the hall, drowning out the decreasing conversation. A lone trumpet bleated a mournful tune.

An escort of elves and dwarves, the best of the Old Guard, marched onto the stage, resplendent in their dress uniforms. Rows of campaign ribbons, the idea likely stolen from the human military, decorated their chests. Polished silver helmets with crests of red running from front to back concealed their faces. The stomp of boots combined with the thump of silver capped staffs as they took their places. Strapped to each was their magic imbued sword, earned upon achieving their status.

Daniel watched them with rapt fascination. He held

no doubts over their lethality, despite the pomp and flair of their dress uniforms. Though this ceremony was unprecedented in recent history, the Old Guard remained prepared to handle any threat should it arise. Massive individuals, each served for a period of one hundred years, often called upon for clandestine missions reminiscent of special forces. Having witnessed their work firsthand and learned about their history earlier, Daniel knew the twenty men and women on stage were more than enough to neutralize the dourest threat.

An ancient rlf followed them. He wore flowing robes of clashing colors. Bones and fetishes decorated the front. A wreath of feathers lay around his neck, flowing down over slender shoulders. Deep lines gouged his face. Dark spots peppered his flesh. Wizened, the elf bore a skull crowned staff. He moved with a fluid grace Daniel didn't expect, taking his position a step to the left center of the stage facing the crowd.

The man rapped the staff twice and silence fell. The ancient swept his gaze over the crowd, boring into their souls with clouded eyes. He opened his mouth. Thin strips of saliva connecting his lips that had Daniel wincing.

"Her august majesty, Morgen Elloirise of House Hightower. Last of her name and first on the throne. Bow your heads and acknowledge." The thunder of the staff striking well-worn tile echoed through the room.

On cue, two thousand voices shouted, "Hail!"

Goosebumps ran up Daniel's arms. He'd seen his share of ceremonies, but nothing compared to the authority on display as the queen of the dark elves swept onto the stage. Had he not known her he might have assumed her a god for all the reverence given. He swallowed the lump in his throat, suddenly eager to see what came next.

The queen took her position beside the ancient and knelt. He reached into the faded leather pouch on his waist, dipping two fingers in before drawing two lines down each of her cheeks in a thick red liquid.

Morgen closed her eyes, shuddering as waves of power coalesced within her. The spirits of her forebearers were with her now. A quiet lament entered her mind as she felt Alvin, fallen king of the high elves and her husband of many years, join them. *If only you were here. I don't know if I am strong enough to do this alone.* When she opened them, she stared back at the shaman. Thousands of years old and he looked the same as he had when the clan split.

"The queen has been blessed by the dead. Rise accepted and take your rightful place at the head of the clans," the ancient said. Though whispered, his voice echoed like crashing waves upon the shore.

The smell of incense filled the hall, adding to Morgen's nerves as she obeyed. Years of fear and doubt settled in her mind. A heavy blanket threatening to swallow all. She closed her eyes and slowed her breathing. Morgen needed to present herself with confidence and in full control, otherwise the leaders might reject her despite the proclamations of the ancient. This was her moment. Her time to leave her mark on the clans and, if the gods decreed, elevate her to the voice of unity her people so desperately needed.

Opening her eyes, she saw not subjects but opportunities.

TEN

"For too long the clans have been divided by ideology, rhetoric, and vitriol. I make no denial for the role I have played in the past. Nor do I shirk from my duties as your queen. Through our division we fall behind, diminish. I have concluded this is no longer a viable lifestyle. It never was. We stumble to ruin through our arrogance. Blinded to the larger world squeezing us to oblivion.

"How many generations have fallen to nothing more than our ignorance? My late husband and I began this schism long before many of you were born. Many of those reasons why are lost to time. You all know Alvin's desire to reconcile our differences. At the time I fought against it, believing my cause was just. Much has changed since his passing. I no longer see purpose in those old beliefs. The time has come to step into the present. Each day we linger behind our masks of prejudices we suffer. Our children suffer."

She paused, letting the words sink in. A handful of attendees shifted, uncomfortable with her implications. Others bobbed their heads or nodded. Morgen felt the old authority resurface, strengthening her. She had the crowd on the verge of turning in her favor. All she needed was a little push.

"We have all grown complacent in the degeneration of our once great society. We are all guilty, though none more so than myself. For that, I shall stand judgment when the time comes. The rest of you must look deep inside and determine your culpability. But before you do, I must bring a dire situation to your attention. Many of you know of the recent action against the Ok'tal'med Nest. The goblins violated our treaties and took human captives. Had they been allowed to bring their plan to fruition they would have struck at the clans and driven us into total war.

The threat has been neutralized, for the moment. How many other goblin nests follow their example? How long before we are faced with a swarm of goblins hungry to devour our world?"

Morgen strode to the edge of the stage, content that all eyes were glued to her movements. She made a show of sweeping her gaze across the shadow darkened crowd from left to right, pausing on familiar faces as well as those whom she had not interacted with for too long. A subtle reminder of who and what she was. She took another step. The click of her heel loud, authoritative.

"The time of division is ended. I hereby propose the reunification of the clans. Together, we can usher in the future where all may once again prosper." She raised her voice so the farthest row could not even mistake her words, her meaning. The sternness in her gaze wilted some opposition and stiffened others.

"I put this to a vote," Morgen continued. She knew the risks of appearing weak, of letting them fester too long with their thoughts. A council of elders could vote for her instant removal should they determine she no longer represented the best interests of the clans. Morgen prayed her efforts leading up to this conclave, the months spent attempting to sway those important figures to her side, paid off.

The fact that several council members were dead did not go unnoticed by her. Most of the casualties were among her allies. Their votes would have ensured her motion passed. Morgen could do nothing about that now. She only had her impassioned speech that came from her soul. She prayed it was enough to sway those still on the fence. Change was always resisted, at first. She wished there had been more time to meet with the others before tonight, but the combination of goblins, lycans, and assassins forced her hand.

To her surprise, the newly appointed Baron Visilias stood first. Gone was the trademark piece of straw from his mouth. His severe features aged him; Morgen knew he was still young, but duty often came with a price. Clasping his hands before him, Visilias raised his head and Morgen held her breath at the intensity she saw.

"The Visilias family stands with the throne. I second reunification."

Several gasps rang out before a round of scattered clapping danced around the assembly, growing in intensity the longer it lasted. Morgen knew that Visilias had just placed a target on his back. She didn't care. Her need for allies trumped all other considerations. One man was not an army, however. Morgen needed more.

Her prayers were answered when a slender high elf woman rose and offered her support. One by one the gathering stood. She fought back the wave of tears threatening to break free. Plenty of nobles remained seated, their dour looks clear even in the gloom. Not enough though were opposed to turn the vote. Morgen clenched her fists to keep from smiling.

Chants began throughout the auditorium. Demands for reunification and a handful of calls for more time. She felt like a queen once more. An alien sensation that had been missing for too long. With it came her old pride. Imbued by the show of support, Morgen raised her hands for quiet. It took the ancient slamming his staff to produce silence.

"My friends, I cannot tell you what your support means. Together we shall bring forth a new world. Free from the old hates that have left us bereft of honor. Wolves have gathered, threatening to tear us down and feast on the ashes of our empire. No more shall we be dependent on the goodwill of others. Today we take the first steps to the freedom we have so long been missing! The time has come to reclaim our rightful place in this world! A time to work hand in hand with the humans and restore all that was lost!"

Her gaze hardened with a fierceness she hadn't felt in too long. Morgen thrust her fist in the air. "Today we return as lords of the earth!"

Morgen absorbed the cheers. Her heart swelled. From the corner of her eye, she caught movement. That's when all hell broke loose.

Sara stood just off stage, concealed from the throngs of staring faces. With Aislinn by her side, she watched Morgen step into her own. Until now, Sara wondered what made a woman a queen. This day, Morgen showed her. A power to be reckoned with and, if Sara was any judge, a force for the future the elves had been lacking.

"I wish our politicians had that presence," Sara whispered. "Maybe then it would be fun to vote. I've never heard anything like this."

"The queen has returned," Aislinn agreed. "Long have we awaited this moment, Sara Thomas."

"Do you think she can pull it off? This reunification?"

"She is the only one who can."

"I think—" Sara stopped when Aislinn tensed, her eyes on the far side of the stage. "What is it?"

"I thought I saw movement," the elf replied. "There, behind the curtain. Do you see?"

Sara squinted but failed to make out any distinguishable characteristics. She did notice the air conditioning vent in the ceiling and attributed Aislinn's concerns to nerves. "It's nothing but the AC. Must have kicked on and moved the curtain. Relax. Daniel and the others have this place extra secure."

Aislinn kept her focus on the curtain. "Perhaps you are correct, but we cannot take chances now."

She summoned one of the Old Guard not part of the ceremonial detail. After a whispered conversation, the elf hurried around behind the stage to inspect the curtains for Aislinn's boogeyman. Sara looked back to the stage where the queen launched into an invigorated plea to garner the support necessary to see her motion pass. Elves, dwarves, trolls, and gnomes began standing. Chants of Morgen's name reverberated but Sara felt an uneasiness settle against her spine.

The world exploded when Morgen raised her arms in triumph. Aislinn caught a glimpse of the Old Guard she dispatched as he peeled the curtain back—he burst apart in a puff of ash.

The assassin, covered from head to toe in dark rags preventing her from getting a good look at his face, stepped into sight before the ash settled. Right arm raised, he began firing from the wrist born bow. Foot long daggers slashed into the Old Guard that surrounded the queen. Several fell before they could react.

Aislinn screamed, "Your majesty!"

She burst onto the stage as screams rose from the crowd. Aislinn caught images of several bystanders dying, their long lives left to ruin.

The Invisible Hand had struck.

Panicked, they fled for the exits, preventing Max Schneider's teams from moving in.

A second killer leapt onto the stage, unconcerned with the sole surviving Old Guard battling his companion. Light danced off his silver blade as he stalked toward the queen.

Aislinn closed on the man, kicking him in the left knee. An audible pop followed by an agonized roar turned heads. Dropping to his good knee, the assassin held up his hands as if pleading for his life. Aislinn ignored him and went for the kill.

The killer moved in a whirlwind of rags and energy. He was back on his feet and plunging his dagger in her chest before she could blink. She grunted, eyes going wide, as he dropped her to the stage. "Your Majesty, run!"

Shocked, Morgen stepped back. All she worked so hard for now slipped from her grasp. Arrows sped through the audience, their rate of fire intensifying as more of Max's security forces barged in. The crowds were thinning, enough to provide open lanes of fire. From the corner of her eye, Morgen saw two more assassins go down, filled with arrows. Others sprang up from the crowd, striking at will. Morgen tensed as Aislinn's attacker stalked toward her with blood dripping from his blade. Rumors of the Invisible Hand being heartless, autonomous agents proved true. She caught the darkness of his eyes. Soulless. Emotionless.

Refusing to beg for her life, she stood her ground, prepared to meet whatever end destiny demanded with the dignity of her station. "Come, scum. You will not get the satisfaction of hearing me scream."

Movement from the corner of her eye had her glancing down, she was surprised to see Aislinn still clinging to life. Her assistant had managed to roll onto her stomach and was now crawling toward the assassin.

The killer reached for Morgen when Aislinn snatched him by the ankle. She had just enough strength to pull him off balance—the killer fell off the stage. An Old Guard rushed him, power sword raised above his head.

Morgen dashed to her assistant's side. This lone elf who had stood by her side through the darkest moments. The one who sacrificed her life. "Aislinn."

Blood trickled from the corner of the elf's mouth. Her face contorted in time with the spasms racking her body. Aislinn raised a hand and touched Morgen's cheek. Her fingers were stained with blood. "Your majesty, it…it has been…my…honor."

She burst apart in Morgen's arms. Ash and dust piling at the queen's feet.

Morgen yelled, a unique combination of rage and sorrow. Aislinn deserved better. She should have been a head of family, not the victim of an assassination attempt.

The queen was pushing off the floor when head exploded in pain.

ELEVEN

"Something's going right in there," Daniel commented upon hearing the chorus of cheers.

Max grunted, continuing to pick his teeth as he focused on the crowd still milling about the lobby. His gaze never settled, constantly moving from one person to the next in search of targets or potential threats. His natural distrust of everyone made him the perfect person for the job. Daniel couldn't help but admire the dwarf, not that he would ever tell him that.

"Heads up, soldier boy. We're about to get a visit from the head man himself," Max pointed at the figure striding through the lobby.

Daniel wasn't in the mood for more dignitaries or nobles. He needed the conference to end so he and Sara could go home again. "Great," he muttered. He vaguely recognized the man approaching. Something about the surety in his step reminded Daniel of...? He wasn't able to reach a conclusion before the man stopped before them.

"Schneider, good to see you again."

"Constantin. Been a long time."

An unreadable look in his eye, he turned to Daniel. "Constantin Andros. We met in New York, did we not?"

"More or less." Daniel found himself impressed despite the urge not to be. Thought they hadn't spoken to each other in the aftermath of the raid on the Fainting Goat Inn, Daniel recalled the martial assault he and the other Old Guard exhibited after dropping from the sky.

"Your team did good work, from what I recall," Constantin continued. "It would have been nice to recapture

Xander and the princess, but their fates were out of our hands."

"They got what they deserved," Daniel agreed. "A shame. Xander and I crossed paths more than once."

"The champion fell far before the end," the elf replied. "He has become another stain on our great history. Better he met his end on his feet than in a cell, though. I can't imagine what those people in the Grinder feel. At any rate, you and your people did good work. I'm glad to see you here now. We need reliable men to oversee this criminal."

Max scowled at the dig. "That was a long time ago and you never had proof." Daniel really wanted to ask about this apparent crime, but the dwarf continued. "What's the word from your side?"

"The queen is convinced the Invisible Hand is going to make a move, but I have not found any evidence to support it," Constantin replied. "My people are stationed outside and in the ceremonial honor guard. Intel hasn't picked up any significant threats. You?"

"Same. We have this placed locked down so tight a fart couldn't escape," the dwarf said with pride. "Nothing is ge—"

The chorus of cheers turned to screams. Daniel's heart clutched. *Sara!* He drew his pistol and chambered a round. Shoving his way past the ring of nearby elves and dwarves frozen in confusion, he sprinted toward the entry hallway. He made it halfway before skidding to a halt. Two figures in black blocked his way. Each wielded a curved dagger a foot long. The one on the right gestured.

Daniel raised his weapon and fired.

The first attacker dropped, clutching his stomach. Blood spread. The dagger slipped from his hands. He fell, striking the carpet. Daniel's eyes widened when the body failed to disappear. They were human! He spied the faded tattoo on the back of the dead man's hand and froze. The second man used the distraction to lunge at Daniel's throat.

Constantin crashed into him at the last moment.

The two fell in a heap of flesh and fury. Fists lashed out.

Daniel regained his senses and leapt over them. Sara was in danger and nothing was going to stop him from reaching her.

He ran into another wall of Invisible Hand killers. Three.

He opened fire.

They scattered. His shots went wide. Daniel kept firing until the telltale click of an empty magazine resounded in his ears. Old training kicked in. He charged the enemy, slamming the pistol's handle on the nearest man's forehead. Bone cracked. Daniel followed up with a pair of blows to the nose and temple, driving the man back off his feet.

Pain lanced through Daniel's ribs: a razor's slash into his body armor. The force of the blow drove him to his knees, gasping for breath. He ran a hand over the area, surprised to find no blood. The subsequent kick to his ribs had him swearing as a rib snapped.

"Get out of the way, you damned fool human!"

He was fighting to his feet when blurred shapes, two men, launched into the two Invisible Hand operatives.

The fight grew in the hall around him. Bodies collided. Blood flowed. Bones snapped. Muttered curses and vented oaths poured forth. Daniel noticed the Invisible Hand were silent even in pain.

He blinked. Where did the third go? Daniel, still on the floor, found one of the curved daggers within reach. So did the last assassin who was crawling forward. They went for it simultaneously. Daniel edged him out, curling his fingers around the hilt and pulling away as the man slid on the carpet. Daniel threw an elbow to his face, worsening the damage done on his initial strike.

The rush of feet escalated the battle. DESA agents and elves rushed to assist. Soon the hall became a melee. A puff of ash drifted over Daniel. An arrow riddled body fell. He lost track of who fought who, instead focusing on the wounded man still confronting him. He was dressed in dark, lightweight clothes complete with a head covering and face mask concealing all but his hate filled eyes. *Does this guy think he's a fucking ninja?*

Daniel slipped inside the man's defenses after they traded another set of blows, driving the dagger he still held up into the man's chin and through the brain. The killer's eyes rolled to the back of his head, ropes of drool spilling free as he died.

Dniel struggled to his feet. Stepping over the corpse, Daniel grabbed his pistol he'd lost during his battle with the assassin and reloaded. Pain lanced up and down his side, forcing him to clutch with his free hand. He caught Max's eyes.

The dwarf shook his head. Blood stained his face, crimson streaks funneling down to his beard. "Go! Save the queen!"

Daniel paused, torn between duty and desire. A quick surveillance of the battlefield showed his allies had the numbers, but many were already slain. He didn't know what sort of fighter these Invisible Hand were, but they proved a force to be reckoned with.

Max took a ridge hand to the side of his neck, felling him with a muted groan. Daniel took a step toward the stricken dwarf before one of Blackmere's people moved in to protect Max. It was that moment he decided he would be of more use trying to reach Morgen, and Sara, than here.

Sprinting down the gradual slope, Daniel stepped over the ash piles of those who had fallen. One of the doors stood ajar, marked by the flicker of light dangling from the ceiling. Steel arrows lay in the ash piles. Daniel thought he spotted a pool of blood, but the patterns of the already dark carpet prevented him from being certain. All signs pointed to an ambush. Tucking his pistol into a ready position, he crept to the edge of the door, shifting to get a glimpse inside.

He leapt back as a flood of escapees poured out. Hundreds of bodies desperate to survive. His fears rose. The egress confirmed the worst. The Invisible Hand was within. He needed to move fast if any of the royal bloodline was to survive this night, but the way remained choked off. Frustrations threatening to boil over, Daniel caught the sign a little further down announcing the entrance for crew. There was nothing he could do for those fleeing the hall. That stampede would soon run into the battle in the lobby. Raw chaos threatened to bring the roof down.

Daniel elbowed the man blocking his way just hard enough to make him move and hurried to the behind the stage access point. Unguarded and with no sign of struggle, he stepped inside. Dim lights created a host of shadows capable of hiding one of the black garbed killers. Daniel ignored the nagging doubts questioning his moves and plunged forward without regard. Saving Morgen was a secondary consideration. His thoughts revolved around ensuring his wife survived. Nothing else mattered.

Movement at the far end of the stage drew his eye. Daniel raised his pistol, searching for a clear shot. Fire discipline kicked in. Regardless of his urgency in finding Sara, he needed to ensure he had a viable target. He quickened his pace, doing his best to keep his steps light to avoid giving his position away.

Crates of stage props created a natural obstacle course while also providing cover. Daniel wove through them and reached the end without issue. Kneeling by the last crate, he had a view of the stage. One man fought against a handful of Old Guard. Another assassin stood over Morgen's stricken form. Sounds of battle came from the audience. He looked around but could not find Sara. *Okay, first thing first. Neutralize the threat and begin recovery.*

Daniel slowed his breathing. His right hand trembled. Any man saying he had no nerves before stepping into a firefight lied. Years of combat experience and the sensation never went away, even after a decade in retirement. Daniel raised his weapon and crept forward. He was too late. The assassin slung Morgen over his shoulder and sprinted toward the exit, using the confusion and diversion of his companion to break away unseen.

Daniel took aim but didn't have a clear shot. Too much of Morgen was in the way. Cursing, he watched the assassin leave the stage. He hurried after the assassin, desperate to keep Morgen from dying.

"Don't. It's a trap!" a familiar voice shouted.

Daniel scanned the area. A haggard Nevada Slim pointed in the direction the assassin fled. Around him, a handful of dark elves subdued the last assassin in the audience.

The battle, in his mind, was finished. Daniel lowered his pistol and dashed to Sara's side when he saw her hiding behind a stack of crates. She looked up with tear filled eyes. Her mouth moved but no words came forth. His heart broke. She was one of the strongest people he knew. To see her in such a state robbed his strength, threatened to render him impotent. Knowing no words were good enough, he wrapped an arm around her shoulders and touched his forehead to hers.

They were safe, but so much had gone wrong. Ashes filled the stage. Dirtied the seats. How many had been killed would not be known for some time, but he estimated the numbers high. The side doors flung open. Max, Constantin, and Blackmere rushed in. They were battered and bruised, but far from broken. He had never been gladder to see them.

"Where's the queen?" Constantin demanded of his Old Guard.

"They took her," Daniel spoke up after none of the elves answered. "That door."

Constantin nodded. "We need to move. Now before they get away."

Daniel realized he still had a choice to make. Sara

clutched him tighter.

TWELVE

Nevada Slim shed his torn jacket as he stepped over the body of the man he just killed. The dark elf leapt onto the stage, joining the already odd combination of men and dwarves. The shared a look before Daniel returned his attention to the commander of the Old Guard.

"You have enough men," he said. "My place is here with my wife."

Constantin's face darkened. He balled a fist.

To Daniel's surprise, it was Sara who spoke. "Daniel, you can't let them take her. You can't. Don't let them do to her what they did Aislinn and all the others." She pulled away and looked down at the ash near her feet. "She deserved better. So does Morgen."

Max glowered. "We are wasting time."

"I will take care of your wife," Slim announced, moving to stand over her like a guardian of old. "She will be safe with my people."

Fuck it. They're not going to let up until I join their death race. "Fine. Let's get this over with."

Blackmere slapped a fresh magazine into his pistol and stepped to Daniel's side. "I'm coming too. The Invisible Hand needs to be stopped."

Constantin drew his sword, the blade glowed yellow with eldritch magic. "Too much talking. We go. Now."

"Wait," Daniel called even as he took a step to join them. "Won't they be expecting us to follow? I don't feel like walking into a trap."

"He's got a point. Any enemy worth their salt would have the exit points watched for pursuit. The potential of ambushes or traps was high. They cut through us with little effort," Max reluctantly agreed and then added, "even if they did strike like cowards. There'll be hell to pay once we determine how they infiltrated the delegates so easily."

Daniel watched as Constantin clicked the earpiece then spoke, "Overwatch, this is Andros. Enemy personnel have abducted the queen. Shoot on sight. I repeat. Shoot on sight. Whoever lets them escape with her majesty will suffer a decade in the Grinder."

Finding the punishment severe, Daniel wondered what the elf thought about his own failures. None of them did what they were assigned to do. The Invisible Hand walked into the middle of the conference, through a thick blanket of security, and abducted the queen from under their noses without effort. Many were dead, but there were no prisoners. Dedicated fanatics. Reclaiming the queen wasn't going to be easy. If she wasn't already dead. It didn't take much imagination for Daniel to envision several of them joining the ranks of the dead. Fallen heroes in a legacy of disgrace. He had no plans of dying this day, Invisible Hand be damned.

A radio attached to Constantin's hip squelched. "We have movement. Target is fleeing on South Wilmington Street. On foot and alone."

"Confirm he has the queen," Constantin demanded.

"Affirmative."

"How did he get past the outer security cordon?" Daniel asked. He sensed the eagerness for Constantin to charge headfirst into danger and aimed for a more cautious approach. "Ask if they can spot any potential escape vehicle. There's no way one man is going to run all the way into hiding with a body on his shoulder."

Unless these monsters had superhuman strength. If that's the case, we're all screwed. He knew, if the assassin reached a getaway vehicle they had almost no chance of saving Morgen. They listened as Constantin relayed the message, all of them waiting with baited breaths for the reply.

"Roger. Headlights spotted in the lot across the

street. Target is moving to that location."

Max cursed.

"It's not over yet," Constantin rebuked. "Overwatch, do you have a clear line of sight on the driver? I don't want that vehicle escaping us."

"I got him!" Goran's deep voice broke in.

The sound of an engine gunning echoed through the mostly empty auditorium as the radio cackled. Daniel's eyes widened. Only one person in Raleigh had the firepower to produce so much chaos.

"Stand down, Goran," Constantin ordered. "You are jeopardizing the mission. I repeat, stand down."

The giant either ignored him or did not hear over the roar of his vehicle.

"Goran…"

The bark of twin heavy machine guns opened up.

"We need to move!" Daniel shouted. He grabbed Slim by the arm. "Keep her safe, Slim. Please."

"You have my word," the dark elf vowed.

Satisfied Sara was in good hands, he leaned over and kissed her forehead. "I'll be right back."

"Kill that bastard and bring her back."

He grinned.

Goran cut the sharp corner and pulled the handle above his head. Twin .50 cal machine guns, a steady workhorse of the U.S. Army since World War II, swiveled on target. Locked and loaded, he waited for the enemy truck to line up without jeopardizing the queen. Each bullet had enough power to shred a man to pieces and were known to penetrate armored vehicles. He had not had the opportunity to use them in a long time. Tonight, his guns would drink once more.

The giant broke into a toothy grin and fired as an opening appeared. Goran figured by destroying the getaway vehicle he was doing his part to save Morgen. The rear of the target vehicle rocked when his guns found it. Metal melted and burst apart under the withering assault. Goran began singing his favorite Grateful Dead tune above the roar of the guns. Normally secluded deep underground and forgotten by almost everyone, the armorer reveled in the destruction. The ping-ping-ping of empty shell casings bouncing off the roof added to his symphony of destruction.

Blinded by glory, Goran failed to see the trio of men step out from behind trees across the street. As one, they lowered the RPGs on their shoulders and fired.

The assassin with Morgen disappeared behind the bole of an old oak, safe from the violence his peers unleashed. Daniel watched in horror as a trio of RPGs flared across the street to strike Goran's truck. They had just made it outside in the hopes of stopping the kidnapper and now it all lay in burning ruin. Snipers eliminated the threats quickly, but the damage was done. Old Guard raced to see if the armorer lived while Daniel and the others followed the line of carnage to the crippled escape vehicle.

He caught a glimpse of a man's head, rather what remained of it, slumped over the steering wheel. The entire side of the vehicle was shredded from the dual .50's but there was no sign of Morgen or the man who had stolen her. A block down the street another vehicle's lights flared to life and Daniel looked in time to see Morgen being thrown into the backseat before the vehicle peeled out with a screech of tires. *How in the hell did he carry her that far on foot?*

Constantin strode past Daniel and sighted his rifle. He fired once then turned away.

The vehicle kept moving and was soon out of sight.

Daniel rounded on the elf. "What was that?" he demanded, not caring how loud he was.

"Good shooting is what it was," Max snorted.

Daniel glared at him, surprised to find a long rifle draped over the dwarf's shoulder. *Where did he...?*

Heads turned. Several of the Old Guard stepped

forward, but Constantin held them off with a finger as he answered, "There was no way we were going to catch them, and this rifle doesn't have the necessary stopping power. Thirty rounds won't do much damage to a fleeing vehicle, even if it isn't armored." His voice was smooth, impossibly calm.

"So, you're just going to let them get away? With your queen?" Daniel fumed.

Constantin snatched him by the collar and jerked him close. "Listen to me, human. I swore my life to the throne. To the queen. If by saving her means sacrificing my life then I shall do so gladly. She earned that much. When have you ever been forced to give up so much for so little?"

Daniel stumbled back after being let go. The question stung. Sure, he'd deployed multiple times to different combat zones, but did he do it for himself or his country? A thick vein of patriotism ran deep, but no soldier worth his weight fought for much other than the person on their flank. Would he sacrifice his life for the elf queen? Daniel wasn't sure he wanted to know the answer. He caught the anguish in Constantin's eyes and his anger faded. *Sara's still inside and she's still in danger. How would I feel if no one wanted to help me?* The answer stung.

"What's our next move?" he asked.

Constantin gestured in the direction the vehicle fled. "I put a tracking round on it. We'll have the techs pick up the trail. Hunt them down and rescue the queen."

That sounded good, but Daniel had enough experience with the elves to know nothing ever went according to plan. At least there were no ghosts to deal with this time. Just hate filled men determined to bring harm to the elf world.

"He's still alive!" one of the Old Guard called out.

Daniel watched them drag an unconscious Goran from the wreckage of his prized possession. One problem solved. A dozen more to go.

Dejected, they hurried back inside.

Daniel found Sara and Nevada Slim already in the command center.

No one spoke.

He looked to see James Corman surrounded by computer screens and techs rapidly typing as information filled their screens. Three laptops flashed a series of mugshots on an endless loop but none of the government systems were picking up any of the assassins.

"Ghosts in the machine. This debacle threatens to undermine everything our two societies have worked so hard to protect. All of you should be ashamed of your actions," the government director suddenly lashed out. "Where is the queen?"

Blackmere stepped forward and took the brunt of Corman's fury as he explained what happened. "I didn't see any of your peo—"

"I want every available agent on this, Blackmere," Corman cuts in. "We must get her back before the Hand completes their plan."

"Sir, we don't know their plan," Blackmere countered.

"Could be ransom, could be capitulation if these people are as fanatical as it seems," Daniel added.

"It doesn't matter. Nothing they do will be pleasant. I have the techs running facial prints through the recognition systems but have no positive matches. Whoever they are, they are ghosts."

"Sir, there has to be—"

"How many dead?" Constantin asked, in no mood for pointless banter.

"One hundred and twenty-three confirmed," Nevada answered. "I have my people trying to get an accurate headcount. It appears most of the casualties were collateral damage. Morgen was the prize. The rest were a distraction."

Daniel looked at his friend in a new light. He truly had filled the role of Baron Visilias and was a far cry from the renegade trying to keep his feet out of prison.

"Director, we have them."

As one, the group crowded around the tech. They followed a red blip moving across the city.

Daniel noticed the direction and route first. His stomach sank. "They're heading for the interstate. If they get on that they'll be an hour ahead of us."

Corman tapped a finger on the desk. "Don't worry about that. I have air support ready to go. Blackmere, pick your team. You're leading the recovery operation. I don't want any mistakes this time. Get that woman back here and eliminate all viable threats. Am I clear?"

"Crystal."

Daniel looked at each with suspicion. To have been infiltrated so thoroughly suggested any of the people around him might be a traitor. The idea appalled him, for it all but rendered their efforts moot before the mission started.

THIRTEEN

For Daniel, the seconds rattled by. Here he was, again, absorbed by the elves. If only he wasn't so excited by the fact. The truth was he enjoyed the rush. The thrill of the hunt. Meshing with the elves and government provided an adrenalin boost unfound in the life of an author. This reluctant admittance threatened to upend all he once thought he understood. He protested each encounter and yet he craved them.

Daniel swept his gaze over the small assembly. Man, elf, dwarf. Disparate faces meet him before looking away. The elves and dwarves were in distress. The government agents looked a combination of angry and afraid. Only Sara showed her true emotions, meeting and holding his gaze.

No one spoke as Corman's cell rang and he moved to answer the call.

The levels of rising mistrust kept the groups separate. Daniel failed to see how remaining apart would help Morgen. Joined by Fritz and Angus, the dwarves now paced like caged animals, ready to draw axes and lash out at any affront. He really wouldn't put it past Max and his sons to do so. Blackmere was wise enough to stay quiet, choosing to go through names of people he trusted for this mission. Daniel worried Corman might blow their fragile alliance apart with his Washington gusto even as he whispered to whoever he was on the phone with. Men like him belonged behind a desk, not in the field with those who rolled up their sleeves and got their hands dirty for a living.

As if on cue, Corman hung up and slipped his phone inside his jacket. "Helicopter is inbound. I gave instructions to land in the parking lot across the street. Agents are clearing out the cars now."

"Then what?" Daniel asked. Not that he wanted to

step up, but with the divisions widening, he was the only one without any skin in the game. Besides, he had worked with everyone assembled, making him a common denominator if not an unwilling participant. *Just like old times.*

The glare Corman fixed him with would have withered a lesser man. The man's nostrils flared. "Next is you and this team of misfits, get on the bird, and hunt down the queen. We must stop them before the Hand unleashes whatever dark plan they have in store for her."

"Did he say misfits?" Max rumbled to Constantin.

The Old Guard planted his feet and squared off on Corman. "He did, but he couldn't have been talking about us. We're the only sensible ones here."

"Right," Max agreed. "After all, it was his fuck up that let those murderers in here in the first place. Morgen would be safe and sound back in her lair if not for the helping hand of the federal government."

"Gentlemen, enough. Please. This pointless bickering will not help save the queen," Blackmere sidled between them and his boss. "Are any of the weapons from your armorer's truck salvageable?"

Glowering, Max shifted his jaw to the crack of bones that had Daniel wincing. "Aye. Enough. But I figure you government types have your own arms room nearby."

"I have enough for my men, but no heavy weapons," Blackmere replied.

Daniel noted the color was returning to the agent's face. His body loosening up, as did the dwarves. *Crisis averted.*

"You can discuss all that enroute to finding Morgen," Corman snapped. "Find her and bring her back. And try to bring back one of those damned assassins alive."

Daniel raised an eyebrow. Given how difficult the Invisible Hand he encountered fought, he doubted there'd be any opportunity for prisoners. He glanced down at Corman's covered hand again, hoping to find the remains of a cut or scratch warranting the band aid. Something about the Washington bureaucrat felt off but he couldn't figure out what. Maybe it was the situation. Shaking his in the hopes of clearing his thoughts, Daniel focused on the task at hand.

"You want to risk a firefight in public? Because I don't see any way to use to the bird without drawing too much attention," Daniel said. "And as long as they are on a major artery and moving among civilians there isn't any way to anticipate their route to cut them off."

"You have all the answers I see," Corman mused. Some of the sting had gone from his tongue but that made Daniel wary of what the director would say next. "Very well, hot shot. What's your plan?"

Doing his best to keep the smug look, one Sara could not stand, off his face, Daniel pretended to give the question some thought. In truth, he knew exactly what he'd do and, in his best estimation, saw it as the only viable strategy.

"Use your tracking and stay at a respectable distance. We don't know where they are headed or how many may be waiting for us at the destination. I'd keep a vehicle borne force on the road to reinforce us whenever we land. Once the Hand reaches their destination, we drop in and swarm them with minimal risk to civilians and property. In and out before local authorities know we were there and let you government boys cook up the usual story to turn heads in the opposite direction while we return with Morgen."

Sara stared at her husband, seeing him in this light for the first time. They'd spent years avoiding talking about his time in service and if this was any indication of the man he was, she never felt safer.

Corman's eyes narrowed. "You're a dangerous man, Mister Thomas."

"I do my best," Daniel said.

"Very well. I approve." Corman turned back to

Blackmere. "I want you airborne ten minutes after that bird arrives—stay in constant communication. Save the queen and you'll have the long overdue promotion waiting on your return."

"Yes, sir," Blackmere concealed his surprise. "Who's coming?"

Max jabbed a finger at him, gold ring shining in the light. "Me and the old elf here. What more do you need?"

"I didn't figure I could keep you away," Blackmere replied, relief on his face. "Daniel, you and me." At Daniel's nod, he scanned the room, stating, "The bird can handle a few more."

To Daniel's surprise, Sara stepped forward with a fierce look of determination. "I'm in. I want revenge for what they did to poor Aislinn."

Daniel's mouth dropped open but before he could tell her absolutely not. His eyes pleaded with her to keep quiet. Change her mind. Anything but add more pressure to the burden he already bore.

Blackmere said, "That leaves room for one more."

Giving up on catching Sara's gaze, Nevada Slim pushed himself off the wall where'd he been lounging. Somehow the piece of straw had returned to his mouth. Daniel questioned whether or not he kept a pack of them hidden somewhere for easy access. "I promised Daniel I would take care of his wife. What good is an elf who can't keep his word?"

"That's six. I have two men I can trust as well. Head down to draw weapons and ammo. Meet me out front in five… Oh and Slim, you might want to think about a change of clothes. You can't stay hidden in a top hat and tails." Blackmere grinned at Slim's groan.

Everyone but Blackmere and Corman headed for the door. Daniel moved to Sara's side, ready to argue that she stay behind.

"Sara—"

"I'm going, Daniel."

"This isn't a game, Sara."

She stopped, staring up at him. That fire in her eyes blazed hotter, taking him aback. "I know. Don't think for a moment I'm going to sit her like some damsel in distress while you go off risking your life once again."

"You're not made for this kind of life," he protested with a shake of his head. "We have kids. And the dogs."

"I've already made arrangements for the dogs yesterday just in case and the kids won't be back until the end of the week. We have time."

Fear made his chest hurt. "I'm serious, babe. This is going to be dangerous."

"What? I can't handle myself?" she demanded. At his wince, she continued. "Who fought werewolves? Werewolves, Daniel. Not some freak in a furry costume! Oh, and don't forget that sword that wanted to kill me. Look, I know it will be dangerous and that's ok. I've sat home and worried about you too many times. I'm doing that again. We're in this together. Just like we promised."

"Nothing I say is going to change your mind, is it?" he recognized the pointlessness of continuing his protestations.

She shook her head. Sara reached behind to put her hair up in a tail. She looked down at her skirt and frowned. "Not even a little. Let's go get Morgen back and be done with it, but I need to change my clothes. This isn't going to work. Maybe we can drop the kids at my sister's and take a nice long vacation after."

While a vacation sounded wonderful, since it had been so long since they found the time for one, he still couldn't quite shake the urge to protect his wife and stop her from going. The notion of locking her in a room until they left amused him but there'd be hell to pay upon his return. He had no doubts about her capability. She'd proven herself a warrior on numerous occasions. But he had enough problems defending himself. Splitting that worry between himself and her robbed him of the wholeness he was going to need.

"Sara, I think—" At her straightening of shoulders, Daniel stopped talking. Once she put her foot down and decided it took an act of God to get her to change her mind.

She started walking, completely ignoring him, and he sighed. "Fine, but I want you sticking to my side like glue. I can't watch over both of us at the same time."

She turned back around and laid a hand on his arm. "Daniel, I'll be fine. I have Slim to look after me if I need it. Those bastards need to pay for what they did. We're the only ones who can do it."

"I'd feel better if Norman was coming along," he admitted. Not much bothered the gargoyle, and for good reason. Norman Guilt was built like a tank and could take as much punishment as he doled out.

Sara offered a tight smile. "I have a feeling he'll be there when we really need him."

"Hey, you two done making out like a pair of horny teenagers or would like a little more privacy?" Max called from down the hall.

Daniel, not Sara, blushed.

"See," she said. "This is already exciting!"

All armed with full kit and body armor, they hurried to meet Blackmere outside. It didn't take much for Daniel to slip back into soldier mode, again. He found the ease with which Sara followed suit remarkable. Somewhere along the way she managed to convince a female DESA agent about her size to swap clothes, leaving the agent out of place. *Give a woman one little firefight and she turns into Chuck Norris*. He laughed, soft and filled with mirth, causing the others to glance at him in question then away. The dull thump of approaching rotors rumbled across the Raleigh skyline and had him reaching for his gun.

Local authorities, in conjunction with DESA and Max's security contingents worked to keep crowds down, though Daniel still spotted a news crew from a local station. He had heard the agents chatting amongst themselves about a story already circulating of a gas leak in one of the older buildings resulting in the subsequent explosion of a pair of vehicles. Invisible Hand bodies were already hauled off to the morgue and cleaning crews worked tirelessly to remove the bloodstains on the carpets, broken glass, and repair any other damage to the building where Goran's bus rested.

Blackmere was huddled with a pair of agents in full battle rattle. Daniel checked out their gear the closer he got and was impressed to find a worthy arsenal on each man.

The DESA agent acknowledged them with a clipped nod as the helicopter hove into view. It was an older model UH-60 Blackhawk. The workhorse of Army aviation for the past thirty years and successor to the UH-1 Huey famous for shuffling troops into hot landing zones in Vietnam.

Daniel rolled his shoulders to adjust the weight of his pack. *Just like old times. Man, I've missed this.*

"You good?" Blackmere asked him, raising his voice to be heard over the Blackhawk.

"I should be asking you that, old timer," Daniel shouted back. "This isn't part of your Navy boy operations."

Blackmere snorted.

The bird touched down and they started forward. Daniel's eyes never left his wife.

FOURTEEN

Pain. The back of her skull throbbed, sending spikes down her spine and into her forehead. Opening her eyes proved a greater task than it should have been, leading her to believe she suffered from internal injuries. But the assassin knew his trade. He struck her in the precise place to render her unconscious without crippling her. Morgen supposed she should be thankful for that but could not get past the deep hurt in her head.

She suspected a minor concussion based on her blurred vision. Knowing her life depended on her next action, Morgen tried raising a hand to her aching temple. She couldn't. Through the haze she spied the course ropes binding her wrists, only now feeling them too. Frowning at herself for not expecting this, the queen of the dark elves seethed. The thought of chewing through the ropes entertained her dazed mind until she realized the foolishness of it. No doubt they were watching her, the treachery of elves was known far and wide.

Unable to move and trapped in a desperate situation, Morgen's thoughts turned to Aislinn. Her loyal servant and, dare she say, friend of many years. The elf had given up her life to save Morgen and it was all in vain. The look in her eyes as she breathed her last before collapsing into ash mocked Morgen's conscious. A grand ruler, wise and powerful, yet unable to prevent her friend from dying, kingdom from crumbling.

She shamed the spirits of her ancestors. A steady string of bad judgments had reduced the elf clans to a mockery of their former glory. It all began with turning from her husband. Alvin was the ruler the elves needed, not her. Wise and strong, and compassionate when necessary, he provided the necessary backbone to keep their people in order during humanity's rise. What had she done but bring them to the point of ruin? Her greed and inability to control their daughter led to Alvin's demise, further fracturing the clans by removing the balance of power. She wished he was with her now.

Each attempt at halting the divide proved futile. The clans were at each other's throats. Nothing she tried worked. And this last show of power ended in a disaster from the assassinations to her now kidnapping after the pointless killing of those in the meeting. The end of the clans, she feared, was fast approaching. The look of despair in Aislinn's eyes crept back into her mind: Morgen vowed to never allow another of her subjects to suffer again should she get free of her captors.

Her focus turned to the wicked men who brazenly attacked them. How many of her best were now dead remained unknown, though she feared the worst. She recalled several of her Old Guard slaughtered. Remarkable, considering how few the Invisible Hand sent. Old enemies, they shredded her sensibility with subtle ease. If her best couldn't stop a meagre handful, how was anyone expected to rescue her?

Growing frustrated, Morgen flexed her forearms and clenched her fists. Pain flared anew. The pressure in her head threatened to render her unconscious. Morgen ceased struggling as the floor bumped beneath her. *In a car, there's still time.* Unable to do much and unwilling to cry, she closed her eyes and centered her thoughts as best she could. The time was coming when she would be forced to stand on her own and she needed to be ready.

The drone of wheels soothed her aching skull.

For now, she remained captive to an organization few knew existed. *Fitting, all things considered.*

Daniel leaned his head against the cold metal frame and closed his eyes. The childish grin he felt creeping onto his face as old memories of conducting night raids accompanied him helped him find the perfect place to focus his inner storm. His trigger finger tapped a beat on the magazine well as he cradled the gun in his arms. This was what he missed, almost as much as the unique camaraderie only found among service members. He despised the loneliness of civilian life. No one stuck together they way they did in a squad or platoon.

Daniel's revelry was disturbed by the smaller figure of his wife shifting closer. He tried to keep her away from this life. Yet here she was and enjoying it too. He would never say it aloud, but Sara continued impressing him daily. Her mastery with the children, a job, and putting up with him left him in awe. Throw in her working with the elves to destroy a ravenous pack of werewolves and he began questioning his own conviction.

Maybe, just maybe, they could work well together as a team. Blackmere's offer to join DESA remained on the table. Working for the government might not be the bad thing he made it out to be, especially with Sara at his side.

The decision before him, Daniel turned his focus back to the mission. The agents seated across from him wore varying looks of worry and determination. He questioned anyone he hadn't worked with, even though he had approved of their appearance earlier. Then there was Blackmere's efficiency in the field. The agent had a desk for most of his career now and might prove a liability when the bullets started flying. Daniel didn't recall him being involved with the fighting back in New York. *Would he be able to hold his own when it came time or was he nothing more than a liability waiting to happen?*

Unfortunately, that was a question only answerable when it was already too late to alter the answer. Disturbed by the direction of his thoughts, Daniel turned his focus on the Invisible Hand. He hadn't believed them when they first mentioned the group, not that it would have mattered if he did. They proved the ultimate killers. Competent. Lethal. Unrelenting from what he experienced. They moved with a fluid grace seemingly impossible for anyone. Killing them proved problematic. He'd only done so thanks to the confusion and massed bodies fleeing the scene. Curiously, none of those who fell wore any type of protective armor. The audacity, or was it raw confidence?

He lowered the mouthpiece to his headset. "Blackmere, what do you know about this Invisible Hand?"

The older agent gave him a thoughtful stare. "They are rumored to be over a thousand years old. Supposedly originating sometime during the Crusades. No one remembers their beginnings. I suspect all accounts and records were tracked down and destroyed by their leadership."

"Making them the perfect boogeymen," Daniel supplied.

Blackmere nodded. "They always strike in groups of five. Never more and never less. It is unusual, from what little we managed to gather, to have so many hands working in conjunction. I think that has to do with the target."

"She's the queen, human," Constantin's dour voice scolded. "She will be treated with respect."

Daniel ignored him. "Why now? And how did they know about the conference? Security was tight."

"The answer is simple," Blackmere started and licked his lower lip. "We have a mole."

"Not among my men," the Old Guard leader stated. His voice took on a dark tone. "They are all loyal beyond reproach."

"No one is questioning the Old Guard's loyalty," Blackmere soothed. "It's everything else we can't be sure of."

Max used the opportunity to chime in, "Meaning what? My people are spies?"

Daniel wondered if the pilots were rated to deal with a brawl midflight.

"Or mine."

Mentioning the deep rifts between clans was stating the obvious. What mattered was discovering the source of the leak and eliminating it to prevent the Hand from striking again once they rescued Morgen. "How about we focus on our next move?" Daniel suggested. "We need to know how much support we have when hitting these bastards."

"My team takes point when we hit the ground. That's not negotiable," Blackmere said. "Constantin, you take the rest in a secondary assault. We strike fast and get out before they can summon reinforcements."

"Where do Sara and I fall in on your plan?" Daniel asked.

"With them. I need our combat strength spread evenly."

"More like you want us to have a babysitter," Constantin snapped.

"Relax, old man. Thomas is good, for a human. I vouch for him," Max commented. "He can hold his own in a fight."

Daniel masked his surprise with a cough. Sara nudged his side, smiling.

"Hopefully it will not come to that," Blackmere continued. "We don't want any prolonged engagement. The longer we are on the ground the more danger there is for the queen. My team will keep the Hand operatives busy while you find and secure her. Extract her and retreat to the chopper. Ground forces will secure the perimeter and clean up. Understood?"

No one spoke. There was no need to. Like it or not, Blackmere laid out a plan that did not offend any party and should be actionable enough to minimize friendly casualties. Everyone but Sara was experienced enough to know detailing a more thorough plan provided opportunities for it to go wrong. Bare details left them free to adjust and operate as necessary without jeopardizing the mission. Just as Daniel liked it.

Each ignored the obvious questions. If they retrieved Morgen alive, what was to prevent the Hand from making another try for her? Why did they choose this moment to end their long war with the elves?

The Blackhawk raced forward, tracking the fleeing Invisible Hand vehicle as it sped west on Interstate 40. Already beyond Raleigh's city limits and approaching Durham and Chapel Hill, they would soon be in the middle of nowhere for a good stretch of road. Perfect for intersection should Blackmere decide the moment right to assault. He made the call for the ground teams to move out.

That orange glow of city lights slowly turned to country dark marred by weakening flows of traffic. Daniel stared down at the road far below. One of those cars held Morgen and her captors. But which one? Were they within visual range or had the pilot been ordered to pull back to avoid giving the pursuit away? He wished he knew, but command decisions remained above his pay grade. Not that he was getting paid for any of this.

So, what the hell am I doing it for? Can't be just the thrill. What sort of dumbass does that? Wait, do I really need the adrenalin rush to validate my life? She is definitely paying off the mortgage after this. Not having any answers, Daniel focused again on the road and caught his first aerial glimpse of the 15-501 intersection approaching. This was central North Carolina's main artery, made famous by the cross-town basketball rivalry of Duke to the north and the University of North Carolina to the south.

Basketball aside, Daniel enjoyed this part of the state. He and Sara once thought of settling down close by, until they saw how much it cost to buy a home in the area. Now he soared over both towns feeling like a god. He hadn't felt this free since his first deployment to Iraq all those years ago. Tonight, he was an avenging angel, bound for retribution and the chance to prove his worth one final time. Or so he hoped.

FIFTEEN

Sara found herself staring down at the world speeding by disappointed that she had never been in a helicopter before now. People like Daniel took them for granted. She lost track of how many times he mentioned riding in them in during his army time. For her, this was the ride of a lifetime. Far better than any carnival ride or rollercoaster. Thankful for the dark, she soared across the sky with a childish grin. Maybe being sucked into the world of the elves wasn't so bad after all.

But no amount of giddiness proved capable of reducing the fear growing inside. Sure, she'd battled werewolves and had an unbelievable adventure while Daniel was gone, but she never truly felt in total danger. Not like now. Whoever the Invisible Hand was, she had trouble believing Thaddeus' explanation at face value, they inspired her deepest fears. Not only was accepting elves trying enough, she now found herself faced with another improbable threat. Worried the terror might fully take hold, Sara glanced around the cabin to see if anyone else looked ready to break.

She'd heard a little about Max. The dour dwarf patriarch reminded her so much of his sons, Angus and Fritz. Sara remained on the fence about whether she liked the dwarf or not. In her limited experience they were a difficult people to bond with on a good day. Since regrouping outside of the performing arts center he hadn't said a word to her. The sidelong glares he gave weren't personal. She watched him do that with everyone. And he had at least supported Daniel earlier.

The elf beside him was an enigma. Constantin Andros was a legend among the elf clans. She heard all about him through whispers before the meeting in the hall even started. Strong, taciturn, and deliberate it was said. His actions were tales passed down through the generations. He had stood at the edge of the storm for centuries, always doing what was right for the clans and the monarchy. She caught glimpses of pain etched on his face when she glanced at him now, for he took the recent downturns as personal failings. Somehow, Sara felt a level of comfort the commander of the Old Guard.

Then there was Daniel, who remained her rock. He was the last person she worried about. She once joked how he was a 'do right' man and always rankled when it came to breaking the rules, even if for his benefit. Tonight, she found that foundation more than comfortable. She knew, without doubt, he would never let her down. Convincing him she belonged right alongside the others remained a difficult nut to crack, no matter how hard she tried.

Finally, her gaze turned to Thaddeus Blackmere and the pair of men flanking him. Whereas Daniel and the others referred to the man by his last name, Sara thought he had an endearing quality and deserved to be called by his first. He was like an older uncle who helped raised her. She found him to be stalwart when necessary and compassionate at other times. Sara usually bought into the not trusting the government since she seen enough to sour her mood when Daniel was still in uniform. Yet for each negative experience there were a dozen positive ones.

Thaddeus never talked down to her or openly thought her lesser. That alone bolstered her confidence enough to sit straighter. No level of confidence or thrill upon seeing mile after mile speed by in a blur of car lights could reduce her thoughts of the impending fight. *Battle?* Her one solace rested in the professionalism of those around her.

The last time Sara recalled involvement with a helicopter had been that harrowing night when she was thrust into the middle of a coup attempt. That night began with a helicopter crashing into a church and their flight to the North Carolina Zoo. Thinking of the chaos of it all did little to calm her already volatile nerves. For the first time tonight, Sara considered staying in the helicopter to let the boys be boys. But she made a vow to avenge Aislinn.

She still didn't know where that came from. One minute she wanted little to do with the elves and the next she promised to avenge the fallen. Not that Sara held any grudges against Morgen's people, but the mental struggle of balancing humanity and elfkind threatened to send her thoughts into a spiral. Without being able to articulate it, Sara knew this felt right.

"We have a target," Blackmere announced through his headset link.

They'd been airborne for almost an hour. The hunt for Morgen's captors taking them halfway across the state. Sara didn't know where they were, but the longer the chase continued the more certain she was they were headed for the presumptive safety of the mountains overlapping the North Carolina-Tennessee border. Should the Hand reach those winding hills and deep valleys Sara saw no way any helicopter could catch them.

"Intelligence is picking up chatter. Looks like they are headed for a rest stop to link up with another team," the agent continued. "Probably looking at switching vehicles as well."

"How reliable is that?" Daniel asked. His concerned look spoke volumes and put Sara on edge.

"Enough. Besides, it makes sense. Add a second vehicle to confuse potential pursuit and eliminate Constantin's tracking device."

Max made a show of spitting a wad of phlegm out the side door. "How does this change the plan?"

"It doesn't." Blackmere's reply left no room for discussion. "We strike as planned. Adjust as necessary."

Sara wasn't sure but she thought she caught a slew of profanity whispered from the dwarf. At her side, Nevada Slim cracked a grin.

"You stick right behind me," Daniel ordered her as they readied to land.

Sara knew better than to debate. Plus, any confidence she might have had fled as the Blackhawk descended. All around her safety belts were unbuckled, except she hesitated with hers. Weapons were locked and loaded. Constantin and Max slid to positions with their legs dangling from the door. The DESA men did likewise on the opposite side.

Her heart thundered in her chest, threatening to rip free before they touched down. She couldn't keep her hands from clenching even as she undid her belt. The weapon in her hands felt small. Insignificant. How was she expected to defend herself with it? Her left leg began bouncing. Eyes wide, she nodded to Daniel who was watching her with a grim expression. They touched down before he could speak to her. She looked to him for reassurance and received it through a wink.

"Go!"

They exited the Blackhawk with skill, Sara coping the others. Crouching to stay well under the spinning rotor, each raised their rifles and dashed across the grass and pavement toward what she assumed to be the Invisible Hand vehicles. The prop wash almost landed her on her face. No one warned her about that. Seeing none of the others so much as stumbling, Sara did her best to halt her forward momentum and maintain pace with Daniel who stuck to her side. It took a few steps to regain her footing but soon she was almost sprinting. Somewhere in the murk of night were the men responsible for so much murder and mayhem and the one woman capable of calming the storm. Steeling herself for whatever might come, Sara tried slipping back into the mood that saw her through the night against the werewolves and prayed it was enough.

Several cars littered the rest area parking lot. A handful of tractor trailers loomed in the back lot, giant shadows inspiring nightmare scenarios. Daniel glanced at those then away. Truckers were no doubt already bedded down for the night and far enough out of the way to avoid being in danger should confrontation grow heavy. It was the other cars and SUVs bothering him. He hadn't accounted for civilians on the battlefield at any stage of their operational planning. Should the Hand take additional hostages the night threatened to get out of control fast. He put nothing past the depths of their nefariousness.

He caught Blackmere and his agents slipping toward the far side of the small bathroom structure. The thought of a hot coffee enticed him from inside the low light building. His eyes felt heavy. They burned. Daniel knew his adrenalin was fading fast. There had been too much downtime in the Blackhawk after the hall battle to maintain his intensity. Threatened with burning out, he picked up the pace. He had a job to do and his wife to protect. No time for weakness tonight.

If Max, Slim, or Constantin felt similar, they didn't show it. Their certainty echoed with each step. Elf and dwarf working together for the future of the clans. He wished he had that level of conviction. Unable to match them with their shared goals, he settled for the honor in their purpose.

They crossed the first parking area without incident or detection by any civilians. Daniel counted seven cars scattered up and down the quarter mile lot. A dog barked at their passing of one. A random head turned, obscured by night and windows. Daniel hoped they remained in the relative safety of their vehicles.

He brought his barrel up as they converged on their target vehicle. Constantin nodded, confirming the tracker was on this car. Daniel exhaled and found his calm. *Blackmere, you better be right about this. Otherwise, a lot of people are going to get hurt.*

Sara was a step behind him as they circled around the building's near side. Whether by chance or purpose, the

Hand parked in the rear away from most civilians. Any relief he might have felt evaporated as soon as his team rounded the corner. A man stood on the sidewalk, sword in hand. Sara flinched at the sight, old memories sneaking back. His face remained concealed behind swaths of black cloth; eyes darkened with kohl. Strong and imposing, he blocked their way forward. Daniel skidded to a halt and clicked his safety off. She followed suit, a question on her face. *How did they know we were coming? This can't be coincidence*

"This one is mine," Constantin's roared. "Go, find the queen."

The elf lowered his rifle and drew his own sword. The yellow glow of magic shined bright in the night.

"Come on." Daniel grabbed Sara by the arm.

She gestured back toward the combatants as swords clashed. "What about Constantin?"

"I have a feeling he'll be fine. We need to move."

Thaddeus Blackmere felt the familiar ache in his joints. His knees burned. His chest heaved. He was wondering how long it had been since he last ran the gauntlet course at the DESA training facility. Between the additional weight of body armor and weapon, he felt sluggish. Heavy. A side eye look showed he was the only one. The other agents were younger, better trained for this. He suspected neither had sat behind a desk, much less being trapped in an office in obscurity. None of that withstanding, Blackmere strengthened his resolution to see the mission through. The fate of multiple worlds rested on their success this night.

Movement drew his focus. Shadows slipping through the night close to a trio of tractor trailers. A pair of SUVs were parked nearby. Neither had plates. *Bingo!* He slipped back, halting his team. They took a knee and trained their weapons on the vehicles. Rules of engagement prevented them from firing until targets were confirmed.

Blackmere trusted his men to do the right thing. It was the secondary team he had doubts on.

Neither Max nor Constantin were accustomed to taking orders, especially from a human outsider lacking knowledge of their hierarchy. Either of them could blow the entire operation on a whim. Only Slim had no qualms against taking his lead. Blackmere felt fortunate he worked with at least one of this crew before. Jurisdiction falling to him, Blackmere needed to move fast to prevent disaster from striking. A second look showed the figures still moving between vehicles. Blackmere and his team hadn't been detected. Yet. He frowned, knowing the only way the Hand could be prepared for them was if they were tipped off. But by whom?

Reaching for his earpiece, he whispered, "This is Blackmere. I have the targets in sight. No sign of the queen. Converge on me. I repeat. We have them."

A shot rang out. Blackmere whipped his head around to the sound. Agent Lamas pitched backward with a muted groan. Blood flew from his mouth. Weapon and body crashed into the parking lot simultaneously. To his left, Agent Talley opened fire. Muzzle flashes broke the serenity of the night. The bark of rifle fire made birds take flight. Small animals in nearby bushes dashed away for safety. Chaos ensued.

Blackmere gave Lamas a last look, ensuring the man was dead before breaking for better cover. Any thoughts of taking the Invisible Hand by surprise were gone. This had devolved into a race for survival. No longer a rescue mission, Blackmere prayed their quick reaction force arrived in time. Otherwise, this was going to be a short night.

"Thomas, get your team over here!" he barked over the headset and opened fire.

Silence came from his headset. *Come on people, where are you?*

SIXTEEN

Sara clapped her hands over her ears to dampen the roar. They were fully engaged with the Invisible Hand. Any notion of catching them in a trap evaporated the moment the first shot was fired. She wanted to scream. Get back on the Blackhawk and leave. Anything other than stand, well crouch, in the line of fire. It was too late for escape. Alone, they were forced to battle it out until Thaddeus' reinforcements arrived. *If we get through this, I'm going to go back to pretending none of this is real.*

The ping of bullets continued striking the metal trash cans Daniel had shoved her behind for cover. She thought she caught several cars speeding away Squinting, she saw Daniel choosing his targets with a calm she could never emulate. Seeing him in action was a far cry from listening to snippets of his stories down at the local American Legion post. It had suddenly become real.

With everyone engaged, Sara was the only one who might save any innocents caught in the line of fire. Forcing down the butterflies in her stomach, she shifted her pistol to her firing hand and crouch walked back into the concrete building. She only rose when it became clear the Invisible Hand either did not see her or failed to view her as a threat. Using that to her advantage, she sprinted the rest of the way to the parking lot, intent on warning those remaining in their cars to flee while they still could. She caught Daniel's bark, muffled by gunfire, begging her to return. It was too late. She was committed once she left.

Sara watched another car race away with a sigh of relief. Every life saved meant one less victim for those murderers in black. It wasn't until she approached the nearest car that she realized she had a weapon in her hand and would likely give whoever was inside a bigger fright. Chagrined, she tucked the pistol behind her and started gesturing for the occupants to leave. Instead, they just stared at her.

"What's going on here?" a portly man with five days' worth of unshaven facial hair demanded.

The car smelled of body odor and road food reached her. Sara failed to keep a look of disgust from showing. *Why is there always that one guy who has to know everything? Just go, mister. Before it's too late.* "Sir, I need you to leave. This is an active shooter operation."

"I don't see any flashing lights."

"Just do as she says, Harold," a woman chirped from the passenger seat.

"Quiet, woman," he snapped. Turning back to Sara, he said, "What sort of trouble y'all in? I was in the army for a bit. I can help. Jenny, get me the Glock from the glovebox."

Of course you were. Frowning, Sara said, "Sir, we have the situation under control, but I need all civilians to evacuate immediately. The government thanks you for your service and support."

She stormed off before he could reply. Shaking her head, she headed for the next car, muttering to herself, "Thank you for your service? If that wasn't the dumbest shit I could think of."

No doubt Harold thought himself a hero and probably never been in a true battle. The thought produced a chuckle. Arriving at the next car, Sara discovered a panicked woman clinging to her steering wheel, knuckle white. Tears streaked down her face.

Putting on her best smile, Sara spoke, "Miss, I need you to calm down. You're going to be fine. I promise."

"Wh…who are you? What's happening?"

"I am a federal agent," she lied. "Please, put your

car in reverse and go. It's all right. We have the situation under control."

Gunfire increased, as if to dispute her claims. Sara rolled her eyes before offering a small wave and another smile as the car slowly began to back out. "Two down. Two to go."

The next minivan she found a middle-aged man with a typical stomach and thinning hair pacing frantically up and down the length of his car. His worried look made Sara walk faster. She recognized a spooked parent when she saw one.

She slowed her approach, placing her empty hands out for him to see she posed no threat when he spun to face her. "Sir, I'm going have to ask you to get back in your car and leave."

Shock mixed with fear in his eyes. "I can't. Emily is out there. I shouldn't have let her go, but she wanted to be the one to walk the dog one more time. She gets so happy with that. It should be me. Not her!"

Shit. What do I do now? No time for second guessing, Sara closed the distance and touched his left arm. "It's all right. Tell me, where did Emily go? Which direction?"

His jaw quivered. The man was verged on a nervous breakdown; no doubt fueled by guilt. It took little imagination to see both his daughter and their dog getting killed and him blaming himself. Her heart went out to him. "Back there, toward the trees by those trucks."

Sara wanted to groan. Of course, the child would have gone into the woods as the dog had plenty of places to sniff. At least she wasn't out in the open and at a higher risk of being shot. "Get back in your car. I'll go and find her. I need you to leave as soon as we return. Do you understand?"

He nodded.

Sara heard the door slam shut behind her as she hurried towards the woods, hoping to stay out of the field of fire and gain the safety of the trees before she was noticed. It dawned on her she had no clue how to find the missing child without shouting her name like a lunatic in the night.

Constantin rolled his shoulders. Gunfire echoed in the distance. His power sword felt good in his hands. An extension of himself; it helped him survive countless duels and battles over the course of his life. This night found him sorely pressed. The Invisible Hand assassin was strong, anticipating all of Constantin's attacks. Both men bled from a dozen wounds. Neither gave an inch of ground. Small, wet circles scattered the pavement as they bled. Torn scraps of clothing littered the bushes, blowing away on the soft breeze carrying the smell of gunpowder.

His opponent stood six paces away. Dark, almost crimson eyes glared at Constantin from beneath the veil. Anger. The elf grinned, knowing he had thrown his foe off guard. An angry opponent did not think clearly. This might be his one shot at ending their duel with speed. From the sounds of things, the others needed his help.

Constantin pointed his sword at the assassin and bellowed an ancient war cry. The assassin crouched, preparing to strike. Constantin didn't give him the chance. The elf attacked, channeling as much strength as he had remaining and unleashed a flurry of blows at the head and shoulders. Each strike was deflected but Constantin refused to back down. Swinging a massive backhand at the assassin's neck, he arrested the swing at the last moment and brought the power sword up in an uppercut.

The ruse worked, splitting the assassin's torso from stomach to neck. Blood fountained. Constantin stepped back to avoid the torrent. He never broke his opponent's gaze. Not until the man's eyes rolled up in the back of his head and, mouth slack, dropped with a wet thud. Constantin wiped his sword, cleaning little blood drops the magic failed to burn away in the process and offered his slain foe a look of raw disdain before turning away to rejoin the fight.

Daniel saw the body on the cold asphalt. He couldn't tell which of Blackmere's men it was. It didn't matter. They were down one and had no accurate way of determining how many enemy combatants opposed them. Daniel bet on there being more than one hand. Forcing concerns of Sara aside, he dove into the fight. Nevada Slim ran at his heels, eager to cut his teeth.

He and Slim slid behind the tree next to Blackmere. "What the fuck is going on? I thought these guys liked knives."

"I don't know. They opened fire as soon as we came into view. Lamas took a round to the heart. This is bad."

Armor penetrating bullets? Daniel's heart sank. *This was beyond bad.* "We need to flank these sons of bitches. Get them firing at each other. Any sign of Morgen?"

"Not yet. We've been pinned down." He gestured toward Talley, who was trapped behind a dumpster riddled with bullet holes.

The bark of a light machine gun disrupted Daniel's thoughts. He saw Max charging behind a stream of red tracers. A hundred bullets shredded the front end of the second vehicle. Daniel winced, praying the queen was nowhere near that fury. Fearing the situation was getting out of control, he knew he had to take charge. Blackmere was ineffective, a dazed look in his eyes, and Max, engulfed with that famous dwarven rage, was now a liability.

"Where's Sara?" he asked Nevada Slim.

The dark elf's eyes widened as he spun. "Still hasn't come back. She was clearing civilians from the other side of the lot."

"Damn it!" Daniel retorted. He turned on his earpiece. "Sara, where are you? Talk to me, lady. Are you all right?"

A wall of incoming rounds forced them to take cover. Cursing, Daniel refocused on the firefight.

"Max!" Daniel bellowed as the dwarf took position behind another tree to reload. "Direct your line of fire between the two vehicles. Do not shoot at either! We don't know where Morgen is."

"That dwarf is going to get us killed," Slim shouted when Max began firing again.

"Probably," Daniel agreed and did another sweep of the area.

Betting on the Invisible Hand using her as a shield, he guessed she was off in the surrounding woods. Several bullets snapped by his head, forcing him to take cover. He cranked off three shots at the man who stepped around a nearby SUV. Sparks danced off the asphalt. A taillight broke, red plastic fragments scattered.

"Blackmere, you and your man lay down a base of fire. I'm taking Max and Slim to the left flank. Don't stop firing until we sweep through," he ordered. Hitting his earpiece, he asked, "Max, you read me?"

The dwarf let off another then dropped the empty drum. Max rummaged through his pack before giving Daniel a thumbs up.

"Copy! Reloading," Blackmere replied.

The plan was shaky at best, but Daniel had no other choice. He couldn't be in two places at once and there wasn't any time to wait for Constantin to return. "We move on two."

"Go. Blackmere, cover!"

Two rifles opened fire. The trio sprinted left, making for the front of the nearest tractor trailer. Daniel hoped the DESA agents knew enough about small unit tactics to execute a proper movement to contact engagement. Otherwise, this was going to be the worst mistake of his life. Blowing out the frustrated, he slammed into the front bumper and readied to advance.

SEVENTEEN

Dense tree cover combined with thick undergrowth dampened the sounds of battle coming from the rest area. Not that she could hear much over the pounding in her head. Each heartbeat felt like a cannon in the corners of her mind. Nothing she did proved capable of calming her nerves. Sara tried. Oh, how she tried. A frightened little girl was depending on her for rescue. A dog too. That alone sparked her conviction. She had to keep going. *For Emily.*

The ridiculous of the situation was not lost on her when she tripped over a tree root. Sara knew this was a tale she'd never be able to tell her friends over drinks. Not unless they were drunk enough no one remembered the following day. No, she decided this part of her life was best left private. After all, who would believe she had Daniel and elves and a dwarf and government agents for companions as they battled assassins while she searched the forest for a missing girl and her dog?

Resisting the urge to laugh, Sara scanned everything in her field of view from left to right as Daniel taught her. She thought it foolish at the time, but the artform of staying alive in a combat zone, that had once been pretend, suddenly became prudent and very real. Sara kept her pistol at the ready, barrel pointed at the ground in front of her as she advanced.

This far from the battle she found the natural sounds of the forest taking command. The rustle of wind through the trees. The snapping of dead branches she failed to spot before stepping on them. A rustling of leaves. Each sound amplified with the night, making her wince. The last thing she needed was to give her position away. Admonishing her lack of focus, Sara slowed her pace and took deliberate steps.

Nothing moved, disheartening her and leaving her with no other choice. "Emily," she whispered. "Emily, your father sent me. Can you hear me?"

No answer.

Stay calm. Think, Sara. What would you do if you just watched a war movie break out in front of you? Guessing Emily to still be little, Sara started looking into every bush and behind larger trees. The possibility of the girl laying down to hide was high, but not likely with a dog. She should have thought to ask what kind of dog it was. A scrap of fabric on branches caught her attention. She stopped midstride, peering into a cluster of holly bushes.

"Emily? Is that you? It's ok. I'm here to take you to safety," she said. "You can come out. I promise to take care of you."

The dog's growl confirmed her suspicion when she took a step closer. "Emily, I know you don't have any reason to trust me, but I made a promise to your father."

"You're with them," a timid voice called from the dark. "Leave me alone!"

Sara sighed and tucked her pistol away. She should have expected the little girl, frightened and in danger, would be guarded. Crouching to appear less menacing, Sara held out her empty hands. "No, sweatie. I'm not with them. Those are the bad guys. My friends and I are here to stop them. They are very bad people."

Silence mocked her. She paused to consider her next move when Emily said, "That's what the bad guys always say. My daddy says never to trust a stranger."

Good man. Too bad that works against me. "Your father sounds like a smart person. He is very worried about you. He was crying when I left him."

"Daddy was crying?" Emily asked, her voice so low yet loaded with emotions that tugged at Sara's heart.

"He was, but if I take you back to him now the three of you can leave."

"Three?"

Sara broke into a smile. "Yes, silly. You wouldn't want to leave your dog all alone in the woods in the middle of the night, would you?"

The comment produced the desired effect. Emily crept out from her hiding spot with a giggle on her face. At her side stood a gray-faced black lab with his ears pinned. *Son of bitch. I would have stepped right on her without noticing. Good job, kid.*

Sara remained still as the dog marched up to her, that look of determination she found in her dogs whenever a stranger was present. She held out her hand and, after sniffing hard, the dog began wagging its tail. Test passed.

"Come on. We need to go. My friends are in trouble, and they need my help," Sara told her as they started back toward the parking lot.

She hoped they were okay. *Daniel I'm coming.*

Bodies lay scattered across the open area. Red pools spread. Several small trees along the parking lot were broken, splintered from the heavy barrage of Max's machinegun. Debris and trash tumbled with the wind from a pair of destroyed trash cans. The clang of bottles rolling down the small slope to the storm drain felt surreal in the middle of a fight.

Blackmere watched a bottle roll passed his left side, between him and Agent Talley's body. Lament resurfaced. As mission commander, it was his responsibility to ensure his people were safe. He failed. Both men were now dead. The second barely fending off the striking assassin before Blackmere drilled three rounds into his forehead.

Alone and cut off from the others, Blackmere's imagination ran wild. If one assassin could get so close without being seen another must surely be on the way to finish him. If he died, Daniel had no protective flank. They would be overrun and destroyed in short order. Falling back on his initial training and remembering how long he had served his country, Thaddeus Blackmere reloaded his rifle and tapped the forward assist to ensure the round seated properly.

Movement drew his attention. He swiveled toward the threat, finger lingering over the cold metal trigger. Blackmere blinked to clear his vision. Constantin Andros' battered form staggered into full view. The yellow glow of his sword appeared less somehow, as if defeating his last foe robbed some of the magic away. While he professed not to understand or even accept magic, Blackmere thanked God for the Old Guard.

The elf halted. A wary look in his eye as he crouched and surveyed the damage. "How many are left?"

"I don't know." Blackmere shook his head. "We never got an accurate count before they attacked."

"I killed two. A second leapt from the shadows after I slew his friend. They will not trouble us further," Constantin said. His voice projected the confidence Blackmere wished he had. "You took another. I counted two more bodies to the left. I assume the others are there?"

A long burst of fire erupted.

"Your count confirms a minimum of two hands," Blackmere said. "We still have no positive ID on the queen."

"Leave that to me. We must move quickly. Stay behind me and do not stop until we secure that vehicle," Constantin ordered.

Blackmere swallowed his doubts and followed the elf into the fray. Every second brought the quick reaction force closer. He just needed to hold on a little longer.

Daniel pulled the dagger from the assassin's neck. Curved and serrated, it matched the other Invisible Hand blades he had seen. How he managed to wrest it from his victim was lost in the whirlwind of their battle. Daniel bled from a series of low gashes to his thigh and biceps. Burning pain lanced through him with each movement. That drop in adrenalin he feared closed on him with each step forward.

Max ran past him, firing as he went. A maniacal gleam twinkled in the dwarf's eyes.

Daniel followed.

The vehicles were less than twenty meters away and resistance was dying down. Spotting movement, Daniel saw an assassin creeping around the back of the ruined car. In a blink, he watched his torso shredded by a string of tracers looking like a laser in the night. Knowing the standard ratio was one tracer to three regular rounds, it took little imagination to picture how many bullets tore through the man.

"Watch the cars!" Daniel shouted at Max.

His warning went unheard. Not that he supposed Max would pay heed anyway. The dwarf bordered on berserker mode. Daniel found himself thankful they were on the same side and for Slim's calming presence. The dark elf fired conservatively, picking and choosing his targets with deliberate intent. Time for thought passed as swiftly as the twenty meters. They were upon the vehicles and fending off a trio of assassins who had been waiting in the safety of the shadows.

Daniel, Max, and Slim were driven back for fear of hitting Morgen with an errant round. The assassins became emboldened by this and swung their blades with ruthlessness. None of them spotted the massive elf until he was crashing into the assassins from behind. The glow of Constantin's sword flashed like lightning. Sensing the tide shift, Daniel lowered his rifle and drew his pistol. At his side, Max had already set down his machinegun and attacked the assassins with his bare hands. Slim, straw in place in the corner of his mouth, pointed at the nearest assassin, leaving Daniel convinced they were all mad.

Soon, Daniel and his team were the only ones still

on their feet. Panting and bleeding from dozens of wounds, they were still alive. Daniel still had not heard from Sara but found his attention drawn to Blackmere opening the back door of the SUV. Bullet holes pinged the vehicle behind the rear doors and one of the tires was flat. Morgen appeared and accepted the agent's hand as she slipped into the open air.

They'd done it.

They had rescued the queen.

Constantin dropped to a knee. He teetered, threatening to tip over. "Your Majesty."

"Get up, Constantin. This is not the time for ceremony," Morgen scolded but offered a slight smile to lessen the words. She cast her gaze around the group. "Thank you, all. Your efforts will not go unrewarded. Agent Blackmere, I trust your agency has answers as to how this all happened?"

"I am sure they are working on that as we speak," Blackmere told her. "But it isn't safe here. We need to get you back to Raleigh before anyone realizes you are missing."

She glanced down at the bodies nearby. Poise. Dignity. Her lips curled in disdain. "Let us go. Where is your vehicle?"

Max broke out in laughter. The gruff sounds worse than gunfire. "Ha! Damned government man! We got dropped off by helicopter and the pilot split the minute the shooting started. There is no exfil."

Daniel noticed the flush of his cheeks as Blackmere replied, "A QRF team is enroute. They should be here shortly."

Catching the scuff of footsteps coming from behind, they turned to face the new threat, guns raising.

Sara froze, raising her hands. "Whoa fellas. Don't shoot. It's just me."

Daniel ran to her, crushing her to his chest. She patted his shoulder and tried to push him away after a minute turned to two.

"I thought I lost you," he whispered into her hair as she squirmed. "Why didn't you answer?"

"I'm fine. Really. I lost my earpiece while I cleared the civilians out of the parking lot once I realized I wasn't any good with whatever you were doing," she said. "I met this incredible little girl tonight. Emily. Brave kid. Her dog was pretty awesome too."

Daniel's eyebrow rose but he said nothing. His pride soared, confirming she was the person for him. As if he needed the confirmation after all this time. They had been together long enough to erase any doubts he might have held. He hugged her tighter, not trusting his words.

"As touching as this reunion is, we need to prepare to exfil," Blackmere interrupted. "The team is almost here."

"Time to go—" Daniel's words and happiness faded as a group of shadows stepped into the light.

They were dead.

EIGHTEEN

The assassins fanned out in a line. Blades waving in their hands. Their faces were concealed, much as the others had been. Imposing figures, they represented the end. Compared to their ragged collection of men and elves, they stood tall. Poised. Ready for battle. Daniel was really beginning to hate them.

Daniel eyed his team; they were on the edge of breaking. They had fought to the best of their ability and suffered for it. Chests heaving from the exertion, each bore a harrowed look with numerous wounds. Each ran on fumes. Only Morgen stood with defiance. He could see she would refuse to be taken captive this time. Her fingers clenched into fists.

Max cleared his throat and spat a mouthful of blood. "Five on five."

"We're dead," Daniel countered. "We barely survived the first three hands. There's no way we can handle more."

"Humans," Max chided, scowling.

Constantin rolled his shoulders. "Daniel has a point. We are sore pressed to hold our ground, Schneider. There is value in retreating to regroup."

"Retreat where? Agent man here sent the chopper away. We're cutoff. Fighting is our only choice."

Raising his power sword, Constantin took a step forward and gestured toward the assassins. "We fight then." He looked over his shoulder, adding, "Daniel Thomas, protect the queen. We will handle this."

Swallowing the lump in his throat, Daniel could do nothing but nod. *Fucking elves. I'm done after this. If we make it out in one piece.*

"I am more than capable of defending myself, Constantin," Morgen said as she stepped forward to join him. "Someone give me a weapon. It has been too long since I last crossed blades with a foe. The time has come to return to my former glory."

"Much as I like what you're saying, this ain't the time," Max grumbled. "These fellas over here don't seem interested in killing you. That's the only advantage we have. We can't let them take you again."

"Enough," Morgen snapped. "I am still your queen. My will commands."

Rebuked, Max fell silent. As if on cue, the assassins raised their blades. Yet instead of advancing in, what Daniel assumed to be a clear victory, they sheathed their daggers and melted back into the night without a trace.

"Watch your flanks," Constantin warned.

Headlights flooded the area, accompanied by the soft roar of engines. The military vehicles rolled in: Blackmere's QRF team had arrived at last. Still Daniel remained on guard. The thought of being surprised by the assassins high on his mind, he tracked his rifle across his immediate field of fire in search of any movement. It was as if they disappeared. No heat signatures. No movement. Nothing but a handful of dead bodies and two destroyed cars puffing smoke.

Three government issue SUVs, black and armored fanned out to cover the exposed places and provide escape for Daniel and his team. Team, he found the concept amusing. They could not be a more different group if he tried writing it into one of his stories. Strange, the idea never crossed his mind to blur this newfound reality with the fantasy that had made him an international bestselling author until now. Some secrets deserved to be kept though. Especially ones capable of ruining his career.

Only when it became evident no additional assault was coming did he lower and sling his rifle across his chest. Daniel took a deep breath for the first time since the battle in Raleigh started. His legs trembled, threatening to give out. Sweat made his clothes stick to his body in an uncomfortable shell. He wanted to sit down, take a long drink of water, and take an even longer nap. He looked at Morgen, surprised to find her standing tall in the middle of the chaos.

"I am no damsel in distress," she glared at the bodies. "That was your first mistake."

"Now they come." Max sneered. "Where were your men when we needed them, Blackmere?"

Ignoring the obvious fact that helicopters moved much faster than any truck, Blackmere focused on the SUVs and decided not to reply to the dwarf. He didn't have an answer, just suspicions. Several agents spilled out, forming a defensive perimeter around Deputy Director Corman who was last to appear. Blackmere couldn't keep the disappointment from his face. His career had been stagnant for so long he wondered how much he had left in the tank. The debacle of the high king's assassination a few years all but cemented his place in the hierarchy. By returning to Raleigh with the queen alive and relatively unharmed he ensured a promotion.

Corman showing up with the QRF cast all those thoughts in doubt. Granted, the man was second in command of DESA and Morgen was a high-profile case, but his presence undercut Blackmere's authority without saying a word. Not to mention the surety with which Daniel took over the battlespace. He wanted to crawl back into the Blackhawk and forget this night ever happened.

"Agent Blackmere, report," Corman called.

There was an intensity in his gaze as he took in the carnage that Blackmere didn't like. Corman was a man who expected competence in all subordinates. From his view of the area, Blackmere knew the current scene lacked any semblance of DESA's standard operating procedures.

"Sir, we have ten confirmed enemy KIA. A third Hand group of five was preparing to attack when the QRF arrived and scared them off. The queen is safe, as you can see," Blackmere stated. "There were numerous civilians in the vicinity when the engagement began, but nothing we could do about that without jeopardizing losing the queen. I chose what I deemed the best course of action and engaged."

Corman eventually bobbed his head. "Yes. Yes, I can see that. Good job, Blackmere. There were no civilian casualties?"

"No, sir." His shoulders dipped slightly.

"Three Hand groups, you say? Bold for them. Damned murderers usually keep their work quiet and low level." He turned to Morgen, "Your Majesty, I think you are still in danger and we must move you quickly."

"This team is more than capable of seeing to my security," Morgen replied, straightening. "I owe them my life."

"Indeed," Corman agreed, "but we cannot allow ourselves to become complacent now. Not with who knows how many more are out there. They want you desperately and I will not be the man to lose the woman the clans are looking to for leadership now."

"What do you propose, Corman?" she asked without deference. For the first time since dressing for the conference, Morgen realized she was exhausted. A woman only had so much fight, after all.

"We move you somewhere safe. Away from the lights and temptations."

She folded her arms, thrusting her chin out. "Absolutely not. My people need me. I will not cower in the shadows while the clans are in disarray. The vote must happen."

"Returning to Raleigh is out of the question. We have already proven we cannot keep you safe there. You have capable heads of state still in control, as well as my agency," Corman insisted.

"He may have a point," Daniel cautioned. "The

Invisible Hand already struck once, right under our noses."

Trapped between honor and duty, Morgen contemplated her options. Neither offered much inspiration. It had been so long since the last time she'd been backed into a corner the urge to fight threatened to overwhelm her.

"What leads you to believe I would be any safer wherever you intend on hiding me? I am still a queen and not subject to human jurisdiction."

"I'm afraid this is not up for debate. I am a representative of the United States government and I have final authority to decide the outcome of this scenario now that human lives have been lost." He fixed her with a look daring her to counter again. "Or perhaps you would like to console the widows of those agents killed tonight? In your royal capacity, of course."

"Mind yourself. This is not the hour," Constantin warned.

The hum of his power sword activating making Daniel nervous. "We just need to take a second and regroup here," he tried, again hoping to keep tentative peace.

Corman backed down, if just. Holding up his hands, he cocked his head. "Perhaps I allowed the situation to get the better of me, your Majesty. But you cannot ignore the threat facing you. All of you. You are in danger, and I need to be able to keep you safe until we can discover the source of these attacks."

"I think that is well established," Sara piped in. She looked at Daniel and frowned. He could tell she liked Corman as much as he did, which was not at all.

"Yes, but not the way," Corman replied, his voice thin.

"He has a point," Blackmere stated. "We don't know why they are intent on capturing you, your Majesty, or who is behind them. Organizations like that tend to work for someone, usually a power backer."

"That could be anyone, Blackmere," Max said, stroking his beard.

"The government men are right, your Majesty," Slim added when no one else said anything immediately. "Your safety is paramount to our survival as a species."

Daniel couldn't help but grin. "Look at you using big words."

Nevada Slim's eyes narrowed but he could not hold a straight face for long before he grinned too. "I may be royalty now, but I'll always be me, Daniel."

"Then get rid of the straw. How did you even keep it with all the fighting?"

"Fine," Morgen interrupted before Slim could reply. "But I do this under duress. A queen should lead her people in times of crisis, not cower. My enemies have much to answer for."

"And they shall," Corman said. "You have my word. I will commit all my resources to discovering the truth behind the Hand."

She unfolded her arms in a failed attempt at looking less hostile. Daniel found her intimidating regardless. "Very well, where do you propose to seclude me?"

"We have a dedicated safehouse in the mountains. Only a handful know of its location. You should be safe there while we investigate and, hopefully, stop the Invisible Hand for good." Corman turned to Blackmere. "I will give you the coordinates. You are to stay in constant communication with me. There can be no more mistakes, Agent Blackmere."

"I understand."

Cleanup teams arrived a moment later and immediately swarmed in. Dressed in white utilities overalls with masks and gloves, they began snatching up the bodies and weapons, taking special care to give honor to the fallen agents while tossing the assassins in the back of a van. Daniel watched with fascination at the clinical disconnection those men and women had as they performed their jobs. He failed to see how anyone could be so dispassionate about wasted lives.

Additional agents began washing away the blood. Still others pulled in with a pair of tow trucks to haul off the wrecks. Soon the area would be sterilized and appear as if nothing had ever happened. Only a handful of confused civilians, now far on the road toward their destinations, would know of a strange event in the heart of North Carolina. None would discover the truth, for the government was adapt in concealing matters it did not want becoming public. Especially where elves were concerned.

Corman stalked off to inspect his people. Though he appeared satisfied with the results of this night, Daniel suspected the man bore a measure of distrust in Blackmere now. A shame. While Daniel had no love for Blackmere he respected the man's commitment to country, even if a level of unspoken corruption festered in the organization's heart. One no one in charge wanted to accept or assume responsibility for. *Who's the threat? Which one of you is going to stab the knife in my back?*

Daniel turned to Blackmere. "I don't like this."

"There's nothing to like," the agent replied. "We all have orders."

Daniel felt Sara slip her arm into his, pressing against his side, before she said, "It's going to be all right."

"I hope you're right," he said without taking his eyes off the Deputy Director and the cleanup teams.

NINETEEN

"I don't like this."

Daniel looked at Sara as she repeated his earlier statement that he had said to Blackmere minutes ago. *You just said…* He said nothing, no reassurance like she had for him. They were forced into the back of the bottle with only a narrow way out. Heaped against rising tides of obstacles and an enemy force striking at will, he failed to see much of a bright spot. Clearly the Invisible Hand held all the advantages. He had no way of knowing how many resources the group had. Judging from the number of bodies littering half the state it seemed endless.

"There's not much to like. DESA has us between that rock and a hard place."

"But why? Why send us to the middle of nowhere, alone and away from allies should those killers discover us?" she pressed.

Admittedly, Sara had a good point. They were sacrificing strength in numbers for secrecy. He failed to recall a time where that worked according to plan. Strained and with most of their ammunition depleted, he accepted their situation with hesitation. A quick glance at the others, spaced apart, did little to assuage his rising trepidation. Elves and dwarves may appear as allies at first sight, but their differences simmered beneath the surface. Daniel knew it wouldn't take much for that alliance to splinter and devolve into battle. Across from them stood the DESA agents. He saw Blackmere in a new light but refused to give the man his full trust. It was James Corman who sparked doubts.

Cocksure and arrogant, the man bordered on open hostility toward the elves, especially Morgen. Why go through all the trouble to protect the queen if you hated the species? Daniel marked Corman as trouble and decided the best way forward went through not trusting him. Ranking officials often fell prey to opposing forces. He'd seen it before. Loyalty stretched as far as a man's limits before temptation snuck in. The possibility of Corman being corrupt was there, but yet unfounded.

"We've been to the mountains before, Sara. You know how easy it is to disappear if we want to," he told her. "That doesn't mean I like it either, but it was Morgen's decision. She accepted and here we are."

Sara fixed him with a glare. "But Valle Crucis? It's in the middle of nowhere."

"That's the point."

"Daniel, cell phones hardly work up there. We'll be cut off from everything."

He placed a hand on her shoulder. "Sara, if our friends can't find us neither can those assassins. We have to trust someone or we'll be eating our own before long."

"We should get more guns," she grumbled. "And definitely more bullets."

That was the smartest thing he had heard all night. He grinned like a lovestruck fool.

"Are you certain that is wise?" The piece of straw was gone, as was his Nevada Slim persona. He stood before Morgen as Baron Visilias, a loyal subject of the crown and staunch supporter. When or how that transition took place was lost on him. One day he served in DESA's secret group of strike teams. The next he stood in his father's place with a family and kingdom to rule. At her frown, he looked down at the stained and bloodied suit that cost more than he was willingly to admit.

"I am unused to being questioned so, Baron. Too many jump when I command."

"Perhaps it is a sign you need someone to balance your thoughts," he replied.

"Perhaps. To answer your question, no, but there is a measure of wisdom in sequestering where our foes cannot strike. I do not like the idea of leaving our people to fall apart in my absence. The clans have suffered from too many different thoughts." She swore, straightening. "What we need is unity. It is the only way we will survive the future."

He nodded. Growing up, he was taught Morgen was filled with vitriol. This night proved all those lectures wrong. Visilias realized he backed the right person.

"There may be a way to salvage your dream, your Majesty," Constantin said, joining them. "You won't like it though."

"Constantin Andros, while I trust your judgment implicitly, I have always considered your suggestions with a grain of salt. It leads me to question whether your addiction to danger is a threat to the crown or just yourself."

The Old Guard blushed. "I am a loyal subject."

"Your loyalty has never been in question, my friend," she said. "Please, continue."

Constantin cleared his throat before replying, "We send the Baron back with to gather the nobles and continue your work."

"Say what now?" Visilias asked, stiffening. "I said the queen has my full support, not that I wanted to fill in for her until she returns."

"He has a point," Morgen admitted. "You have been with me since I anointed you, but that is the recent past. Still, you are the only one to come to my aid and thus, the only one I trust. I repay loyalty, Baron. Do this for me. I beg you."

"I'm not that person, your Majesty," he protested.

"It is time for you to become that person," she replied. At his hiss of panic, she continued, "Baron Visilias, I charge you with this task. Do not let the clans fall apart. Build the alliance in my absence."

"Your Majesty, I think—"

She stayed his protests with an open hand. "Nay, I will not accept no from you. Nor do I ask you to lead the reformation. Just hold it together for me. Can you do that?"

Every instinct screamed for him to run. How he longed to return to his old days where he roamed the world at random without worry or concern as Nevada Slim. The burden of leadership nearly took him to his knees, forcing him to think of more than himself.

"How? I am not well versed in the ways of nobility," he asked. Even he heard the resignation in his voice which signaled her victory.

The slightest twinkle of mischief entered in her eyes. "Oh, I am sure you will find a way. Perhaps use some of that Nevada Slim charm that worked so well with our DESA friends. I will draft the orders." She turned to the silent, Old Guard. "Constantin, I want you to return with him and reorganize security."

"But your Majesty! Duty compels me to remain by your side!" the Old Guard fumed.

"Funny how that works," the Baron smirked.

"This is my command," she said, her voice hard. "Do not disobey me now." At his nod, she smiled. "There is another task I have for you upon your return to Raleigh."

"What do you suppose they are plotting?" Corman mused as he and Blackmere watched the elves huddled together near a transport vehicle. Only the dwarf stood apart, out of earshot, content with breaking down and cleaning his weapon while the others dithered over the next course of action. "Elves. Have you ever known a more divisive or contemptable species?"

Blackmere stood, uncomfortable with the line of questioning. He vowed to serve his nation at the expense of keeping the greatest secret mankind ever had. That didn't mean he believed humans were superior. They were just different, and both occupied the same planet. "Sir, she is the queen. Her entire world stands upon the brink of collapse. I should think they are working through their issues to save elfkind and keep to our treaties."

"Bah. We should never have been forced to care for

them. I feel more like a warden than a bureaucrat. It would be better for all if we had the power to shove them in one country and guard the boundaries," Corman retorted.

Knowing to hold his tongue, Blackmere listened to his superior's tirade with a blank expression. He had suspected Corman's bias, bordering on open racism, for some time but this was his first true encounter. Did others in the senior leadership feel this way or was Corman an outlier? He wished he could peel back the layers and discover the truth, if for no other reason than to find a measure of peace of mind. He would've liked to know just where everyone stood as the echelons of power were confusing enough without privately questioning those in charge.

"No comment, Blackmere? I should have thought all your years of service might loosen your thoughts. "

"It's not my place, sir."

"Nonsense. I asked your opinion. You've worked more closely with these people than I. What is your gut telling you?"

Biting the inside of his cheek, Blackmere said, "Morgen will do what she must. The clans are in disarray at the moment. She needs to find a way to calm matters before they spiral out of control. I don't envy her."

"It is better to sit beside the king than be a king, eh?" Corman contemplated. "This is a dangerous time for them and us. Our careers are in the noose if we fail to keep her alive. Personally, I don't give a damn about elven society or their troubles, but this assault has brought us into it. You will remain with her until I recall you back to Raleigh. Is that clear?"

"Yes, sir," he replied. "What further orders do you have for me?"

"None. Keep them alive. Keep them safe and beware of the Invisible Hand." He tossed a set of keys to Blackmere. "Here's your vehicle. I'll be in touch when you can return."

Blackmere knew his time with the elves had entered the most dangerous phase. One he might not survive. The only question remained who was going to be the one to do him in.

Max guzzled the Mountain Dew until the last drop popped onto his tongue then let out a massive belch. He tossed the empty bottle aside and wiped his lips. The dwarf passed silent judgment on his companions as they continued to ignore him. Though they counted among the best for their roles, he longed to have his sons beside him once more. He hoped they were well amidst the confusion and violence. Few forces could prevent the fury of a trio of dwarves when unleashed. He knew they were going to need the additional help before this event resolved.

"So, this is it?" he asked when the others, minus two notable members, joined him.

"It would appear so," Morgen confirmed. "Visilias and Constantin are to return in my stead."

Max poked at a piece of meat lodged between his back teeth with his tongue before replying, "Eh, could be worse. What's our move?"

"The Deputy Director has provided me with coordinates to the DESA safehouse he mentioned before. It's about two hours away. We should be getting on the road before dawn," Blackmere said.

Knowing the agent was holding something back, Max held out his hands for the keys. "Fine, I'm driving." He caught the keys and headed for their SUV without delay.

When no one else moved, Morgen offered, "It appears we are going to the mountains. Best hurry before that stubborn dwarf drives off without us."

Daniel watched her go, wondering once more how he had gotten himself into this mess. With Sara too. It was then he noticed the off look in Blackmere's eyes. "What aren't you telling us, Blackmere?"

Startled, Blackmere hedged, "Nothing. We had best get going."

Daniel wasn't thrown off but shrugged because picking a fight right now would be pointless. "Keep your secrets, but if they wind up putting us in danger, I promise I have a round saved for you. This isn't just about the elves, Blackmere. This is about my family."

Sara at his side, they left for the SUV.

Thaddeus Blackmere wanted to throw his hands to sky and bellow his frustrations at the top of his lungs. He gave James Corman and those remaining behind with him a final look, as if contemplating how much to keep to himself before stepping after the queen. *How do I tell Daniel this is about far more than just our lives? This is about survival.*

Too much went wrong this day for any sense of comfort. Blackmere struggled trying to piece the puzzle together but ran into a dead end in every direction. While he could have used the additional firepower the Old Guard and Visilias provided, he knew moving in a smaller group increased the odds of escaping detection long enough for the people on the ground in Raleigh to get to the bottom of who betrayed them to the Invisible Hand. And if they didn't…

TWENTY

Far from the ideal crew to have at his back, Daniel forced himself to think beyond the obvious. Survival was paramount and, despite the lack of evidence, he suspected they were stumbling into another trap. The night evolved too conveniently to accept at face value. He trusted each of those in the SUV and knew they were loyal, but the unknown threatened to unravel his thoughts.

Most concerning was Deputy Director Corman's involvement. Daniel didn't know where the man fit into the scheme, only that his presence felt off. Sure, he knew plenty of commanders who insisted on being in the middle of the action. They served no real purpose other than being in the way or shifting concern off the mission to ensure their safety. For the second ranking member of DESA to be in the field, even on a night such as this, smelled bad to Daniel. But how to approach the subject with Blackmere without rousing the agent's ire?

Their relationship already tenuous, Daniel couldn't afford to alienate the government man altogether. Not yet. Not until he was certain where the man's true loyalties lie. Thankfully, Blackmere was soon snoring in oblivious sleep with his head against the doorframe.

He hit his fist against his thigh, willing himself to concentrate. The slapping continued until Sara placed her hand atop his, stopping the action.

"What's wrong?"

Where do I begin? I feel the noose tightening with each passing hour: have since Morgen summoned us to her lair. I used to think this was fun and games, a chance to relive my old life, but here I go and drag you into the middle of it. Shit!

"I know that look. You're thinking too much," she scolded.

How many times had he heard that before? Certainly not from any of his high school teachers. They were more than happy to funnel him up to the next grade and then out the door. None of his squad leaders thought him stellar material during those early army days either. He proved himself in the field then others took notice and began to listen. Daniel rose through the ranks before retiring a senior NCO.

Not that that meant much to his current predicament. Sara was the sort who forced a conversation and, given the tight confines of the truck's cabin and Daniel's reluctance to play his hand in front of the others, was wedging him into a bad spot.

"Daniel?"

He placed his other hand atop hers and squeezed softly before letting go. "I'll tell you when I figure it out." Seeing her mouth open, he shifted away to call up to the front seat, "Hey Max, how much longer before we reach the safehouse?"

The dwarf's jewel-like eyes glittered in the fading darkness as he glanced into the rearview mirror at him. "An hour and a half according to the nav. You should be sleeping."

"Too much to think about," Daniel replied, disgruntled it had only been thirty minutes since they pulled out. "We're going to need supplies once we get there. I don't imagine DESA keeps their bolt holes fully stocked."

"Water and standard military rations only usually," Blackmere chimed in. Daniel glanced at him to see him wiping a spot of drool from his chin. "I don't recall having one in Valle Crucis though."

"Looks like they don't tell you everything either," Daniel muttered with a snort. "You and I need to have a serious conversation when we get there."

"Agreed."

That was it. No argument. No sense of concern. Just a simple confirmation. *Why does that bother me even more?*

"And I also agree with stocking up with provisions," Blackmere added after Daniel failed to reply. "There's no telling how long we're going to be here."

"I will not hide for long, Agent Blackmere," Morgen interjected. The strength in her tone left no room for suggestion, as did her claiming the passenger seat despite their protests. Daniel figured they had three days max before she'd leave on her own. "My kingdom stands upon the brink. I allowed your Deputy Director this night and one more to settle matters. Cowering in shadows doesn't suit a queen. The time is soon approaching where the elves will take the fight to this Invisible Hand."

Not even three days. Ha. Daniel grabbed Sara's hand when she shifted in her seat.

"Your Majesty—"

Morgen twisted around, giving Blackmere an intimidating glare. "My word is final, Agent Blackmere. Treaties be damned."

Rebuked, he still refused to back down. Daniel almost felt sorry for him. "You risk everything our two societies have built for revenge? I don't understand."

"Perhaps once you have been pushed against the wall and given no other option than to surrender you might begin to. This is a desperate hour, and I will not be the one to allow my people to fall. Not now, after all we've endured."

The SUV fell into awkward silence. Daniel held Sara's hand a little tighter and stared out the window.

Disgust. Raw and deep-rooted filled him at each item Max tossed into their shopping cart. Daniel's stomach clenched at the thought of what a box of Slim Jims and energy drinks would do to his poor stomach. Add several bags of spicy pork rinds, packets of noodles, and a bag of rock gut coffee and Daniel found himself transported back to his days as a private where anything tasted better than

MREs. He failed to keep the sneer from his face as the dwarf ambled by, squeaky wheel and all, with a wide grin.

"You all right?" Sara asked as she rounded the corner with an armload of vegetables.

The difference of her choices and the dwarf's caused him to laugh. "Yeah, though I think my stomach feels bad for what Max is buying."

She winced. "I saw that. I guess he has a better metabolism?"

"Or an iron stomach," Daniel agreed. "Get everything you wanted?"

"I'd love to say yes but without knowing how long we are going to be here…" She shrugged. "Do you think there's a grill?"

"You want me to throw some steaks on for dinner?" At her second shrug, he sighed. "Sara, this isn't a vacation. We're laying low and have to be prepared for another attack."

"We still need to eat."

"And go to the bathroom."

She made a face. "What?"

Daniel grinned. "Nothing. More of a private joke. I was thinking how you never read a character having to take a bathroom break in the middle of the big battle scene."

She reached up to cup his cheek. "That's why it's called fantasy, silly. I'll get the toilet paper. You know, just in case."

"Fine, I'll hit the meat section," he relented.

"Oh, you still owe me an explanation of what's bothering you," she called before he turned the corner.

"Outside, when we are alone," he grimaced.

"Promises, promises."

Daniel cornered Blackmere in the Food Lion parking lot as the others checked out their various food choices. The agent bore a haggard look that Daniel chalked up to the combination of age, stress, and fatigue. Knowing that did little to stem his rising anger at the man. *Am I angry at him or at having the rug pulled out from under me? I don't need to be here. I could have said no and gone home at any point. This is as much my fault as anyone's.*

"What's the word from back in Raleigh?" Daniel did his best to sound neutral.

Blackmere put his phone away and faced him. "Nothing new. Corman is back on the scene. Cleanup is still underway. Baron Visilias, I still have trouble thinking of him as anything more than Nevada Slim, is gathering the remaining nobles and heads of families. Constantin is rallying the surviving Old Guard to retaliate."

"No word on who sanctioned the assault?"

Blackmere gave him a queer look. "What are you getting at, Daniel? It's not like you to beat around the bush."

Daniel leaned against the SUV and stretched before admitting, "I don't trust Corman."

"Neither do I."

"He's the sort who storms in with secrets and…. Huh?" Daniel paused as the agent's reply sank in. "What do you mean you don't trust him? He's your boss."

Blackmere looked around to ensure they were alone before leaning in closer. "Yes, but he's hiding something. I don't know what and that worries me."

"You think he's working with the Hand? Funneling their efforts?"

"I don't know. I don't think so. He's been in the agency for as long as I can remember. The man has earned his stripes, Daniel. What purpose would it serve for him to switch sides now?"

Every year in the army his unit sat through security briefings, most of them ending with a detailing of soldiers who gave away sensitive information to enemy countries for a meager sum, ruining their lives forever. Greed and hate offered opportunity for those with weak conviction. Then there was the bandage on Corman's hand. If that wasn't a sign Daniel didn't know what was. Too bad he lacked proof.

"Maybe Corman thinks he's the one to not get caught," Daniel suggested. At Blackmere's huff, he rushed to continue. "Before you get all defensive on me, I'm not saying he's a spy. Just that the possibility is there. Whether we want to admit it or not."

"You're talking about the band-aid on the back of his hand."

Daniel barely avoided grinning. "You saw that too."

"Of course I did. I am a professional," Blackmere snapped. "He said he got a cut doing yardwork."

"And you believe that?" Daniel rolled his eyes.

The agent shrugged. "I don't have any way to disprove it."

"We could—"

"We're focusing on the wrong thing," Blackmere interrupted. "We need to be trying to think ahead of the Hand. If they should discover us, you and I both know that's a fight we might not win."

"We need backup." He almost wished for Angus and Fritz, despite their proclivity to entice violence.

"From where? Bring in more elves or dwarves and we'll have another mess to clean up, or worse. And too many federal agents will force the enemy away, allowing them to choose how and where to strike." Blackmere shook his head. "You said it yourself, we don't know who we can trust. I'm afraid we're in this alone."

"Then you better hope we have enough ammo and this safehouse is in a defensible position," Daniel said, avoiding stating the obvious 'otherwise'. "The others should be coming out soon. We need to get this carnival on the road."

They had stopped in the college town of Boone, home to Appalachian State University, for supplies and the opportunity to decompress from the previous night. Sleep beckoned, burning his eyes and reducing him to feeling and acting sluggish. Though Daniel had argued against stopping. After being shouted at, he gave in. He learned long ago not to go against the tide and did his part to facilitate the process. That did little to keep him from feeling exposed right now.

"I'll go get the others."

Leaving Blackmere, Daniel sauntered back toward the store entrance, pausing to let a young mother pushing her baby stroller go ahead of him. He smiled down at the child, knowing it had no clue what kind of world it was in. His steps were jarred by the rest of the group emerging and Max nearly running him over with the cart.

It was Morgen who gave him pause. He never imagined seeing a queen leaving Food Lion, much less any grocery store. People like that didn't drive or shop for themselves. They relied on the subservience of others to see to their needs. At her look of disdain, he shook his head. *And look where that landed her. Smack in the middle of a shit storm she can't escape.*

Daniel fell in line beside Sara, only half hearing her argument with Max on the importance of vegetables for a healthy diet. After helping load the groceries, he tried to think of it as supplies, Daniel closed the hatch and watched Sara excuse herself to make two quick calls to ensure the kids and the dogs were fine. He didn't blame her. Once they got up into the mountains there was no telling what sort of cell signal they'd have. Best to leave with everything in order. Any reassurance was worth its weight in situations like this.

She returned with a guarded look.

"Everything all right?" he asked.

She nodded. "Yep. Norman has been playing with the dogs. Says he's covered in fur."

"That's…nice," Daniel replied with a hint of doubt on his tongue. Given the gargoyle's uses in a fight, he found it odd the big guy was sitting this one out. "All right let's get moving before it gets too late. I don't like the idea of being caught in the open. If that's fine with you, your Majesty?"

Morgen, dressed more appropriately in a sweatshirt and yoga pants from the Target across the street, arched an eyebrow but gestured with her hand rather than reply.

TWENTY-ONE

To say they were in the middle of nowhere was an insult to nowhere. Pulling away from the quaint mountain town, they quickly left the trappings of civilization behind. Houses turned into fields and mountains. Pavement became dirt roads. Up and around they drove until they were all lost—besides the GPS.

Daniel admired the view. There was tranquility to be found among the mountain streams, lakes, and endless fields he rarely got to enjoy throughout his travels. It reminded him a little of home. He stared out at the endless sea of trees as they made another turn. It was a world that didn't know strife or the hardships of the elves. Almost primal, this was where people went to escape. Daniel's eyes found the shimmering waters of a clear pond, now several hundred meters below, as the morning sun reflected.

He assumed it was the last time he was going to get to enjoy himself before the assassins found them. How could they not? Every indicator suggested the Invisible Hand benefited from a vast intelligence network. They knew every move Morgen made, well in advance. Daniel knew any victory was fleeting and, if not rooted out at the source, meaningless in the grand scheme. Especially if the government was working against them. He couldn't shake the feeling Corman was involved more than he admitted.

"Didn't we stay around here once?" Sara asked as they continued into the deep mountains.

He nodded. "Not too far. I think the old Mast Store is nearby. It's been years." They hadn't spotted a building in a while. "Remember when we—"

"I trust you are studying the roads, Daniel," Morgen interrupted. "It wouldn't do for us to be trapped without an exit point."

"Study the roads? Morgen, I have no idea where we

are," Daniel replied, irritation showing in his tone. In truth, they were fortunate their route was still being picked up by the nav. "The only benefit is in our enemies not being familiar with this area."

"Meaning if we are lost they must also be?" she questioned.

He smiled. "Something like that."

Max wheeled the SUV around a sharp bend that went up. Daniel could pick out a red metal roof of another house on the adjacent peak. Foliage obscured any other possible structures. Just the way the owners intended. Many of the houses were rental properties and vacant most of the year. Tourists and city folk seeking to 'rough it' for a weekend found the lure of the mountains romantic and mysterious. Daniel thought they were idiots but couldn't fault them for wanting to get away. He longed to do so right now.

"Looks like we're here," Max announced over the sound of tires crunching gravel.

Craning his head to get a better view, Daniel took in the expansive log cabin. It had three levels, with the highest having a single window. The lower level was wrapped with a deck overlooking the downward slope and the road below. He could still see the pond and the driveway was on the opposite side of the road leading up to the red roofed house. Defensible, though not ideal.

The hillside practically dug into the back of the house, preventing all but a suicidal charge from coming down from above. Daniel imagined the mountainside swept around the home, funneling any attack from either below, where they would be forced up a steep hillside, or through the front door. He liked their odds.

"You can't possibly expect me to stay in this?" Morgen asked. "Here? I would think DESA would spring for better accommodations."

"What's wrong with this?" Max scratched his cheek as he looked around. "Seems cozy."

Morgen rolled her eyes.

"Sorry this isn't a five star hotel, but we need to hide, not advertise our whereabouts," Blackmere said without looking at any of them.

"We can hold here," Daniel said before the opportunity to devolve into another argument arose. "I need to sweep the property. Verify all entry points and figure out where to place the heavy gun, but this isn't the worst place to be."

"I'll come with," Max added. "Need to stretch my legs and all."

Daniel nodded and gave Sara a quick kiss. "Be right back."

"Stay safe," she replied.

"They are an odd pair," Blackmere said after they disappeared from view.

"Perhaps the best among us," Morgen corrected. "We are in good hands, Agent Blackmere."

"Thaddeus, please. I don't feel much of an agent these days. It's been a long time since I got into a fight."

"We do as we must," Morgen said. "I don't expect you to throw yourself in the line, Thaddeus. That's what those two are foe and woe be unto our foes should they stumble upon the defenses."

"It's a lovely day," Sara threw in. She had never felt like she didn't belong more than right now. Surrounded by a regent and warriors. For so long she relied on hearing tales from others. Listening to Daniel reminisce of his army days or work through a book plot. Now she was thrust into the middle of her most harrowing adventure, a real one at that. Nothing she did against the werewolves felt comparable to the danger levels here in the quiet of the mountains. She almost laughed at herself. Over a year trying to convince herself the werewolf escapade wasn't real and it was all washed away thanks to evil ninjas trying to kill them all.

She caught Morgen studying her. Passing silent judgment. Sara steeled herself beneath that haughty gaze. The queen may rule an entire people, but she was still a woman. One Sara had come to learn how to handle without compromising her integrity. A secret part of her thrilled at the confrontation. She once dreamed of mingling with royalty. Reality proved far different from fictional meetings, however. Sara put on her best smile, though it killed her inside.

To her surprise, Morgen replied, "Yes, I believe you are right. Would you care to walk with me, Sara? It seems a shame to waste this glorious morning trapped inside."

"Do you think it's safe?" she asked, glancing at Blackmere.

"Oh, I doubt the Invisible Hand will have discovered us this soon," Morgen replied. "Don't you agree, Thaddeus?"

"I don't see how they could. I'll go check the interior and start unloading the truck."

Sara folded her arms. *Then why don't I feel safe?*

Max stepped around the end of a fallen tree as Daniel shifted around a wide trunk of another nearby. They had circled around the house and kept going a few hundred meters to get a better idea of the lay of the land. Though neither spoke aloud, both were establishing escape routes should the safehouse fall. Daniel and Max would exchange the occasional nod or hand gesture before slipping through the forested slope.

Daniel halted when he could no longer see any part of the house or the road below. He leaned against a tree and took in the view. Lightly forested and steep enough to prevent all but the most determined foe from assaulting, the mountainside presented a natural obstacle cutting off escape without difficulty.

"Looks like that dry streambed is our best option if

it comes to that," he said and gestured to the gully plunging down.

Max grunted, stopping beside him. "That's a lot of rocks. Plenty of chances to twist an ankle in the dark."

"Is there a choice?" Daniel countered. "We're in a tight position. The safehouse is remote enough to prevent the Hand from striking with ease but that advantage is lost the moment they realize they have us trapped."

"Beats being in the goblin nest," Max replied.

Disgust twisted his face. "Don't remind me. It took weeks of washing before I got that stench from my clothes."

"I burned mine," Max laughed. He tugged on his beard, looking around once more. "This blows."

Daniel agreed. He hated having his options taken away. There seemed little doubt their enemy would find them. He felt it in his bones. That sense of surety one couldn't shake. The noose drew tighter, trapping them. And for what? Secluded from the rest of the world, with limited communications and no foreseeable back up.

"What do you think about Corman?" he asked.

"That suit? He's in the way. Stormed into my command post and started making demands while you were with Goran." The dwarf shook his head. "I think he weakened our position just enough to let the assassins slip in undetected."

"On purpose?" Daniel didn't like the implications of Max thinking the same.

Tugging his beard, Max looked thoughtful. "Maybe, but how can you prove it? Look Daniel, I don't like humans much and he's one of those who fights a war from behind their computer screen while trying to be the big star. That doesn't make him evil. Could be he's a bumbling idiot more worried about which tie to wear than saving lives."

"Right. Still, I don't like it. He's too involved," Daniel replied with a puffed out breath.

"Relax. We'll know for certain if the Hand shows

up before dusk. Until then, we continue recon and secure the house. By then it will be lunch and I'm already starving."

"Does your wife know about the junk you eat in the field?" Daniel asked as they started moving again.

"No and you're not going to tell her," Max said with a glower. "It would be a shame to have to cut out that tongue of yours."

Daniel chuckled.

"I miss Aislinn," Morgen said without warning.

Caught off guard, Sara tried to stop the memory of watching the elf die resurface in her mind. "She was a good woman."

"More than that, Sara. She was my conscience during dark times. Everything has fallen apart since my husband died. Aislinn kept me on task, guiding me without accepting credit. She stood against my fury. Never batted an eye. If only I had others who felt similar."

"I can't believe you've lived all this time without developing your web of allies."

Morgen hummed. "Allies I have aplenty. You misunderstand me. I speak of those willing to speak up when they think I am wrong. Those who jeopardize themselves for the greater good of the clans. Aislinn was rare, even among elves."

"Rare among humans too," Sara added. A male cardinal chirped from a branch above them. His bright red feathers in sharp contrast to the shades of green. She cracked a smile. "They say cardinals are angels sent to watch over us. This one could be Aislinn."

"A comforting thought," Morgen whispered, studying the bird.

Sara was happy the queen accepted her words as a peace of mind. The image of Aislinn lying at Morgen's feet a moment before disintegrating flashed in her mind.

"This is good land. Quiet. Secluded. Perhaps I

should move the seat of my kingdom here, away from the chaos of city life."

"You'd give up all you've work so hard to build?" Sara balked.

"What would that be, Sara? A crumbling empire pressed in by the greed of humans and the decay of my own people? As much as I am loath to admit it, I cannot rule the clans alone."

Sara narrowed her gaze. "Are you speaking of abdicating?"

"Let us not talk foolishly here," Morgen chided. "I merely suggest moving the heart of the kingdom to a location better suited to the clans. Human cities have ruined our society. They made us soft. There was a time when we thrived in nature. We were attuned to the world and knew harmony unlike any since. I miss those days, simple as they were."

Sara laid a consoling hand on Morgen's shoulder. "Perhaps this is the storm you need to cleanse the land. I've always imagined what it might be without cell phones or cars."

"It is easy to look back on the past and think those days were better than now," Morgen added. "The nostalgia is a powerful lure. Progress demands we look forward rather than back. The past has its place, Sara."

"Just not here."

"No, not here. Come, let us continue our walk. I fear there will not come another time soon," Morgen suggested.

TWENTY-TWO

An unmitigated disaster. There was no other way to describe the previous night's events. Jams Corman stormed through the remaining carnage wearing a perpetual glare of disgust. He expected better, from all parties. The sheer sloppiness of the Invisible Hand assault coupled with the inability of the dwarves to counter without minimizing damage left him astounded. His career was built upon a bedrock of competency, mingled with the right amount of aggressive selfishness so many in Washington thrived on. That was the path to true power. Not bowing before the false monarch of a species that shouldn't exist.

Corman held no love for the elves and their unending stream of drama and problems. Funneling them away to secret prison facilities like the Grinder brought him the most joy he'd had in years, perhaps since joining DESA. To think any creature other than humanity should walk the same planet with indifference toward the true rulers offended him on fundamental levels. A piece of Corman wished for the end of the elves to happen already. It was an inevitability. They weakened with each new generation. Their blood diluted to the point of becoming mundane. The sooner the elves faded away the better for all humanity.

A trio of agents spotted his approach as they stood outside the command center door. One slipped inside to likely warn the others before he arrived. He didn't mind. Better to find a scene prepared for him than otherwise.

The door opened for him and a voice greeted, "Welcome back, Deputy Director."

"Agent Andres. Status report."

He hand-selected her straight out of the academy over a decade ago. Corman knew her to be capable in most aspects and willing to do the necessary on command. The perfect tool to weaponize should matters devolve that far.

Since rising to his current position, Corman accumulated assets loyal to him.

"Sir, all human bodies have been removed. Crews anticipate having this facility fully restored by nightfall. Media teams are still spinning the narrative we first discussed to cover for us."

"What of that van filled with weapons out back?" Corman asked.

"Gone. It appears the elves removed it sometime during the confusion of the night."

So, they managed to keep their arsenal and armorer out of my hands, again. Very wise, but futile. "I want an edict issued to all channels. The elf clans are to stand down. They will shelter in place until the threat has passed. Anyone found breaking curfew will be arrested and sentenced without trial for violation of the treaty. I want the armorer brought to me. He will be punished for his careless disregard for life and secrecy. This is non-negotiable. Am I clear, Andres?"

A whisp of her black hair slipped over part of her face as she nodded. "Yes, sir, though the elves will not like that. There is bound to be dissent."

"I don't care what the elves like. This is a human matter now, and I am in charge," he growled. "Where are the remaining nobles?"

"Most filtered off during the night," she replied after a pause.

He stiffened, glaring down at her. "They did what? I gave strict orders for no one to leave."

"Apparently they did not feel your decree pertained to them, sir," Andres said with a slight shudder.

Corman clenched a fist. The veins on his neck popped but he held his tongue. He hated being ignored and had since the first time he was slighted by both king and queen several years ago. But Andres was not the problem. She served the agency loyally for many years and did not deserve his ire. No. Another example would need to be made. One not forgotten for years to come. The elves needed a reminder of who ran the world today.

"I want every available agent brought before me immediately, Andres. Do not disappointment me again."

She saluted and hurried off to obey.

He watched her go, slightly amused at her actions. He was contemplating his next move when his cell phone rang. Seeing the number, Corman slid back into his official role and answered it. It was a call he had long been expecting. Perhaps the day was not lost after all. He stalked off in search of privacy.

"Something smells good," Daniel commented as he and Max strolled through the front door.

"In the kitchen!" Sara called.

Sharing a look with Max, their gear was piled just inside, unceremoniously dumped and abandoned. Daniel felt a measure of shame for not coming back in time to help Blackmere with the other gear that was also piled nearby, but the man never asked.

Daniel found Sara and Blackmere with coffee and a heap of bacon ready. Hash browns and eggs were on the stove. To his surprise, Morgen manned the stove, apron on and spatula in hand. She kept a steady eye on the old cast iron pans Sara likely found while rummaging around.

Daniel's stomach growled in anticipation. "I could probably eat all of that by myself."

"Sorry, big fella. The doctor won't be pleased next time he checks your bloodwork," Sara teased.

He frowned, noticing she too was wearing an apron. She wasn't the one to spend her days in the kitchen. Sure, she cooked, but she wasn't keen on it. A woman on the go, she called herself. Daniel didn't mind. He liked the freedom of creating that the kitchen offered with every recipe. Besides, retirement did nothing for his mind if he wasn't busy writing or editing.

"Fine, be that way, but I have dibs on the shower,"

he replied, convinced she was busying herself in the kitchen to take her mind off their predicament when she avoided his gaze. "Unless that's spoken for too?"

"There are two. One's at the end of the hall. The other is downstairs."

He caught Blackmere staring at him over the rim of the coffee cup and raised an eyebrow in question.

"Don't worry, I already brought everything inside," Blackmere muttered with sarcasm.

Max beamed. "There's a good man! I call the downstairs shower. I have enough grime on me to shame a pig."

Daniel went to sneak a piece of bacon from the tray.

Sara slapped his hand. "Not until you shower. You smell like a compost pile, Daniel," she chided and shooed him out the kitchen.

Daring the slap, Daniel snatched a piece of bacon and shoved it in his mouth before holding up his hands and backing away. A devious twinkle brightened his eye.

She watched him with a fond smile before turning back to the stove.

Chuckling, Blackmere reached for a rifle that was sitting on the chair beside him and got to his feet. "I'll pull first shift on the deck. Try not to eat everything before I get back."

"I'll have your plate in the microwave," Sara promised and topped off his coffee as he made a grab for it.

"Thank you."

"He is a conflicted man," Morgen commented after he left. "Sworn to uphold his oaths yet struggling with the duplicity of his orders. A man trapped by his sense of duty."

"That's way over my head," Sara commented, stirring the hashbrowns. At Morgen's sigh, she added, "Look, I get it, Morgen. I do, but we can't let our personal feelings create divisions. Otherwise, those creepy killers will run right through us. I would very much like to go home and see my children and dogs again."

"It doesn't end here, Sara Thomas," Morgen reassured her. "Our stories have more to go before that fateful last breath."

"You really know how to have a good time," Sara joked to lighten the mood. "Do you think we should make pancakes?"

"You speak of more cooking at a time like this?"

"I know Daniel can eat and just looking at Max leads me to believe he could eat half a cow himself. Anything is better than thinking about any future attacks."

She felt Morgen studying her again but didn't have it in her to confront the elf queen. She was just exhausted.

"Of course. Dwarves are famous for their appetites. Show me how to make these pancakes of yours," Morgen finally said.

"That was tasty," Max stated and pushed his empty plate away with satisfaction. A dribble of maple syrup lingered on his beard. "Best meal I've eaten all day."

"It's the only meal you've eaten," Sara retorted, shaking her head. She had trouble telling where the dwarf's lighthearted jokes ended and seriousness began.

"Still the best."

Sara rolled her eyes. "What's the plan now?"

"Sleep. Inventory and clean weapons. I'll go relieve Blackmere. Everyone else bed down. I don't want to be caught exhausted if these guys show up tonight," Daniel suggested.

No one argued. Not even Morgen, which he found interesting.

A few minutes later Daniel gathered their plates. Daniel insisted on taking care of the cast iron and left the rest. He once had let a former team member clean his favorite pan at home and had then spent months re-seasoning it. He hadn't gotten mad, per say, not even when the guy broke out vinegar to scrub away the food residue.

At the time there was little Daniel could do other than stand in shock before trying to thank the guy for helping. Lesson learned: Trust no one with his cast iron.

"Daniel, maybe you should go sleep for a while first," Max offered, his arms covered in soap to his elbows. "Dwarves have greater stamina than humans. We can go days without sleep before it starts to wear on us."

"Are you sure? You did most of the heavy fighting back at that rest stop," Daniel said. His eyes were already half closed and his mind begged to shut down, even if for a few hours only, but he wouldn't shirk from his duty.

"Positive. I'll come get you in a few hours. No need to push yourself until you have to."

"Thanks, Max."

"Don't mention it."

Max grabbed his machinegun and a cleaning kit and head for Blackmere's overwatch position.

Exhaustion struck Daniel as the dwarf disappeared through the doorway. Daniel's knees weakened and it was all he could do to stagger down to the room he and Sara shared. He found Sara pulling back the blankets.

"I thought you were going on guard?" she asked, looking concerned. "You look terrible."

"Max offered to switch shifts. I can't say that I fought him too hard. I'm beat," Daniel admitted.

"Then it's time for bed."

Closing the door behind him, Daniel sauntered up to her with a gleam in his eye.

"What do you think you're doing, mister? I thought you were tired?"

"What?" He played innocent. "Can't a guy appreciate his wife? I mean, we are in the mountains. You love coming here. Who knows when we might get another chance for…you know."

She grinned despite herself. "You're incorrigible."

"I try."

They melted into each other's arms with urgent

passion. Survival remained in doubt and there was just enough time to express their love…

Except both were snoring minutes later.

TWENTY-THREE

Too few remained. The Invisible Hand successfully eliminated over half the ruling nobles and clan heads.

Visilias stared at the fractured remnants of their once proud society and wept inwardly. Combined with the disaster in upstate New York when his father and a handful of other prominent family heads were murdered by the former Prime Minister, the elf clans were in complete disarray.

He liked working in the shadows better but had spent centuries learning the game before ascending to head of family. Visilias knew he was more than capable in rallying his broken family to regain their rightful place at the top of the hierarchy. He not only had Morgen's ear, but now her trust and confidence. Visilias assumed she meant for him to go higher, perhaps to the office of prime minister itself, making him her right-hand man. He shuddered at the thought.

I don't want any of it. All that mattered was pulling the survivors together and repaying the assassins for their sins. Revenge in his heart, he strode to the center of the room. Chatter faded to murmurs as heads turned his direction. They noticed his disheveled look. The torn and bloody clothes. A few saw the piece of straw jutting from the corner of his mouth.

The room was in total silence as he hopped up on a table. Never one to back down from a fight, Visilias opened his arms. "My friends and fellow nobles I come before you at the behest of the queen. She had been recovered from the assassins and is enroute to a safehouse. Last night we suffered for the sin of arrogance. Many lives were lost in that cowardly ambush and, I fear, many more are still to come.

"The strength of our people is being tested like never before. To those who still stand opposed to the unification of the clans I say this: We will not go quietly back to the caves and forgotten places on the world. No. We will stand. We will unite. And we will fight!"

"What is there left to fight for?" a short female elf asked. Her golden locks had long since faded to grey. Lines worried her face and hands. "The clans are defeated!"

He recognized her from one of his father's lessons. "Only if you choose it to be so, Lady Milland. I know your family well, for we often warred against each other. You have great honor. Do not let a setback determine your fate.".

"Setback. We were slaughtered!" a portly dwarf whose name escaped him barked. "This is not war. This is murder."

"Humans have a saying: an eye for an eye. I am all for getting revenge on those cowards who dared destroy us, but there is work to be done before we can charge off into that battle." He held up his hands for silence when the muttering started. "We must continue what Morgen began."

"What are you saying man? Speak plainly!" another elf, one fully unknown to him, demanded.

Visilias took a deep breath. This was the make-or-break moment. Their future rested on the next few moments. Rested on him. "We must unify the clans! Here. Now. The only way forward is by eliminating our divisions and presenting a strong front."

Protests erupted, as he expected. Far from royalty, Visilias lacked the charisma to sway those hardliners putting self-interests over purpose. *Fools and cowards.* He made notes of who spoke the loudest. Those who required additional pressure. Yet for each voice in opposition two cried in favor. Perhaps the day was not lost after all.

"Quiet, quiet please!" he shouted when he gave them enough time to squabble.

Yet silence did not come. The arguing continued. Frustrated Visilias tried again, "Quiet, please! We have much to—"

"SILENCE!"

Visillias blinked. Heads turned. Shock widened eyes. The crowd parted as Constantin Andros stormed through them with his power sword held at the ready. The Old Guard was proud. Determined. He would not be cowed by any. Taking his place on the floor beside Visilias, the elf swept his baleful gaze over the crowd. Many shrank away. Others cast their eyes down in shame or guilt. Visilias was grateful the elf was on his side.

"Your queen stands in harm's way and here you are, bickering over her last command," the Old Guard barked. "This man has been selected by Her Majesty to bring an end to your internal strife and return the clans to lost glory. He fought all night for you and your families. You dare rebuke him in this hour of need? Were I not sworn to defend the crown I would take this sword and lay waste to you all. And I would be right to do so."

Buoyed by the support, Visilias returned the nod he was given and addressed the crowd once more. "What say you? Will you begin the process of unifying the clans and field a force capable of defeating this Invisible Hand once and for all?"

"This cannot happen overnight, Visilias," Milland countered. "Agreements must be made. Treaties enacted."

"I am not expecting miracles, Lady Milland. I am expecting cooperation and a harkening back to the time where were we allied," he told her. "All Morgen seeks is our survival. You are the chosen of your families. Men and women from across the globe. A new world is dawning. The only question is will be here to greet it or be swept away under a tide of violence?"

Noting their silence, Visilias jumped down and, Constantin at his side, strode away with all the confidence he could muster. The wheels were turning. The bait set. He prayed they reached consensus before it was too late.

"That was foolish," Constantin told him once they were alone. "They easily could have turned on you."

"No. You saw the looks in their eyes. They are broken. A remnant of whatever glories they once thought they had," Visilias replied. "I pushed them. It was the only way. Elsewise they would stew in their failures and be picked off one by one until none remained."

"Do you think you were enough to sway them to the cause? Morgen has placed all her hopes on this act, Visilias," the elf reminded.

For some reason the name irked him. If he was going to take charge, then he wanted to be addressed with the name he had chosen himself. "Enough with the Visilias. I prefer Nevada Slim. Or just Slim. It's bad enough I must wear suit and tie. Don't make me languish beneath false titles."

"You are your father's son," Constantin replied to Slim's amusement.

Minutes later they were slumped in chairs at a small bar, half empty glasses before them. Slim felt the fatigue settling in. Gone was the adrenalin of the night. They had stood against their foes, earning honor for their deeds. Saved the queen from her kidnappers. But there was still so much to do. He eyed his drink then his drinking companion.

"Can't always escape our pasts, can we?" Slim raised his glass and drained the rest of his drink. "To think I'm sitting with a high elf of the Old Guard. It would be laughable but a few months earlier. We need their army."

"What army? The clans have not had one since before the schism. And for good reason. The best we can manage is house guards and private security forces." Constantin shook his head and followed Slim's example. His empty glass clanked on the bar counter.

"I'm no tactician, Constantin. How do we convince a handful of nobles who think they are on the brink of annihilation to give up their only line of defense?"

"That is your arena now, my friend," the Old Guard replied. "I wish you luck. You're going to need it if those complaints are any indication. I will detail a squad of Guards to protect you. Don't trust that human. James Corman is a man of many secrets. I fear he is working against us."

"I thought the same thing when he showed up at that rest area," Slim agreed. "Are we fighting a war on two fronts?" The possibility of DESA turning against the elves, in their darkest hour, chilled him.

"Keep doing that and you'll have lines creasing your forehead," Constantin mused. "Not a good look for one of our senior leaders."

"Tell me you're not thinking the same thing."

Constantin poured another round. "This is the only chance we get, Slim. Get these bastards in line. Thanks to the tracking device I put on their vehicle before we left, I know the queen's location. I will take the bulk of the Guard and protect the queen. We are not losing this battle."

"But what—"

The Old Guard took the shot and slammed his glass on the counter before storming off.

Slim watched him go, muttering, "This isn't a battle, Constantin. This is a war."

He was about to take his shot when one of the doors opened and Lady Milland slipped out. Alone, without her guard, and with an unreadable expression, she smoothed down her dress, the same one she wore the night before, and joined him at the makeshift bar.

"Come to tell me the nobles refuse to see past their noses and work shit out?"

Milland's expression changed. A new energy lit her eyes. "Quite the opposite, Baron. Most of the nobles have agreed to begin talks. Enough to sway the others. There will be unification, though it may take time. Elves do not work quickly, you know."

"That's what I'm afraid of," Slim admitted. He

didn't know if they had time.

Four ranks of ten stood at attention before him as he entered the room. They were the best of the Old Guard. Elves and dwarves who placed the needs of the clans ahead of their lives. Constantin eyed them with pride. A military force unmatched by most nations, human or elf. He hoped they were up to the challenge of defending the queen one more time.

Some were missing though, killed during the last battle, and that gave him pause. The Invisible Hand presented a unique challenge and, unless he deciphered the riddles concealing the killers, they were fighting a losing battle. Constantin needed more answers. Better intelligence. Something tangible to work against.

"Captain Rory, report," he ordered after reaching the makeshift command table littered with maps and charts.

Rory was a slender elf with centuries of experience. Her dark hair and skin clashed with the golden hues of her tactical armor. The tip of her left ear was missing, clipped by a goblin's sword from one of her first fights. She never forgot that shame, using it to steel her resolve and prove herself time and again in combat. Constantin trusted her without question.

"Sir, we have recalled three full companies with another two in reserve. The facility is secure. We await your orders."

"Five hundred will not be enough to stem the Hand's tide," he theorized. "How did they achieve tactical surprise last night?"

"We are still working on that. Best guess, they had someone on the inside," she said.

"That's what I'm worried about. I want a list of names of everyone on duty. Everyone who had an inkling of the security plans." The notion one of their own had been turned chilled him.

Rory gestured to the stack of documents. "Already

done. If there is a traitor among us, we will find them. I promise you, sir."

"Did you lose friends last night, Rory?" Constantin softened his expression at seeing the grimace she failed to conceal.

"Too many."

He placed a hand on her shoulder. "We do this for them. Avenge the fallen and restore our honor. Come, there is much work to be done."

TWENTY-FOUR

Thaddeus Blackmere suffered from a crisis of conscience. The debacle in Raleigh fell on his shoulders. Heads were sure to roll. Corman's unexpected arrival cast the operation into disarray and continued rippling waves of discord in the wake of the disaster. He needed answers. Solutions. Squirreling away to the mountains provided a brief respite but did little to resolve the situation, making it easy for Blackmere to wallow in defeat.

Showered and placated, he paced the hallway in search of clarity. Blackmere felt like they were on the cusp of a greater conflict. One neither society was fully prepared for if it erupted. How to stop it? He wished he knew, but answers weren't forthcoming. A lifetime of dedicated service placed him in this unenviable position. The only thing in his favor was his proximity to the queen. As long as she lived, they had hope in preventing a war.

A dozen scenarios played out in his mind. None of them good. The Invisible Hand proved an elusive entity to track. Their headquarters remained hidden. No one knew the identities of its members. They were anonymous. A microcosm of human society slipping through the cracks for years. Not even DESA had been able to break the wall of mystique.

The one constant Blackmere knew was the Hand had vowed to see elfkind destroyed. How or why were unclear. He couldn't understand how anyone could hate another so much. Life was already short enough, why waste it devoted to bringing others to their knees? While he failed to comprehend the motivations behind his foe, Blackmere knew the inherent danger threatened to unravel all his organization worked so hard to establish.

Millennia of elven rule meant something, at least to those who knew of their existence. Blackmere kept his personal feelings on who or what deserved to dominate the planet private. He learned long ago personal opinions drew unnecessary attention at the wrong times. No, Blackmere was more astute than that. Alone and in a considered hostile environment, he needed to focus on the present.

What he needed, more than anything, was allies.

Max was out of the question. The dwarf, when he did speak, provided nothing but irate bits with an aggressive personality. Morgen remained untouchable, as befitting of her station. That left Daniel and his wife, both of whom he endured tenuous relations with. His previous bid to sway Daniel over to the agent side fell on deaf ears and, though Sara viewed him kindly, like an uncle or absent father, her vote tended to follow along with her husband's. Still, Daniel was his best bet. The only question being how to get him fully onboard.

Frustrated, Blackmere strolled into the kitchen for another cup of coffee. His doctor complained he accomplished nothing but eating away his stomach lining from his caffeine addiction at every checkup, but Blackmere continued to ignore him. He needed the push.

To his surprise, he found Morgen standing over the sink, staring out the small window.

"What?" she asked after noticing him. "Have you never seen a queen washing dishes?"

Blackmere blushed. "My apologies, your Majesty. I didn't expect…"

"Nonsense, Thaddeus. The problem people have today is they want to apologize for everything. No one is allowed to speak their minds anymore from fear of offending someone."

"There was a time where we could respectfully disagree and still be civil," he agreed as he poured the coffee into the same mug he'd used before. "I think those days are long behind us now. Still, I didn't expect to find a queen washing dishes."

"Sara left your plate in the microwave," Morgen

said. "It won't do to go hungry. Besides, it gives me something to do. An unoccupied mind is a terrible thing, Thaddeus. You may address me by name, if you please."

His blush deepened. Despite his misgivings, Blackmere found her to be a breath of fresh air. "I appreciate that. You're the only royal I know. Breaking a lifetime of discipline is easier said than done."

She set down the soap covered plate in her hands and looked at him. "Thaddeus, do you think I am doing the right thing?"

"Cooking? Like you said, one of us had to do it." He took a large swallow of coffee.

"No. I am speaking of unifying the clans."

He offered a sad grin. "I know. Given the circumstances, I fail to see how you could not."

"There are plenty enough failings to go around, Thaddeus. Do not blame yourself for elements beyond your control," she chided.

Are you feeling the same guilt? I wonder, can a queen reduce herself to common emotions without compromising her regal integrity? He took another sip of coffee, luxuriating in the hot sensation flowing down his throat. "That doesn't change the fact we are in a bad place."

"You suspect our enemies know our location as well," she speculated and resumed washing.

"How can they not? We're but a handful. Should the Hand attack in force there is no way for us to beat them back. This safehouse will fall."

"We are not as defenseless as you assume. Take heart, Thaddeus. The night is never as dark as you might think."

Max slid the charging handle forward, enjoying the metallic "schraak" of clean and lubricated weapon parts operating smoothly. He repeated the process several more times. Like any weapon, he treated the machine gun with utmost care. It had saved his life more times than he cared to admit and would be needed for the coming fight.

And soon. There would be another round with the cowardly assassins. He was certain of it. Skilled as they were, the assassins died like everyone else. A few well-placed rounds ended their efforts in short order. Getting them to stay still long enough was the problem.

He'd fought on a hundred battlefields against myriad foes. None proved as elusive as the assassins. Max clicked the safety off and squeezed the trigger. The upside to battling the Hand came from how good it felt when he made contact. Satisfied the machine gun was ready to go after another round of inspection, Max slapped in a fresh drum of two hundred rounds and laid the first few on the feed tray before closing the cover.

The M240 machinegun entered U.S. Army line units in the late 1990s and became the go to weapon for infantry squads, replacing the heavier and larger caliber M60 used throughout the Vietnam War. Max enjoyed the versatility of the weapon despite the small round. Capable of firing two hundred rounds a minute, it provided enough stopping power to stall any assault. His problem stemmed from losing himself in the moment and firing too fast for too long. He lost track of how many barrels he'd melted over the years.

Chuckling as he remembered the first time it happened, he paused to check the two spare barrel bags they brought with them. He had more than enough ammunition. Several thousand rounds in a pair of assault packs stashed in the two positions he picked out.

Max settled back into the rocking chair and pulled out his pipe. The sweet aroma of tobacco soon filled the covered deck. He tilted his head back and closed his eyes.

The calm before the storm unsettled many warriors. He usually found peace. A chance to clear his mind while preparing for the fight to come. The tobacco helped too. Max ditched the long-stemmed pipe dwarves were famous for in favor of a shorter, human model. Every time he saw a movie depicting dwarves he frowned at the nostalgia of the old ways when they produced their pipes.

Max exhaled a mouthful of smoke, enjoying the taste before reopening his eyes. The surrounding landscape reminded him of home. Not Raleigh, but the lands where his bloodline originated from. Nothing calmed him like being in the mountains. There was contentment to be found among the trees and mountain streams. A peace all but eliminated amidst the towering skyscrapers and narrow city canyons.

He longed for the feel of grass between his toes. The smell of dirt and clean wind. Max wanted nothing more than to be home with his wife. He carved a small world for himself in what he thought was far from civilized lands. Being here now made him rethink that decision. The flatlands of southern North Carolina were a far cry from the mountains bordering Tennessee. He wondered how his wife would take it if he mentioned picking up stakes and moving here.

Wind tossed the branches about, creating a wave of undulating greens and browns. He smiled. This felt right. A shame it was little more than illusion. Max knew hunters were out there, hidden and unseen among the trees. It was a matter of time before they narrowed down their search and began preparations for their next attack. Scanning the trees, he spied a trio of female deer grazing on the opposite hillside next to the pond's edge. What he would give to enjoy that innocent freedom. He took another puff.

As nice as the current surroundings were, Max couldn't help but refocus on the Invisible Hand. The killers proved worthy opponents. He hadn't felt so far behind an enemy in years. What was it ab—

The crunch of tires grinding down the dirt road broke his thoughts. He sat up, right hand snaked down for the machinegun. Max watched a beat-up pickup ramble up the incline then keep going past the driveway without slowing.

Unwilling to rule them out as a threat, he tracked the truck until it disappeared around the bend. He caught the pink of exposed flesh of hands. The flare of a denim jacket. Knowing any good unit conducted an intelligence prep of the battlefield before engaging, Max wouldn't put it past the Hand to alter their appearance and tactics to lull him into a false sense of security. He had lived too long to fall for simple tricks.

"Keep moving. Nothing to see here," he said to himself as the truck moved past his field of vision. He gave his weapon a loving pat. "Just an old dwarf and two hundred rounds of whoop ass waiting should you decide to turn around."

"Talking to yourself, Max?"

Startled, the dwarf grumbled and gestured to the empty chair beside him at seeing the agent just hovering nearby. "Might as well take a load off, Blackmere. I have a feeling we're not going to get too much more time."

"No, I don't suppose we are."

Blackmere settled into the chair, gesturing at the handcrafted woodwork. "Nice work. I could use one of these at home."

"We craft better. Just rocking away on your Washington home, eh?" Max countered. Dwarves had better pieces, he had a few in his own home. "I don't see you as the relaxing type."

"I'm not, but my wife keeps telling me I need to learn how," Blackmere admitted. "How are your boys?"

"Obstinate as ever. They get that from their mother. I swear that woman will be the death of me. We could use them here."

"I hope you have a good life insurance policy."

Max snorted. "Funny." When Blackmere just sat there, staring, he prompted, "What brings you down here?"

"I couldn't sleep any more. Daniel's snoring can wake the dead."

"Best let the man sleep while he can. We're going

to need him tonight, if not before."

Blackmere reached into his jacket pocket and produced a cigar and lighter. "Do you think they'll strike before nightfall? What? I'm not allowed a vice?"

A look of surprise on his face, Max shook his head. "Didn't say that at all. This is going to be one hell of fight, Blackmere."

"It is. Let's hope they continue underestimating us."

Max raised an eyebrow but said nothing.

TWENTY-FIVE

He stood behind the bore of an ancient oak. Massive and crowing branches thirty meters wide, the tree had likely witnessed the world's turning for centuries. Today it shielded him from view. He had traded in his black fatigues on the way there in favor of a camouflage pattern that blended more into the scenery. Exposed areas of his flesh he'd painted to match his tight clothing. He even chose moccasins instead of his favorite boots.

He left nothing to chance.

Not now.

Not this close.

He had spent years training for this moment. Endless days of pain and punishment under the judgmental eyes of his masters. The torment was about to pay off, for he alone would succeed where so many others had failed. Eyes twinkling with the promise of his reward, the man raised the veil over the lower half of his face and began slipping through the trees toward the solitary log cabin on the side of the mountain.

"Do you smell that?" Max asked. He lowered his voice to a bare whisper, forcing Blackmere to sit forward and cock his head.

The agent scanned the trees. "What is it?" he whispered back.

The dwarf set down his machinegun and unsnapped the holster at his hip and drew his Glock. "Trouble."

Unaware of that dwarf's had a heightened sense of smell, Blackmere drew his own sidearm without trying to look obvious.

The wind stopped blowing, bringing an unsettling stillness to the area. A lone bird chirped but otherwise there was silence. The hairs on his arms raised. He felt cold. Disheartened. It had been a long time since Blackmere last felt this on edge. He found himself missing additional agents. The isolation threatened to gnaw on his nerves.

"There's someone watching us," Max announced.

"I don't see anything." His mouth went dry. Trigger finger beginning to tap his pistol. Blackmere swept his gaze over the area Max was focused on. "How could they have found us so fast?"

"Doesn't matter." The dwarf pointed his weapon. "There. Downslope about thirty meters. Two o'clock. One man. Camouflaged."

"I still don't see him," Blackmere muttered. No matter how many times he worked with dwarves he never got used to their advanced vision.

The click of Max's safety going had Blackmere following suit, though without a target he felt hamstringed. *I'm not*—Images of his two slain agents, their mangled bodies cooling on the pavement, filled him with anger: the need for revenge. It was time to repay the favor.

"Don't worry about. I got him."

Before Blackmere could reply, Max slipped from his chair and, crouching, moved around the back side of the deck. Keeping to the shadow, the dwarf took his time easing down the stairs and into the grass and gravel. Blackmere held his pistol at the ready as Max disappeared.

There is an artform to hunting. One most people never realized. The ability to stalk your prey through difficult terrain without being spotted required years of training, years of failed or sloppy attempts. Hunting humans proved far less difficult than any animal. Humans seldom paid attention to their surroundings. They chose to walk through life with blinders, oblivious to the world ready to bring them down. The absurdity of failing to recognize your potential demise was laughable to him.

For men like him, this hunt lacked the nuance of a

proper chase. He worked through the light tree cover, dancing from one position to the next with ease. His blade was sharp. His mind clear. Orders were to find the queen's location and return… For the first time in his life, he ignored his orders. Having called in the prey's position, he found the opportunity to wet his blade too powerful to ignore to return and wait to see if they'd send him again.

Blackened steel drawn, he continued the slow march toward the cabin where, should fortune be with him, glory and immortality awaited. It was all he could do not to break into a grin. This day belonged to him. His lone regret stemmed from not having the ability to collect trophies. Elves proved no harder to kill than humans, but the manner in which they evaporated upon death left him unsettled. There was no glory in returning a heap of ashes. Not when his masters expected other results.

Consumed by his thoughts, he almost failed to see the approaching dwarf. *Fool. Pay attention.* Stubborn and warlike, dwarves thought themselves superior to all other races. A glaring hole in their strength. This dwarf would soon learn the price for his arrogance. Shifting his grip on the dagger to plunge rather than slash, the assassin narrowed his gaze.

Sweat dropped into his eye, slipping from the protective head covering. Cursing silently, he reached up to wipe his face. By the time his vision resettled he lost track of the dwarf. Scowling, he crouched as he'd done during training countless times, reducing his silhouette to prevent detection. A crow cawed from a distant treetop.

Silence.

Stillness.

The killer slowed his breathing, desperate to locate his target. As arrogant as dwarves were, they did not lack martial ability. Should the dwarf gain the advantage, the assassin knew he was in for a fight—one he might not win. He tried calming his heartbeat next. The enemy was out there, engaged in his own hunt. There seemed little doubt the dwarf knew he was there.

It became a game of cat and mouse.

Years had passed since the assassin's last opportunity to properly test his skills. Killing the dwarf proved the right appetizer for the true price, the hated elf-bitch. *Queen.* He scoffed. No inhuman creature deserved to place themselves over the rightful masters of the earth. Kill the queen and become the hero his people required. Easy as that. But first, he had a dwarf to kill.

Closing his eyes, he listened for telltale signs of the dwarf approaching. The snap of a twig. The rustle of leaves. He heard nothing. This dwarf was good. Perhaps as good as himself. Thrilled at the challenge, all fears of failure slipped away as he found true pleasure in the hunt for the first time.

A branch cracked to his right.

His eyes snapped open.

The last thing he felt was a pair of cold hands grip his throat from behind.

Max held a pistol in one hand and his favorite short blade in the other. He was tired of being chased by the Hand. But knew they wouldn't stop until they were either all dead or they succeeded in retaking Morgen. Well, he couldn't let that happen. Wouldn't. Enough bad things had happened over the centuries. And the assassination of their queen on his watch would make him the laughingstock of the clans. Dishonor would follow his bloodline to the ending of time. Max refused to allow such to happen.

The desire to kill missing, Max decided his best course of action was to incapacitate the assassin and search him for any sort of cyanide capsule or other device he might use to kill himself before he could bring him back to the others for questioning. Naturally, that didn't preclude a little harmless wounding during the capture. Especially if the assassin fought back. Max craved the chance to sink his blade into a thigh or shoulder. A small measure of justice.

The silence was a little unsettling. He knew better

than to take it for granted. The Invisible Hand proved themselves in the field as more than capable. Max remained wary. Where there was one assassin the other four were sure to be close. There would be no ambush this time from the Hand. No hiding in shadows, waiting to strike. The playing field was even and that, Max knew from experience, was more than enough for any dwarf worth his axe.

A hint of movement drew his attention; Max spied the assassin drop and grinned. That trick wouldn't work. Not with a dwarf like Max prowling. Suspecting they were evenly matched as the assassin had noticed him coming, the dwarf holstered his pistol and regripped his knife. He looked forward to drawing first blood. With the assassin now stationary, Max took the opportunity to draw left, down slope on the backside of a thicket of blackberry bushes littered with white blossoms.

Stepping over downed branches and over moss covered stones, Max moved with slow surety. Seconds fled into minutes. He ached from the restraint. The constricted movements burned his muscles. Every instinct begged for release, to plunge downhill and engage. There were times he despised civility. That feral instinct all dwarves had simmering deep within raged in his mind. Swing the blade. Crush the enemy.

He slipped behind the bowl of an ancient oak, pausing to draw one last breath before striking. Max became a blur. Blade in hand, he whipped around the tree.

They looked down on the corpse with a mix of emotions. Max stood indignant each time one of them glanced at him, soon brooding with a twisted his face. The fingers on his right hand danced over his holster, tapping a grim tune.

Blackmere finally sighed. "Really?"

"What?" Max recoiled. "I didn't do it."

"His neck is broken. This man didn't die of natural causes," the agent replied. "You should have taken him alive."

"I had every intention of it. Seems like someone had other ideas." At their various looks of disbelief, Max lashed out, kicking the corpse in the ribs.

"Max, that hardly seems dignified," Morgen chastened. "If you did not kill him, who did?"

"That's the actual question," he replied. "Do we have any allies in this area? Ones Constantin might have alerted?"

"None I am aware of," Morgen said. "This is a mystery indeed."

"One we don't need," Blackmere said. He glanced at the surrounding woods then faced the queen. "Your Majesty, whoever did this might not be our enemy, but that doesn't make him a friend. The only certainty we have right now is this location has been burned."

"Agent man is right. We should leave before others arrive," Max added.

Bristling at the derogative, Blackmere had to take a deep breath before saying, "It's a safe bet to assume the Invisible Hand has all access points watched. The only viable exit would be up and over the mountain on foot. Knowing this, they will have teams scouring the forest for us." He eyed the woods, his shoulders slumping. "Cutoff and on foot, we'd be easy targets… I suggest we hold in place."

"We'd be fish in a barrel," Morgen argued with a frown.

"Defensible ones for the most part," Blackmere told her. "There are only so many ways into this house and we have more than enough guns to cover them."

"Our advantages will shrink with the night, when the Hand is most comfortable."

Blackmere conceded the point. They needed to find an advantage over the assassins if any of them were going to survive. There was only one he could think of. "We take away the night."

"How? We don't have much to work with. This place is bare bones for supplies," Max said. "The only way to keep them at bay would be setting fire to the forest."

"Need I remind either of you this place is constructed of wood?" Morgen rolled her eyes. "We'd be burning down our only defense."

"There might be a way to control the burn," Blackmere insisted.

"How?"

"Gather all the rags, towels, anything flammable and siphon fuel from the truck. We place torches around the slope, ring the house with them."

Max grinned. "That could work. It would at least give us the Hand's location when they try to strike. Might as well string wire with cans between the trees too."

"Do we have any?" Blackmere's eyes brightened.

Daniel pinched the bridge of his nose. "Great, now we're the Scooby Gang."

TWENTY-SIX

Dusk approached. That quiet darkening of the world that was headed to sleep. Shadows crawled into those empty spaces abandoned by the fading sunlight. A cacophony of insects and

toads awoke, bequeathing their songs for all to hear. Inside the cabin, Daniel and the others sat around the kitchen table. It was the calm before the storm. A last opportunity to fill their bellies and work the kinks from their plans. *I can't believe we are Scooby Dooing this.*

Nerves ran high, so Daniel took the time to grill steaks for them. No longer concerned about remaining hidden, they had already been found, he figured they deserved a fitting last meal before the coming battle. Soon the smell of roasting meat filled the kitchen through the open deck door. He didn't know who had the foresight to grab steaks back at the grocery store, but they were going to go well with the handful of potatoes he had on the grill beside them.

He cast a glance through the kitchen window. The news from the day troubled him, though not for the obvious reasons. Whoever killed the assassin, there was no doubt that's who the man was, the person or thing responsible for killing him proved equally deadly. Daniel knew better by now not to discount any fantastical creature lurking in the quiet places of the world where men dared not look. Any sort of creature might be watching them from the security of the surrounding forest. That unsettled him. He failed to see why none of the others saw the same issue.

They stripped the body of his uniform before disposing the corpse in a small ravine nearby. He and Blackmere covered the body under a scree of rocks and debris amidst the elevated protests of Max. The dwarf didn't believe their enemy deserved that honor. Daniel argued it made tactical sense when other Hands arrived to scout the scene. The last thing they needed was the rest of the Hand discovering their companion and increasing their assault. Max relented but refused to help.

He and Blackmere then set about emplacing torches on the downslope, spaced just far enough apart to prevent the darkness the assassins needed from breaching the ring of fire once lit. To his surprise, Blackmere found an old tacklebox in the accompanying shed. He and Max wove a tangled web a foot off the ground through the trees until they ran out of line. There were no cans though. Inside, furniture was placed over the windows deemed unnecessary to defend. The rest of the house was laid out with ammunition caches and supplies. Their defense depended on quick reactions and the ability to displace to wherever the heaviest fighting occurred.

Satisfied they did all they could given their limited resources and time, Daniel got up and went to the grill. It was the only thing normal in this entire situation. The only thing missing was a cooler full of cold beer. After all they'd been through in the last two days, he deserved that much. Not to get drunk, but enough to take the edge off. Hell, they even found a way to get beer in Afghanistan. The empty fridge upon their arrival squashed any thoughts of that happening.

Daniel flipped the steaks, thrilling at the way the flames licked up from the charcoal. Few things beat the smell of grilled meat and his stomach growled. He knew some of them inside weren't going to eat. Their nerves would get the best of them. He'd seen it before and had been that way once himself. Then he learned that there was never a guarantee for that next meal in a combat situation. Soldiers took advantage where they could. The others might not eat, but he planned on cleaning his plate and Max would probably take any leftovers.

No matter how hard he tried to keep thinking positive, his mind insisted on focusing on the unknown killer in the woods. Was their guest watching him now? Salivating at the brazen smell drifting over the house. The uncertainty of it hounded him. He was a man who hated variables. Any good combat leader adapted to changing situations but without an identity he couldn't replan accordingly. It was a nuisance.

"Whose side are you on?" he asked the trees before remembering the window was open and the others could hear him.

"Yours if you hurry up with those steaks," Max called back.

"Yeah, yeah. They're almost done, Max." Daniel couldn't help but laugh.

He often used humor to soften the hard edges in times of stress. This certainly qualified. Daniel blew out a breath and glanced at the rifle leaning against the house. He struggled with the urge to do a little target practice before dinner. Where was the harm? It was a fair assumption the dead assassin called in his position before moving on the house. The odds he hadn't were negligible. Daniel figured firing off a few rounds might give the others pause, forcing them to reconsider their tactics before swarming the cabin when the last rays of light faded.

He opened the grill and was satisfied with the char marks on each steak. Daniel made the ultimate sin by slicing open one of the larger steaks to check if it was done enough. No one, not even Max, well maybe Max, wanted their meat weeping blood on the plate. The bright pink sliver in the center sparked a fresh round of grumbling from his stomach. Daniel started pulling them from the grill. He set the plate down long enough to shoulder his rifle and turned to the door, reaching for the plate.

Headlights shined bright on the road below.

He no longer felt hungry.

Daniel hurried to grab then deliver the food and give a quick warning. Max and Blackmere followed him outside, food forgotten. They just settled behind cover as the car turned the final corner and pulled up into the driveway. Daniel's finger touched the rifle trigger without any pressure.

The car rolled to a stop. The engine turned off.

Daniel reached up to click off his safety. Army rules of engagement stated no one fired until fired upon. He knew Max didn't suffer from any restrictions, but the dwarf hadn't fired yet. *Why?*

The answer came a moment later when the driver's door opened, and the driver stepped out.

Max spat, "Shit. Looks like you're going to need to cook some more food."

Daniel ignored the dwarf and found himself staring into the eyes of a man he hoped to never see again, Xander, the fallen Champion of Light.

Shit indeed.

Stares all around. No one spoke. No one knew what to say. Of all the possibilities to occur this night, none thought to see the exiled Champion grinning at them in the way only a man who had been on vacation for years could achieve. Tall and confident, Xander took them in with a pitying expression that set Daniel even more on edge.

"Well, we're here."

"We?" Blackmere echoed. *You're supposed to be dead. What else haven't you told me, Daniel?*

Daniel closed his eyes. His finger remained on the trigger as he entertained the idea of finishing the job started all those years ago in Raleigh when Xander pretended at being his ally. Their last encounter saw them part ways as no longer enemies, but far from friends. Daniel agreed to let Xander and the princess slip away and told Blackmere that they had been killed in the battle. He opened his eyes when the passenger door opened and Gwen stepped out. *So much for deals.*

Xander hummed. "Norman said this was important."

"Not important enough for either of you to be in my sight," Morgen snapped as she stormed out the door. "Go back to whatever hole you've been hiding in all these years. I want nothing to do with either of you."

"Stop being so dramatic, Mother," Gwen lashed out. "We didn't come all this way for pleasantries or to be turned aside after we had been requested."

"Requested by whom?" Morgen folded her arms and glared at her daughter.

"Her," Xander said and pointed at Sara.

"What are you talking about?" Daniel growled. He rose and stepped closer to his wife. "She didn't call you. No one but me knew you were alive."

"He's right, Daniel," Sara called. "You told me when you got home from New York."

"When? How?"

Placing her hand on his gun barrel, she pushed the weapon down and met his gaze. "Back at the grocery store I called Norman and asked him to send help."

"You what?"

"How was I supposed to know this is who he would call? We're in real trouble and need the help."

"Yes but to do this—"

"Perhaps we can finish this discussion indoors? We've come a long way, and I would very much like to use the restroom," Xander suggested.

"Yeah, you do that, elf boy." Max rolled his eyes, lowering his weapon. "Blackmere, you and I have torches to light. Come on, this is a family matter."

Daniel watched as they hurried off. He wanted to join them, not wanting to be a part of the shitstorm about to engulf the cabin.

"Amusing as ever, that dwarf," Xander mused. "I assume you're expecting company?"

"You already know that," Daniel replied with a trace of bitterness. "Or didn't Norman explain what we're dealing with?"

"Daniel, be a dear and put another pair of steaks on the grill for our guests," Morgen said, having regained her composure. She stepped inside without pause, as befitting of the woman with the crown.

Daniel ground his teeth and followed her in.

"How did Norman know where you were? We had a deal," Daniel asked then stuffed a forkful of meat into his mouth.

"And we upheld our end of that deal. Gwen and I disappeared to a private island on the far side of the world for a time before the lure of returning home became too strong. We were thinking of coming home anyway but had no desire to return to the politics of the court," Xander said.

"And we wouldn't have, if not for the gargoyle," Gwen added. Her gaze bore holes in the queen who hadn't spoken since they sat down to eat. "You just can't stay away from drama, eh Mother?"

Morgen stiffened. "This is beyond me. Once the Invisible Hand finishes with me they will come for you."

"Like Daniel and Xander already mentioned, no one knows we are alive," Gwen boasted.

Daniel barely managed to not roll his eyes when Morgen replied, "Foolish child, did it not occur to you we have been compromised? Or did you think by killing the assassin in the trees that was the end of this?"

Xander perked up. "What assassin?"

"You didn't kill him?" Daniel asked, setting down his fork. That rock in the pit of his stomach reformed.

Xander shook his head. "I haven't killed anyone since that last night in New York. Who are you referring to?"

Daniel shared a look with Sara then explained. When he finished, the former Champion blanched. Clearly seeing that it wasn't Xander, he went back to trying to figure out the missing pieces of the puzzle. His thoughts were disrupted by Max and Blackmere's return. Daniel had trouble meeting Blackmere's gaze.

"Torches are lit. We should have a little advance warning when they strike," Max announced. He paused, just then noticing the tension. "What did we miss and why don't I like it?"

"Xander wasn't the one who kill the assassin," Daniel told him. "Looks like we still have another player to worry about."

"Wonderful," Blackmere muttered.

"Still one less bad guy to deal with," Max added and took an empty chair before reaching for a steak.

They settled into an uneasy back and forth discussion over the now cold meal. Xander explained how Norman Guilt always had his contact, using it as a bargaining chip should the situation ever arise. Neither of them expected to break that glass, but Morgen's kidnapping demanded swift action. He was glad he and Gwen were close enough to reach the safehouse in time. He claimed he wanted to reclaim his lost dignity and, if done right, prevent the end of the clans.

Throughout the course of their conversation one question dominated Daniel's thoughts: How did Xander know the location of the DESA safehouse?

TWENTY-SEVEN

"I don't know what you were thinking having those two here," Daniel said quietly once he and Sara were alone. "They're nothing but trouble. Or did you forget how they plotted to kill Morgen and her husband?"

"It's not like we could trust anyone else," Sara countered, facing him to stand her ground. Defiance shining in her eyes, she said, "Daniel, we need all the help we can get and who better than the Champion of Light? Whatever that means."

Some of the fire left him. He didn't have the strength, or desire, to argue with his wife. "I know. That doesn't mean I have to like it. Xander and I have a bad history. I was hoping to never see him again. Hell, you could have asked Norman or even the Schneiders to come instead of *him*."

"You mean the same elf you let live and convince the rest of the world he was dead?"

The innocence in her tone masked her sarcasm. Barely. Daniel raised his eyes but chose not to speak the first thought that came to mind. "Yes, that elf. Still, I must admit he's one hell of a fighter. We can definitely use him tonight."

"You're certain they will come tonight?"

"I don't see why not. We've already found one on the property. The others won't be far behind." He grimaced. "This is going to get hairy, Sara."

She leaned in to hug him. He wrapped his arms around her and felt the slight tremble in her shoulders and wished there was some way to get her clear before the fight began. "We'll get through this. One way or the other," he told her. "Look at the bright side, at least we'll have another weapon on our side. I guess that counts for something."

"Do you promise?" she asked.

Daniel pulled away enough to look down into her eyes. "As much as I can." He kissed her forehead.

"That's good enough for me," she said. "We should get back to the others before they tear each other apart."

"You'd think they'd have the decency to hold off until after this is finished," he groaned but followed her back upstairs.

Mother and daughter sat opposite each other at the dining room table. The others had long cleared out under the pretense of one excuse or another. Not even Xander seemed willing to get in the middle of their dispute. The click of Morgen's nails drumming on the lacquer of the table added fuel to their silent staring contest.

Unable to take it another longer, Gwen said, "Your usual tricks aren't intimidating. I grew up with you, remember? You're not a queen, just my disappointment of a mother."

"I'm the disappointment?" Morgen snapped. Her hand slapped the table. "You murdered your father and would have done the same for me had other forces not intervened."

"You mean your pet human?" Gwen scoffed. "You both had your chance to be rid of me after Basil had Xander freed from the Grinder. You even sent Viviana to face me rather than doing so yourself. That's love for you."

"Love has nothing to do with any of this, Gwen. Your father and I did what we thought best. He had his methods and I mine. We never expected you to try to eliminate us both."

"His time had come," Gwen countered, remaining defiant. "A new age is dawning, Mother. One where a single point of rule is obsolete. Xander and I wanted to change the clans. Make them better. Stronger. The two of you were in the way."

Morgen leaned back, nestling into the hard wooden chairback. Eyes narrowed to slits, she considered what her daughter had to say. Despite the gaps between them, Morgen knew they were too alike. Perhaps enough to find a hidden advantage in this mess. "Interesting you say that. I have called for the unification of the clans. We will be under one banner again."

"You mean your banner."

"I," she started then paused. Perhaps there was merit to Gwen's argument. The elves were in dire straits, caught between DESA and the Invisible Hand. Maintaining the single point of rule presented unique disadvantages. Morgen knew change was necessary, but how far to take it? "I will take that under consideration."

Argument derailed, Gwen's glare softened. If just. "How have you been?"

Morgen's laughter, strained and forced, echoed through the room. "I'm in the middle of an antiquated home in the middle of nowhere and on the run from assassins. How do you think I have been? This is our worst moment, Gwen. I can't forgive you for what you did, but I am glad you and Xander have come."

"He's more than just Xander now. We were married a year ago."

"What court did you convince to perform those rites?" Morgen demanded.

"A human one. We couldn't go anywhere near the clans. Not with everyone thinking us dead." Gwen's voice was deceptively calm. "Stop acting so surprised. You knew this was going to happen from the start."

"Not by human law," Morgen insisted.

Her daughter shrugged in response. "What's done is done. Now we must focus on keeping you alive long enough to heal the wounds you and father created."

Morgen had no reply.

"Married huh? Why would you do that?" Max asked.

The dwarf sat on his now favorite rocking chair

overlooking the concentric rings of torches he and Blackmere emplaced before Xander and Gwen's arrival. He glanced to where Xander stood with folded arms, leaning against the railing. They weren't friends. They didn't have to be. Regardless of their ideologies and pasts, Max bore a mutual respect for the elf and felt the elf returned that.

"I seem to recall asking you the same thing years ago."

"She tricked me, and you know it!"

Xander chuckled. "Maybe, but centuries later you're still together. Where are those nightmare boys of yours? I expected them to be mixed up in this."

"Bah, lazing around back in Raleigh for all I know. I've been a little busy here," Max replied.

"I heard you three reconciled during the goblin nest incident."

Max tugged on his beard, face twisted. "We did, for a time, but you know them. Headstrong like their mother. Didn't take long before we started butting heads again and I told them off. They never did have any sense." He rushed to change the topic, teasing, "So, married?"

"Last year. It felt right," Xander admitted. "We were betrothed already, before the mess with Alvin. Getting married was the next logical step. But enough of that. Tell me more about the problems here. What have I gotten myself into? Gwen into?"

"The Invisible Hand." He paused as Xander shifted in his chair, a dour look on his face. "They hit us right after Morgen announced the reunification of the clans. They killed plenty of good people two nights ago. Constantin's group got hit hardest. Well, them and the government boys. Almost took out Goran as well."

Xander's mouth fell open. "The armorer left his lair? Impressive. I always had a fondness for him. Is he still alive?"

"Last I heard." Max shifted, toying with his

machine gun. "Look, Xander, we have bigger issues. Those killers have been one step ahead of us the whole way. This is bad. Blackmere says there's a mole."

"Among our ranks or his?"

"We don't know, but we can't trust anyone," Max replied. "This is a mess."

"Do we have enough weapons?"

"That's not the problem," Max replied. "We've already battled several Hands. This has the feel of a major operation. And endgame. Xander, they're not going to stop until Morgen is dead, and the clans are in ruins. We lost plenty back at the conference. It wouldn't surprise me if they already successfully decapitated the leadership. Hell, we could be all that's left by now."

"They were that thorough?"

The dwarf nodded as he kept his gaze on the trees. His focus was jumbled, bouncing between Xander's arrival to the unknown person stalking the surrounding forests to the turmoil of having now two royals to protect. "We're in for a fight and I'm not sure we can win."

"What of DESA? Aren't they providing support?"

"They're part of the problem. Blackmere seems all right but his boss is shady." Max shrugged. "At least that's what Daniel thinks."

"What say you?" A slight breeze swept through the valley, tousling the elf's hair.

"I think he might be right. Everything is all too convenient to make sense. This is a set up."

"Perhaps Norman's summons was a blessing after all," Xander murmured and turned to face the night. "Let them come. We shall show them how sharp our teeth are."

Thaddeus Blackmere slipped into his body armor, frowning at the uncomfortable feeling of it encasing his torso. Technological advancements strengthened the lifesaving vest but failed to mold it better to the human body so as not to be intrusive. As much as he enjoyed staying alive, he was being forced to sacrifice mobility.

"I'm too old for this shit," he muttered to his reflection in the bathroom mirror.

Time had not been kind to him. Where opportunity abounded, time brought waves of aches and pains throughout his body. Lines formed on his face and hands. It felt like yesterday he was the vibrant eighteen-year-old stepping into the recruiter's office to begin his new life. Now, he stalked closer to retirement and the final quarter. Tonight presented what might be his final opportunity to prove his worth in the field.

Strapping his holster to his left thigh, Blackmere slapped a fresh magazine into the pistol and clipped it in place. His vest held six rifle magazines and a handful of pistol ammunition. A single knife tucked into one of the pockets did little to comfort him. Blackmere's hand to hand combat training was years behind him. He prayed he remembered enough to stay alive.

Cupping a handful of cold water, he wiped down his face and headed out. Blackmere met Daniel and Sara in the hall. Both were dressed for war.

"Why didn't you tell me they were alive?" Blackmere asked.

Daniel bit his lower lip. "I made a call. The only way to get everyone to settle down was by making the world believe they were dead. I stand by my actions."

Glare softening, Blackmere made a show of lightly punching the wall. "Doesn't matter now. They're here and I'm glad for it. Xander is a hell of a fighter."

They headed for the lower deck.

"Doesn't this bring back memories?" he tried to joke.

"None I want to relive," Daniel uttered back. "Blackmere, how did the Hand know where to find us?"

"We've been through this, Daniel. I don't have answers."

"I'm not buying it. You and I both know your boss

is the only one who could have betrayed our position," Daniel insisted, opening the door and stepping outside.

"I...I know," Blackmere conceded, suppressing a shiver at the slight chill in the air. "But I need proof to act. Otherwise, he will continue sending these assassins after us. This isn't a game, Daniel. If Corman is corrupt that means the entire agency might be as well. We're not just facing the Invisible Hand."

"Glad I can count on you to spread a little cheer before the fight," Daniel said with a glare.

Sara slapped his arm. "Leave Thaddeus alone. He's putting his life on the line right beside the rest of us."

"Fine," he said after staring into her eyes for a moment.

Blackmere understood Daniel's anger. Tensions were running high. All it would take is one small act to destroy them from within.

"But there will be a reckoning once this is over."

"How much longer do you think before they strike?" Blackmere asked Daniel.

"They know where we are. What's the point in delaying?" Daniel replied. "It's what I'd do—quick strike and cut off the head."

"I—"

The first torch in the outer ring winked out. Darkness flowed into the space where light once reigned.

Blackmere's mouth went dry as Daniel whispered, "Time's up. They're here."

TWENTY-EIGHT

"I want you to stay with Morgen. I mean it, Sara," Daniel instructed. He slipped his rifle off his shoulder and loaded a round into the chamber. "This is going to get ugly fast. Keep your head down and your back to the wall. Don't give these freaks the chance to slip behind you." He gave her a quick kiss, adding, "Oh, and babe, don't shoot me."

She frowned. "As if."

Breaking into a smile, Daniel took his position. Keying his handset, he said, "Heads up. Our guests have arrived."

"Moving into position," Blackmere told him, offering a clipped nod before slipping off.

Suddenly, all the lights in the house were turned off, Gwen reporting that it was her that had turned off the electricity. Daniel took comfort in the small attempt at leveling the playing field. He caught Sara heading back inside from the corner of an eye. It was safer than being out in the open; that and someone needed to stick next to Morgen and Gwen. If she died this was all for naught.

"Movement. Thirty meters downslope. Eleven o'clock." Max's deep rumble sounded like thunder in his ear.

Showtime.

"Schneider," Xander called. The whisk of Velcro snapping shut as he settled into his body armor was louder than he anticipated.

"A little busy, elf," Max replied. Xander noticed the dwarf was repeatedly flexing his firing finger as he surveyed the area.

"I see. Tell me again why we don't have any night vision?"

Max lifted his head, looking at Xander quizzically.

"You know, that's a good damned question. Blame Blackmere. This is his operation."

Frowning, Xander assumed Goran would have outfitted them with everything under the sun… had he not been injured. But they were lacking vital equipment that now put them at a decided disadvantage. One he needed to find a way to overcome before it became too late.

"No more talk," Max announced and handed over a spare earpiece. "Here, last one. I make three targets pushing for the nearest torches. Plug your ears."

"Wait, not—"

"Firing."

The 240 erupted in flame and death. A line of bullets shredded the nearest assassin. Blood splattered from his bullet riddled torso as the dead man pitched backward. Bark flew from the nearest tree. The red line of tracers swept right without pause but the other two assassins were too fast. Max caught one in the shoulder, spinning him around but not killing him. The third man disappeared back into the night.

Round one to us, Xander thought.

"I lost them," Daniel growled. *Fucking Max!* The dwarf always needed to be the first to open fire. His impetus might have cost them the little advantage they had.

Tracking his rifle where he saw the other two assassins disappear, Daniel swept the field of fire. Darkness played tricks on the mind. Shadows became targets. People disappeared behind bushes and rocks. He hated night ops during his army time, and every mission seemed to happen in the middle of the night. Of course, they had had night vision and helicopter support. Not like here. Daniel couldn't keep the scowl from his face.

"Got them. Moving to the left," Blackmere reported.

"I don't see anything," Daniel replied.

"Look down to the left of the corpse. They're

moving toward the next torch."

Daniel scanned the area but still saw nothing. He rubbed his eyes, knowing better than to stare too long at one object. "That's your mind playing tricks on you, Blackmere. I don't see anything but trees."

"I'm telling you I saw movement," Blackmere insisted. "There!"

A short shadow burst into the night. Daniel shielded his eyes from the flare of muzzle flashes, instead following the rounds as the body dropped. Another shadow broke away from an old pine tree to avoid being struck by Blackmere's salvo. Daniel fired twice. The assassin dropped and didn't move. A third figure scrambled back into the night.

"Go ahead and say it," Daniel said, both surprised and impressed.

He caught the mirth in Blackmere's tone as he replied, "I don't need to. You just said it for me."

"Wonderful. I can see two down. How many more to go?"

Morgen flinched at the first sound of gunfire. Feeling foolish, she hated being inside with no way of knowing what was happening. For all she knew their enemies had already swarmed the defenses and those rounds being fired were the last of her team falling. Tired of running and hiding, Morgen longed to return the battle to her foes.

Another round of fire had her muttering, "This is ridiculous. I am going out there to help."

"That's insane!" Sara blurted.

Gwen sidled between her and the door. "You are going to stay put and let those men do their jobs, Mother. This is your role."

"Do not think to lecture me on propriety, child," Morgen snapped. "This is not some fool game or fantasy quest. They need all the help they can get."

"They need to focus on the task, not worry about you getting killed or captured. Xander and I didn't come all this way just to see you hand me the crown before my time," Gwen retorted, smoothing down the front of her blouse.

Morgen bit a laugh. "You think you're going to live long enough to wear my crown? Put the armor on."

A burst of gunfire emphasized her words.

Gwen slipped into the vest and glared. "Did you never think to check on me? Not once to come and see how I was being treated? All those months trapped in a cage like a pet in a zoo. Oh, sure, you sent your hand in your stead. Viviana Cal and I might have been friends as children, but she is no hero to me. She did her best to try and kill me that night Basil made his move against you." She paused, head tilting. "Speaking of which, where is dear Viviana this night?"

"She is off on other business and not your concern," Morgen replied. "I put you where you were to keep you from further trouble. The clans demanded your execution, and, for my part, I considered giving it to them. You murdered a monarch, even if he was your father. But at the end of the day, I am still your mother. I chose to keep you alive and under careful watch until I could think of the best solution."

"And then Otero found me," Gwen added. "We nearly died that night. I have never seen anything like what that old inn had within. A nightmare energy that should never have been born." She paused to look at Sara. "Your husband is an honorable man. He did what the others could not. He let Xander and I go in peace."

"Did he make a mistake?" Sara asked.

"That remains to be seen."

"On what?" she pressed.

Gwen broke into a feral grin. "On whether we survive this night."

Another round of gunfire shattered the night. And this time it didn't stop. Morgen gripped her weapon tighter.

She had much to consider before passing any judgments.

"I missed!" Daniel shouted as he reloaded.

"I don't see him," Blackmere countered, searching the tree line.

Three more torches had been extinguished, opening a swath of darkness in their rings of lights. A few more and the assassins would have a clean avenue of approach leading up to the house. Bodies littered the downslope. He settled back behind his rifle and searched for another target.

Blackmere's eyes widened. Less than ten meters away and pushing forward, were two assassins. They were close enough to see the hate in their eyes through the scope—he fired. His burst raked down the spine of the man crawling on the left. Tracking right, the second assassin already rolled clear and rose to a knee. Blackmere squinted, trying to make out the weapon in the man's hands.

The arrow zipped past his head and buried six inches into the pine beam next to him. Ducking to avoid a second shot, Blackmere struggled to figure out when to make another move. The thunk of another arrow striking close to his head broke his concentration. Fire from Daniel's position, followed by the gargled cry of a man mortally wounded, told him the second assassin was neutralized.

The immediate battlefield was clear again, but the enemy continued gaining ground.

Soon, too soon, they were going to either have to fall back or die in place.

"I have had enough of this."

Max looked up from the rear site aperture of his 240. "Are you mad? You leave now and this whole defense collapses."

"We're already being squeezed. Stay here much longer and we're trapped."

We're already trapped, you stupid elf. I guess all those years in prison rattled your mind. "I need you on my flank, Xander. I can hold this sector long enough for Daniel to figure out how to counter these bastards."

Frustration simmering in his gaze, the elf tightened his grip on his sword but remained silent. Max understood his frustration. He knew what was happening, they all did, and everyone hated being powerless to prevent it.

As the dwarf fired, Xander followed the murderous line of tracers and mixed ball rounds slashing into the night. Small trees burst apart. Leaves and bark scattering in the air. But there were no assassins. No bodies other than those already cooling. Xander needed to act before it was too late. *Plan or not, it's time for me to do something. Anything.* Knowing anything was better than nothing, he slung his rifle over his back and gripped the handrail, ready to leap down into the middle of the madness.

The sound of pistol fire, sporadic and loud, coming from inside the cabin chilled his heart. Gwen! A group of five Hand assassins emerged from concealment in the trees. Xander railed at the seductiveness of the moment. He faced his strongest opponents in a hundred years but to do so meant abandoning Gwen and those left inside. Those who were likely now under attack.

"Go! Save the queen," Max roared and unleashed the full fury of his machinegun into the advancing assassins. "I've got these fuckers."

Xander gave the men in black a final look, acknowledging them all with his sword. *Another time.* He clasped Max's shoulder in passing and dashed inside. This night would forever change the elf clans and their relationship with mortal men. Though how remained to be seen.

The only thing Xander knew was his wife, and their unborn child, were in jeopardy.

TWENTY-NINE

Darkness greeted him. Far more confining than the torchlit slope below the cabin, the interior inspired grim promises. Unfamiliar with the floorplan, Xander slowed his approach. He kept his footsteps light as he slipped through the lower floor, passing several closed doors before reaching the base of the stairs.

Gwen and the others were in the den on the main floor. He'd argued against it, stating they were too exposed in the center of the cabin for proper protection should the men on the deck become overwhelmed, but Morgen insisted on having full mobility to see their hunters approaching. He paused, listening for signs of struggle, or worse. Satisfied there was naught but silence, Xander set his boot on the bottom step.

The door to his left opened. A black clad assassin rushed forward, barreling into him before Xander had the opportunity to raise a defense. They exchanged elbows and fists, neither winning enough to use their blades. Caught off guard, Xander was driven into the wall. His head smashed into one of the fake family portraits he had snorted at when he first saw them, glass shattered, cutting him in several places along his scalp. He grunted, throwing an elbow into the assassin's exposed neck.

They toppled to the floor. Xander lost his grip on his sword. Unarmed and off balance, it was all he could do to bring his arms up to block his foe from crushing his throat. They grappled, rolling over one another in a desperate attempt to get the upper hand. Xander grunted, feeling the burn of a blade sliding between the lower edge of his body armor and his belt. His opponent had skill.

"I have you now, elf," the assassin taunted, his mouth all but pressed against the side of Xander's head. "It's a shame you will die before seeing your queen slaughtered but my name will be long remembered as the one who slew the great Champion of Light. We have long waited this moment. Tonight, you fall. Tomorrow, we rise."

Pain lancing throughout his abdomen, Xander summoned his flagging strength. He slammed the side of his head into the assassin's face. A satisfying crunch told him he broke the man's nose. Blood, hot and wet, splashed his cheek. The assassin rocked back, giving Xander the chance to slip free from the death lock around his neck. He felt the blade jerk free, knowing it tore flesh and potentially ruptured a vital organ.

Xander pressed his assault. He slammed the heel of his hand into the assassin's broken nose. Cartilage drove into the skull. His foe died as splinters fragmented into his brain. Unwilling to rest, Xander plucked the same dagger used to wound him and slit the assassin's throat.

Waves of fresh pain jarred him when he rolled to his hands and knees. Xander grit his teeth and pushed to his feet. Blood flowed down his front to drip on the floor. Stars swam in his vision, but he refused to stop. Not with Gwen so close. Step by step, the former Champion of Light marched closer to his family. That is, if he didn't black out first. It was all he could do to stay on his feet.

Sara heard the commotion downstairs and raced to the top of the stairwell, pistol in hand. She trembled. The sudden thought one of the men might be inside prevented her from firing blindly into the darkness. The urge to scream, empty her pistol, and hurry back to Morgen and Gwen threatened to unravel all she and Daniel had rehearsed.

"Who's down there?" she called. Her voice was timid, reserved.

She caught a grunt, followed by the sound of fists striking flesh. Finger tapping the trigger well, Sara forced her foot to stop tapping too. All she needed to fire was one glimpse of positive identification. She jumped when the lone man burst through the front door. Instead of catching his prey by surprise, the assassin discovered not all cubs lacked fangs.

"Last chance," she said and tried toughening her voice. "Who's down there?"

All sounds faded away, bathing the cabin in ominous silence. Sara slipped her finger onto the trigger. A figure stepped from the shadows, taking the first step up. She fired. The bullet buried into the wood paneling to the man's right.

"Don't shoot! It's me, Xander."

Sara pulled her finger away from the trigger but kept the pistol pointed in his direction. "Are you alone?"

"I am now," he said.

She caught a note of pain in his voice. "Are you okay?"

"How did they get inside?" Xander asked, ignoring her question.

Sara shook her head. She knew about the man in the front door but for another to be downstairs... It was then Xander drew near enough for her to make out the red stain running down the front of his trousers.

"Did I do that?" she asked.

Xander looked down. "No. Unfortunately not. I'm going to need a sewing kit."

"Sure, let me just run and grab one real quick," she quipped. At his nod of agreement, she groaned. "Xander, this place didn't even have army rations or water for us. I doubt you're going to find any medical supplies hiding in the spare cupboards."

Grimacing, Xander gained the top floor and brushed her aside. "Fine, can we start a fire?"

"What are you going to do with it?" she asked,

following him into the main living room.

"Cauterize the wound before I bleed to death."

His deadpan delivery inspired flashbacks from old 90s muscle movies Daniel loved watching with her. The sort where muscle bound morons got shot and placed a hot poker over the wound while smoking a cigarette. *No one was really like that, were they*? "I'll see what I can do," she said aloud, ignoring the little voice whispering how much she wanted to watch the display.

"Thank you," he said. "Where is Gwen?"

"Guarding the front door," Sara supplied. "We barricaded the front door with the furniture after the first man broke in. I've never seen anyone move so fast. One minute we were listening to the battle outside and the door crashed open. He was among us before we knew what was going on."

"Who got him?" Xander asked as they entered the kitchen.

A demure look brightened Sara's eyes.

"I killed the scum," Morgen announced. She looked down at Xander's wound and frowned. "I see he was not alone."

"He was not," Xander confirmed and slumped into one of the kitchen chairs. "Nor is he a threat. They will not be the last."

"No," Morgen mused. "They always move in fives. I suspect the other three are lurking just out of sight to see how well the first two did. Are you well enough to fight, Champion?"

"Stop the bleeding and I will be," he said.

Gwen's hushed voice came from the front of the house. "I see movement."

"The fire, Sara," Xander demanded.

"You will sit tight and let us handle this," Morgen returned. "We are more than a match for these gutless cowards."

"I can't leave Gwen alone." Xander tried to rise but collapsed back into the chair with a hiss.

"There is a medical kit in the SUV. Once we deal with this Hand group we will retrieve it." Morgen gave him a queer look when he shook his head. *What are you hiding from me*? "I need you to sit still and cover the staircase. We can ill afford another breach."

"I-I will hold the stairs," he affirmed and took the extra pistol Morgen handed him.

"You have a full magazine. I don't imagine our friends have been forced inside yet, if they still live." Morgen frowned. Xander had been an integral part of the perimeter defense. With him being inside, now there were only three. She knew it wasn't enough to stop the enemy from storming the cabin. *Why did he leave them?* "Aim true, Champion. The consequences of this night will ripple through eternity."

A trio of quick shots sounded from the other room. Morgen gave a clipped nod and hurried off to join her daughter.

Xander watched her and Sara go, his heart aching. The thought of losing both his wife and unborn child combined with the knowledge there was nothing he could about it in his present condition threatened to rob what strength remained. Xander drew as deep a breath as he could and cocked the hammer on the 9mm.

Morgen saw the bullet riddled body of another assassin sprawled in the gravel driveway, a wet pool spreading under him. Facedown, she suspected the man never knew what hit him. A shame: the longer she found herself entangled with the Invisible Hand the more she wanted to make them all suffer.

Vengeance burning in her veins, Morgen joined her daughter near the closest window and searched the night for any sign of the remaining two assassins. Gwen fired again, careful to place her fire through the already broken window.

Morgen heard the footsteps on the roof, faint and almost imperceptible thanks to the soft soul slippers the assassins preferred. "Sara, the roof!"

Sara looked up, surprised to find small trickles of dust raining down. "There's a single room upstairs! If he finds a way in…"

"Go, Gwen and I will handle the other."

No hesitation, Sara headed for the small pocket staircase leading up. Morgen watched her with renewed pride. Humans like that were hard to come by in the modern world.

"Mother, go with her. I have the last man," Gwen said.

"I will not leave my daughter to the wolves," Morgen said, though the words felt hollow.

"If she dies, we lose all support the humans are giving us. Go. I can handle this and, if not, Xander is stone's throw away."

Curious you have yet to comment on him being inside instead of out there with the true fighters. When Gwen waved her free hand for her to move, Morgen gritted her teeth. *You two are hiding something from me and I will find out once this affair is settled.* "Very well," she said with her most regal tone. "Do not die on me, Daughter. There is much we need to talk about."

"More than you know. Dying is the last thing on my mind. Go."

Rebuked, Morgen left her daughter once again. The past was repeating itself. Would Gwen and Xander return to a DESA prison after the dust settled or did fate have a crueler end in store? Would she be able to pacify the remaining clan leaders to avoid a demanding of execution? Morgen vowed to do all within her power to keep her daughter and son-in-law alive. At least until she got to the bottom of the conspiracy suffocating this cabin.

Weapon in hand, Morgen picked up her pace. She

found Sara crouched beside the top of the stairs. Sliding beside her, she followed Sara's line of sight to the small moonlight patch centered above the twin sized bed dominating the loft. The window cracked, pried open by the unforgiving steel of a blade, just enough for the assassin to reach inside and drop a flashbang.

"Sara, get back down!" Morgen shouted and fired. Blood splattered the window, but it was too late.

The explosion rocked the loft, filling the area with black smoke. It wasn't long before the first lick of flames caught the aged bedspread.

THIRTY

Disgruntled and ready to unleash a lifetime of bridled animosity, Max Schneider hammered the downslope with his machinegun. Most of the torches were extinguished, opening wide swaths in the night for the assassins to approach. He didn't know how they managed to get so close without being detected, but they paid for their arrogance once he sighted them. Bodies littered the slope. Close to two full Hands were neutralized. But how many more hungered for their blood?

Max hated being at a tactical disadvantage. With the goblins he didn't need to know numbers. He and his sons were outnumbered substantially and knew it going into the fight. Fortunately, goblins were shit fighters and the danger remained relatively low. These human murderers were far more aggressive, matching their lethality with uniquely branded human cunning. Were they not actively trying to slaughter him, Max might have considered them a worthy foe. As it stood now, his heart held nothing but contempt.

Compounding his frustrations was the fact Xander abandoned his position to race to his wife's side. Max snorted. *Like she needed it.* Gwen always proved the more capable of the two. Ruthless as the night was long, she took after her mother. How else could a woman so easily slay her father and feel nothing? Max thanked the gods he only had sons. Sure, they were obstinate knuckleheads, but neither would so much as consider taking action against him the way Gwen did with her parents.

The click of an empty drum made him fall behind cover to reload. A pile of empty two hundred round drums, lay scattered at his feet alongside the weapon's original barrel. The smell of cordite was a familiar friend, leading him to question how his people survived so long without gunpowder. Intoxicated, Max slapped a new drum in place and loaded the weapon. A quick glance at his watch showed it was just past midnight and he was down to his last spare barrel.

They were running on fumes despite the brief respite of the day. Lack of sleep, since he hadn't gotten any, and constantly standing on the edge riddled him with fatigue. The others had to feel the same. How else could Max accept his own surging lethargy if the humans did not feel the same, or worse?

"Max, do you copy?"

The dwarf, thankful for the unwitting hand, replied, "Send it."

"Looks like you have a trio moving up on your right," Daniel reported. "They could flank you."

Max shifted positions, nestling down on his belly and dropping his weapon's bipod. "Where?"

"Three o'clock. Maybe thirty meters out and trying to skirt around the remaining torches."

Squinting, he switched his scope to thermal imaging and was rewarded by the sight of three assassins preparing to rush his position. "Got em. Thanks for the heads up."

"No pro—"

The bark of machinegun fire cutoff whatever else Daniel was going to say. Max kept adjusting fire to keep the assassins off guard as they fumbled about. Unable to guess which way he was firing, they were easy pickings. He hummed an old childhood tune as he mowed them down.

"Daniel, I got—"

Two assassins leapt over the railing, knives flashing.

"How many more of them are there?" Daniel shouted to Blackmere when Max's words cut off over another round of firing.

He wished they knew more about the Invisible

Hand, but Blackmere's knowledge base proved remarkably limited. The agent had bare bones details lacking strength of numbers, bases of operation, or any significant tactical factor that might put Daniel's mind at ease. With bodies already littering the battlefield, Daniel needed to know how much the assassins had yet to throw at them.

That they continued driving closer to the cabin despite their losses suggested they had arrived in force, with at least platoon strength. He shivered at the thought of fighting off fifty or more of the assassins even while acknowledging the possibility. Daniel was going to run out of ammunition long before the Hand ran out of assets. The mission wasn't supposed to go beyond rescuing the queen from the rest stop. Yet here they were, a day later and on the brink of collapse.

The echo of gunfire sang up and down the valley. No doubt any neighbors or vacationers in the area were either hunkered down behind locked doors or had called the police. Daniel figured Blackmere could flash his badge and talk his way out of their predicament if the authorities arrived before it was too late. At least he hoped so.

"There's no way of knowing," Blackmere called back when the firing paused.

The immediate field of fire was clear, prompting Daniel to look harder. One lesson learned was any lull in the fight meant the Hand was consolidating and adapting their tactics. Thus far, all the action focused on the primary defense, but Daniel was no rookie. He knew it was a matter of time before they slipped around to the front of the house to assault from the weak side. The battle in the back might already be little more than a feint, designed to focus their attention while the assassins slipped in.

The thought unsettling his nerves, Daniel keyed his handset, "Sara, how goes it?"

No reply.

He waited a while more before repeating the question.

Again, there was no reply.

He looked back to the dark windows leering at him. With no lights on and no answer, it proved easy to imagine a scene of slaughter inside. *What if she's...* That's when he smelled smoke. A faint whiff at first but growing more pronounced the harder he sniffed the night air. "Blackmere, I think we have a problem. Do you smell that?"

"A fire," Blackmere concluded.

Had they already circumvented our defenses? He tamped down his panic, letting training and experience take control. Daniel couldn't get a good angle of view from his position. He did a 180 and found himself facing the opposite side of the engagement area. There, to his surprise, moved three assassins with deliberate intent. He marveled at how they exhibited no fear in their approach despite stepping around a carpet of their fallen.

The fire would have to wait. Daniel keyed the headset again. This time for Max. The dwarf was going to have more than enough to handle.

Groaning, coughing up the smoke filling her lungs, Morgen pushed herself off the floor. Smoke burned her eyes. The stinging making her tear up. Ringing in her ears prevented her from catching anything going on around her. She looked, startled to find flames already creeping up the wall behind the bed. Looking higher, she saw an outstretched arm surrounded by a pool of blood covering the moonlight. At least she took out the man responsible for setting the house on fire.

Morgen found nothing to extinguish the hungry flames and focused on the limp figure sprawled out before her. Sara took the brunt of the flash bang: the concussion had knocked her out if not worse. Catching the rise and fall of her chest, shallow as it was, Morgen thanked the gods the woman yet lived. She summoned her waning strength and began pulling Sara to the stairs. She cried out for help, unsure if anyone heard or if any were still alive.

Xander's wound was grave, leaving Gwen the sole defender of the cabin. She needed to hurry. Summoning what strength she had left, the elf queen hoisted Sara onto one shoulder and moved as quickly as possible down the stairs and back into the kitchen. Relief washed over her upon finding Xander still breathing. He had grown quite pale and had his head down, but he was alive.

"Hold on, Champion. Just hold on," she struggled to reassure between breaths.

He coughed in response.

Morgen set Sara down on the chair opposite Xander and, after ensuring the woman wouldn't fall over, went to see how Gwen fared. The fire was already spreading. She deduced it wouldn't be long before they would be forced to abandon their position and head into the woods. Fortunately, this had been part of the plan all along. Break the enemy tide on the anvil before slipping into the night.

She found Gwen prowling between the windows flanking the front door. A pair of bodies were outside. At least one Hand had been dealt with but did little to soften her anxiety. The night was only half done. Heavy gunfire deafened the area though she barely caught the pop of rounds thanks to the ringing in her ears. Morgen traced a finger up her cheek to her earlobe. The tips came away sticky. Blinking, she found herself staring at Gwen who was suddenly in her line of sight.

"Mother, you're injured."

"What?" Morgen shouted. She instantly regretted it. Waves of pain danced through her skull, forcing her to clamp both hands to her rattled head.

Gwen rushed to her side, checking her pupils and then pulling her hands away to expose the bloody ears. "We have to get out of here before this place burns down around us… Can you hear me?"

Morgen shook her head, trying to read her lips. "Not really."

Gwen nodded and talked slower, enunciating her words. "We are taking Xander and Sara out to the SUV. Get the med kit and see about the men down below. Do you understand?"

Morgen stretched her jaw. Pins and needles spread through her flesh. A good sign the nerves were waking up and the brief effects of the flash bang were wearing off.

"Mother?"

Morgen gave her a thumbs up, not wanting to try speaking again.

"Guard the door," Gwen ordered, slapping her pistol into her hands after checking to see how full the magazine was.

Before she could reply, Gwen slipped back into the kitchen. The only way to save Xander was by clearing the threat. Nothing else mattered until then. Well, almost nothing.

Gwen smelled the blood before seeing Xander. How could she not? The very air seemed laced with the iron tang. Her heart ached for her husband but there was little to be done for him until they made it to the vehicle. Smoke began pouring down the stairs, suggesting the cabin continued burning at a devastative rate. Time was running out.

She placed a hand on Xander's shoulder and squeezed. "Stay strong, my love. We're going to get out of this. I just don't know how."

She moved over to Sara, tilting her head back. Foam bubbled on the woman's lips and her face was covered with smoke and grime, but she appeared no worse for wear. Gwen grabbed a bottle of water from the refrigerator and splashed some on the human's face.

She awoke with a start, sputtering. "What happened?"

Gwen explained what little she knew, studying Sara to ensure there was no lasting effects from the blast. "I need you to cover me while I go get the med kit. There's no way Xander can wait for all of us to get out of here."

"I can do that," Sara said, glancing at Xander in dismay.

Gwen refused to look at wound and instead reached for Sara's hand. "Come on. We don't have time to spare."

They headed back into the front room. Gwen felt the sweat beginning to trickle down her face. The cabin was heating up. Soon flames would spread across the roof and upper floor in an unstoppable inferno that wouldn't be happy until it devoured the entire cabin. This was not how she imagined her night going. One minute they were erased from the world, enjoying all life had to offer. The next they were cast upon the shores of destruction with one way out. Gwen cursed silently, knowing she had to choose between the gentleness of motherhood and the tenacity of warrior.

"Where are you going?" her mother demanded as she rushed by and to the front door.

"Xander needs that kit now or he won't make it. We don't have time for a debate," she replied and hurried to the SUV. The thought of losing the father of their unborn child chilled her.

Stepping over the bodies and sending brief looks at the surrounding trees, she reached the back hatch and popped it open. Heart hammering in her chest she began rummaging through their meager supplies for something capable of saving Xander's life.

THIRTY-ONE

Max gripped the assassin by the back of the neck and slammed his face into the wall with a bone shattering crunch. He let go and watched the corpse slither to the deck but there was no respite. The dwarf grunted from a slash across his left shoulder blade. The sting of the knife burned, but the wound wasn't deep enough to cause much injury. Infuriated, Max whirled. He was unarmed, but that seldom left a dwarf at a disadvantage. The remaining assassin glared.

"Come on, fight!"

To his surprise, the assassin set down that curved and cruel blade, now dripping with Max's blood, and pushed his sleeves halfway up his arms. That glare transformed into a grin bearing the same malevolence. He gestured for Max to attack.

Max wasted no time. He launched at the now unarmed assassin and the two settled into a dance of fists and opportunistic kicks. The flurry of motion proved dizzying, for each showed their worth in battle. *A worthy opponent indeed.* Max unleashed a series of blows aimed at the man's head and torso, but the assassin was too fast, almost as if he had anticipated the moves. A second round left Max depleted and confused.

The assassin stepped back, leering, then leapt forward with lightning speed. His ridge hands slapped Max on both sides of the neck. Stunned, the dwarf dropped to a knee and threw his hands up to fend off the blows. A knee caught him in the ribs, bowling him over. Instead of pressing his advantage, the assassin stepped back. Once more beckoning Max to attack.

Swearing, Max coughed up a mouthful of blood. His head throbbed. Breathing was difficult thanks to the precision blows to his throat. The indignity being offered enraged him. It was all he could do to keep his wits, lest the assassin continue dismantling his defenses for a slow, easy kill. Max pushed back to his feet with a grunt and rolled his neck. Pain lanced through his spine. Not a good sign.

Legs shaky, Max clenched his fists and charged again. Instead of wasting time and energy trying to dance with the assassin, he barreled into the man with as much force as he could. They fell to the deck: Max heard the snap of bones, saw the man curl inward to protect his unbroken ribs. Bolstered by the injury, he wrapped his hands around the assassin's neck and squeezed. The man's eyes popped. Blood frothed on his lips, fresh and vibrant.

Max squeezed harder. His gloved fingertips dug into the exposed flesh until the man's face turned shades of purple and blue. Still the man did not die. Still he applied more pressure. The tip of a tongue slipped free, swollen and distended. Anger flashed and Max drove his forehead into the dying man's face. The crash of bone and flesh resounded across the deck. Max got a burst of strength and felt the assassin's neck snap.

Rising once more, he cast his head back and threw out his fists in challenge to any lurkers still out in the night. "Who's next?" He coughed, spitting out blood. "Come on you bastards. Come and see what this dwarf has for you!"

"Max!"

The dwarf waved Daniel off who was running towards him. "I'm fine. Where are the rest of them?"

"Scope's clear," Daniel replied.

Grunting, Max gathered a mouthful of blood and spit again. "What's that smell?"

"That's the new problem."

"Stay with me, baby. This is going to hurt."

Gwen finished wiping the blood off Xander's abdomen with an antiseptic pad and poured half a bottle of saline solution. Doing her best to ignore his dazed and pained look, Gwen pressed the edges of the wound as close together as she could without causing additional hurt. Three inches wide with jagged edges, it didn't appear to have perforated any of his vital organs. The blood was dark and slowing but not enough to let it go on its own.

At her side, Morgen grabbed the spray bottle of silver nitrate from the med kit.

Gwen leaned forward to kiss Xander's forehead one last time before spraying the cauterizing medicine over the wound. He tensed. His face twisted in a rictus of agony as the spray burned his wound shut. Gwen held back her tears. She watched as his flesh turned black around the edges of the wound.

He clutched the table until his knuckles went white. Still, Gwen continued spraying, leaving nothing to chance. The only way they were going to survive the night was by having him in fighting form. At last the bottle went empty. She tossed it aside, knowing she probably hadn't needed to use the entire dose. Ignoring his labored breathing, Gwen next took a small piece of gauze and applied it over the wound before adding a large bandage. Xander winced then gasped.

When she finished, Gwen found herself staring into eyes. "Sorry, but it had to be done. How does it feel?"

"It hurts," he said. Sweat beaded across his brow. A brief look of defeat entertained his face before she watched his features go blank. "Where is the queen?"

"Right here, you pigheaded fool," Morgen snipped, still at Gwen's side. "I understand you are a hero, but I need you to act with a little more care."

Gwen watched as he looked at the queen for the first time, noticing the soot and dust coating her face and clothes. A pair of scratches decorated her scalp and she smelled of smoke. Her mother had given her pause when she had first appeared from upstairs. Seeing him quickly hide his exasperation, he reached for his weapon and commented, "I shall do my best, your Majesty."

Gwen kissed him on the side of the face, relief evident in her eyes.

Satisfied, Morgen gestured to the building cloud of smoke clinging to the ceiling. "We cannot stay here."

"Right, time to move," Xander agreed.

They had all rehearsed the backup plan before the sun set. Xander noticed the handful of gear packs waiting by the front door. With the temperature rising, he knew returning downstairs to the deck to get the others wasn't viable. He would miss their combined firepower in their flight to safety but there was nothing for it. He had to trust they stayed alive and were sticking to the plan.

Rising, he tested his wound. The pain remained prominent. His flesh burned from the silver nitrate—a fire unlike any he had ever felt. It constricted his movements but his confidence in the wound being sealed kept him moving.

A cough drew his attention. Sara covered her mouth, desperate to keep the smoke from plunging into her lungs. Morgen followed suit. Xander frowned. It wouldn't be long before the upper floor collapsed. "We need to move. Now."

Morgen nodded. "Lead on. I for one have no desire to burn to a crisp."

"At least they wouldn't find our bodies," Sara murmured between coughs.

Grinning, Xander led them to the door in a line. He cracked it open after shouldering his pack and scanned the seeable area. The way appeared clear, but he knew that line of thought would see them dead quicker than not. *The plan…*

He paused to look each in the eye. "We can't risk taking the truck. This needs to be on foot."

"On foot? Against them?" Morgen blurted.

Sara added, "Are you insane? We won't stand a chance!"

I know. I know. Xander held up a hand. "They will be expecting us to flee in a vehicle. It's what I would do. If we go on foot, we stand a better chance of shaking pursuit and, hopefully, linking up with the others at the rendezvous point. Your Majesty, you trusted my judgment for so long. I ask you to do so again this night."

All eyes fell on the queen. He saw a woman teetering on the brink of collapse, who's hope dwindled with each passing act yet remained defiant in the face of overwhelming odds. Another burst of gunfire below told them at least one of the others yet lived and with them hope. Morgen stiffened, once more appearing regal. Domineering. The way she was meant to be.

"You hold the hope of us all in your hands, Xander. Lead the way," she commanded.

Thankful the exchange ended with minimal arguing, Xander adjusted the weight of his pack to balance with his rifle and slipped outside. The others followed in single file, skirting past the front of the SUV and down the driveway before reaching a low ditch running parallel to the main road below. Xander shooed them down with Gwen in the lead.

He halted her long enough to kiss her cheek. "Go. Stay low and as quiet as possible. I will bring up the rear and provide outlier," he whispered. "Do not stop until we are on level ground."

"What about the others?" Gwen whispered back.

Sara reached for her handset, only to find it missing. No doubt melted upstairs. It was their only one, leaving them cut off from traditional comms with the rest of their group.

Xander looked back at the cabin, now wreathed in a crown of flames and smoke. He shook his head. "We can't go back, and I don't think there will be any friendlies before us. Not if they stick to the plan. Keep pushing forward."

"I love you," Gwen told him before continuing down the ditch.

He forced out the breath he'd been holding as he watched her disappear into the darkness with the others. Guilt accosted his conscience, for he knew he never should have placed her in such a predicament. Xander gave a final look back at the burning cabin and silently wished the others luck before following the women.

"That's it. We need to displace now," Blackmere announced as he collapsed his position and joined Daniel and Max. "That whole part of the cabin is a raging inferno."

Daniel didn't bother to respond. His heart ached with uncertainty. He stared at the flames licking down over the eaves. Sara was up there, somewhere, and he had no way of getting inside to reach her. Judging from the rising intensity of the flames, a large portion of the cabin was already lost. He prayed Xander made it upstairs and escorted the others to safety. Otherwise…

"Collect what gear we have," he managed. *Trust the plan.* "We head for the exfil and pray the Hand have made their shot." At the dwarf's grunt, he added, "Max, are you good?"

"Peachy, thanks for asking," the dwarf glowered. "We should go now."

One by one they slipped over the railing and clambered down the side of the house to reach the ground. Bodies littered the area for as far as they could see, interspersed with fallen trees. A handful of torches yet burned but Daniel knew better than to approach them. They were going to need what little night vision they had the further from the burning cabin they got.

The sky over the hillside transformed into walls of orange and red. Daniel took little comfort in knowing their foes were robbed of their immediate protection too. Daniel led his team down into the forest where their vehicles sat concealed on a cut off from the main road leading out of the valley.

Daniel could feel the heat of the house fire long after the trees converged on him.

THIRTY-TWO

He watched. Silent. Thoughtful. Scores of black clad men similar to the one he eliminated earlier in the day rushed through the darkness with the impunity of men performing foul deeds. For seventy-five years he wandered the mountain paths alone, content in the knowledge humanity had as little interest in him as he had with it. Now that illusion of serenity was shattered forever causing a quiet rage to simmer within.

He abandoned civilization long ago for a reason. The insanity of the world threatened to bring all to ruin, and he wanted no part in it. Now, far removed from the trappings of power or political intrigue, he had enjoyed a life among the trees and babbling brooks running down from distant mountaintops. A life spent wandering forgotten paths and exploring deep valley waterfalls. Life as a hermit.

Not that he had forgotten how to be violent. No. Once learned it was seldom forgotten. That, he deemed, was the greatest mistake his kind continued making. Never underestimate the man who had known violence, for it came as easy as the flipping of a switch. With a mental finger hovering over the switch, he watched the assassins assault the cabin on the hill and remembered what it meant to dedicate his life to harm.

Yet for all his self-enforced impotence, he did not act until he spied the first fingers of flame licking above the cabin, searching for the delicate lower branches of ancient oaks by which the fire could spread through the valley. The simmering rage became an old hate that quickly resurfaced, and it was all he could do to keep from unleashing the monster chained within. Knowing time was short and his back was to the wall, he drew his hooked blade from his belt and set off into the night.

There was work to be done.

Max planted his barrel square in the middle of the assassin's chest and fired. Being so close the 5.56mm rounds sliced through flesh and bone and kept going. The body jerked, flopping, before the mind recognized death. Max kicked the man away and kept pushing forward. On either side he caught glimpses of Daniel and Blackmere handling their own opponents.

They made it less than twenty meters into the trees before another Hand team beset them in a near perfect ambush. It was only thanks to Max's keen sense of sight that they detected the assassins in time. Three now lay cooling among the fallen leaves. The other two weren't far behind but Max questioned how much left his beleaguered team had to give. They were beaten and pushed to the edge of breaking. With energy stores running low, as well as ammunition, he and the others were isolated from the rest of their group and, in his estimation, the one person who needed to survive the night.

Running out of options, Max took stock of the situation. He caught Daniel evade a swipe aimed at his neck and brought his pistol up to take the assassin in the bottom of the jaw. Max nodded to Daniel as the man died. On the opposite side, Blackmere held his ground despite his age. The last assassin fell to a round to the chest and the forest returned to silence.

"We're not going to make it if something doesn't turn in our favor," Daniel said between pants as he came to stand beside Max. He gave Blackmere a look. "How are you holding up, old timer?"

Blackmere wiped the sweat and grime from his face. "I'm still here, aren't I?"

"We need to keep moving," Max warned, interrupting their banter. "I don't like sitting out in the open like this."

"The vehicles can't be far off," Daniel agreed.

"Let's hope the others have better success than we're having."

The idea of their fight drawing to a close entered the dwarf's mind. Shouldering his machinegun, finally feeling the weight dragging on him, Max replied, "And here I was hoping we had killed the last of them already."

"No such luck," Daniel said and led the way.

"How much further?" Sara asked. She was covered in sweat. Her body ached. Nothing in her life prepared her for the toils of this night, nor could she think of one instance where she might ever have considered the need to prepare. This, she decided, was not normal. Her companions were just as mad as the people trying to kill them. There was no other explanation. What little she knew of the elves came from Daniel's stories, though her time spent with Morgen last year went a long way in helping Sara understand some things just didn't make sense.

Elves certainly fell into that category. Each of them exhibited a reckless attitude akin to a death wish. They stormed after their foes with abandon and seldom paused to look back or consider the ramifications of their actions. Xander was the worst. Perhaps that stemmed from being a proclaimed champion. She failed to see how anyone, immortal or not, might live up to such a lofty title without allowing their head to swell.

Sara very much wanted to live to see her family again. The thought of waking up sandwiched between two giant dogs while Daniel made breakfast threatened to steal her focus and that was the one thing she needed more than anything else. Clutching her pistol a little tighter, she followed Gwen and Morgen into another cluster of trees. Somewhere, at the end of this nightmare, waited a fresh vehicle and the promise of escape. They just needed to get there first. A few meters later and Gwen brought them to a sudden halt in a ditch.

"What is it? Why are we stopping?" Sara asked,

crouching.

"Quiet," Morgen whispered. "We are being hunted."

She caught the dull roar of engines approaching and dared a look. Sara spied the glow of several sets of red taillights glowing in a trail winding up the road toward them. Far too small to be full sized cars, she surmised they were four wheelers or some other rugged comparable vehicle ready to take the fight into the forests. *Of course they do*.

Had the assassins given up on stealth in favor of a full-frontal assault? The idea struck fresh tremors of fear. She raised her pistol, seeking to take a shot at the leader driver.

"What are you doing?" Morgen hissed, her voice burrowing into her ear. "Do not give our position away. If they knew where we were they would not be approaching in the open like this. Let them pass. Sara."

Sara wavered, her grip on her pistol tightening. What if it was a distraction? What if they did know and she wouldn't see her family again?

Morgen sighed, adding, "Trust me. This is the only way. Unless you wish to die in this forgotten ditch?"

Reluctantly, Sara did as she was told.

The first ATV roared within full view, followed by several others. Sara clamped a hand over her mouth. They'd been discovered! Her stomach threatened to rebel as she crouched deeper into the ditch in the hopes of remaining unseen.

The Hermit stepped into the center of an abandoned clearing. A favorite spot he once used to muse upon the creators of the universe and the majesty of the heavens. Now it was reduced to a war-torn shadow of its former grandeur. He struggled to contain his emotion. Seldom one to fall for base tricks or first takes, he preferred deep analysis before offering an opinion or taking action. This night not only robbed him of that capacity, but it also steeled him for what must come next. He shed his cloak of leaves and dark colors, standing in the center of the clearing with arms wide open in a flexible bodysuit designed for ease of movement.

The time for hiding was ended. Now had come the hour of his return and woe be unto the world for what he was about to unleash. His wait wasn't long. Assassins seldom took the opportunity to think through their tasks. These Invisible Hands were no different. Blood running hot from the thrill of the hunt, they were eager to sink their blades into his lone being.

They circled him. Ten men armed with knives and mutual hatred. He let them come. There was no need for haste now. His opponents seethed arrogance. He saw it in their eyes. The way they held themselves. Ten to one had the odds in their favor, they knew victory stood but a moment away. That was their biggest mistake.

Gesturing to the first person he deemed weak, the Hermit invited the assassin to dance blades first. The Hand stalked into the circle, crouching as only one accustomed to murder did. The Hermit let him have his moment. Let him pose for his fellow team members thinking he had the upper hand. It would avail his naught. Moments passed. The assassin taunted him, flashing his blade. The Hermit was no regular prey. The Hand should have just eliminated him—it would be his last mistake.

The assassin struck with blinding speed. His blades crossed, questing for the Hermit's throat. Instead, they met air as the Hermit stepped back and punched his blade through the assassin's throat, twisting and ripping half the throat away in a shower of blood and falling teeth.

Rather than let the body drop, the Hermit snatched him with his free hand and lifted him off the ground in a savage display of dominance. *Challenge sent.* He shook the corpse for all to see and cast the body at the feet of his next target. The Hermit grinned upon seeing the assassin tense.

This stealthy killer who lacked the courage to face his enemies one on one was now cringing from the thought of meeting a similar fate. No matter how much strength the Invisible Hand portrayed, they were just like every other assassin guild in the world. *Cowards at heart.*

The Hermit hummed in appreciation as the man refrained from launching into a singular assault. Perhaps there was a measure of collective sense among them after all.

The circle tightened. Just as the Hermit wished.

He unleashed his full wrath and fury upon them. A blur of motion, he struck with blinding speed. Men cried out. The Hermit wove webs of intricate destruction, cutting through their ranks with abandon. He could not be stopped. Not by the likes of any human agents. It was over in a matter of moments. Ten dead assassins piled at his feet, soaking his clothing in their gore and viscera. The Hermit frowned. He so hated being filthy. An annoyed look twisting his features, he began moving the bodies into a circle, their feet pointing out. He was careful to cross their hands over their now still chests. A small measure of respect for men who sought to match skills with him.

Their weapons he collected in a pile. Those would be melted down and reforged for better purpose by him later. The world had enough killing and violence in it. Perhaps his efforts might sow a bit of good so desperately needed. Perhaps not. Who was he to fight the tide?

Finished, the Hermit sheathed his blade and folded his hands before him. There was little more to do but wait.

They found him standing in his circle of slaughter. Trees and bushes were painted red. He stood with empty hands, for the time to use his blade had long passed. Here, among the cooling bodies and pointless massacre, he was once more in touch with the natural world.

The dwarf lowered his weapon, if just and stepped to the edge of the circle. He admired the dead assassins before asking, "Who the fuck are you?"

The Hermit smiled. "A ghost from the past, Max Schneider."

THIRTY-THREE

Nevada Slim longed to escape. He felt outmaneuvered, backed into a corner. Since returning to Raleigh, he found himself locked in a desperate string of meetings and discussions to preserve the clans. With the wolves at the door, Slim gathered what few allies remained. Those numbers dwindled thanks to the culling the Invisible Hand conducted but was not in vain. He just needed to hold on a little longer.

He and Constantin Andros left the suddenly taciturn James Corman the first moment they could. The human proved most difficult, leading both elves to suspect a hidden agenda. Mistrust rising, it was all Slim could do to get away from the man he found reviling. They parted without a word, though he felt Corman's gaze lingering on his back.

Slim waited until they were far enough away from the Deputy Director before addressing his concerns with Constantin. "That man is hiding something."

"Say the word and I can get it out of him," the Old Guard replied without any hint of emotion. "He will break easy enough."

"I don't want him broken. Not yet at any rate. We need to discover what his motivations are and if Daniel's guess is correct."

"You think he is working with the Hand?" Constantin asked.

"I need to find out. Too much has gone against us to be coincidence."

The first slivers of dawn broke the horizon. Slim quickened his pace. Morgen and the others would be at the DESA safehouse by now. "The burden is now on us to get to the bottom of the Invisible Hand," he mused aloud. "Can we trust Corman?"

Constantin clenched a fist. "He will betray us, if he hasn't already."

"DESA has never let me down before," Slim said. His concern grew over Constantin's dark tone. He didn't want to admit the alternative. Not yet.

"Slim," Constantin called and halted mid-step, turning to face him with a feverish gaze. "We have been behind every step. Corman and his people seem to know more than they are willing to share."

"You have a point, but we all agreed moving Morgen to safety was our best move," Slim replied. "Are you still able to track her?"

A twinkle entered the elf's eye. "I am. She is fitted with a tracking device only I have access to."

"Sneaky bastard. Where is she?"

Constantin checked his phone. "Heading into the mountains. Looks like they are north of Boone."

"That's fairly secluded," Slim added. "Do you suppose it's a trap?"

"I wouldn't be good at what I do if I said no."

"How fast can your strike team get out there?" he asked.

"Not long. I can be out there by the evening," the Old Guard guessed.

"No. I need you here with me. Put your best person on it, Constantin, and let me know when they are ready to deploy. We need to play this one close to keep DESA from getting word of our plans," he explained. "Meet me back here as soon as you are finished."

"What are you thinking?" Constantin asked.

"I can't focus on reunifying the clans while worrying over the queen. Deploy your team and then we need to build one here. People we trust should our friends in DESA decide we've outlived our usefulness."

The captain of the Old Guard nodded and stalked off to find his people. Slim watched him go, passing a glance at the now distant Corman.

"Talk to me," Slim ordered as he swept into the remnants of the fallen command center.

He took in the handful of menials and computer techs, elves and dwarves performing various roles for their clans. Failing to find any familiar faces, Slim centered himself in the room and made them come to him. Knowing optics was everything in times of crisis, he presented himself the authority. None questioned him.

"Sir, we have cleared out all remains and have teams actively seeking out potential survivors who might have fled during the chaos."

"You are?" he stared back at the tanned elf addressing him. Her dark hair matched the hue of her flesh, lending her an exotic look he couldn't place.

"Viviana Cal," she replied.

His eyebrow rose. "The queen's right hand. I was under the impression you were off on other matters."

"I was," she replied. "Then I received word of this debacle and returned as soon as possible."

"I trust you brought reinforcements, Viviana?"

A devious look crossed her already severe face. "One or two. They are outside waiting my call."

"Can we trust them?"

"As much as we can any dwarf."

He grunted. "Wonderful. Anyone I know?"

She folded her arms, silently appraising him before responding, "Perhaps. They are the Schneider brothers, Angus and Fritz."

"What have you done, Viviana Cal?" He rubbed his forehead, immediately recognizing the name. "Ahh. The spawns of Max."

"You know them?"

"Only by reputation," he admitted. "Still, I suppose it is better they are on our side. Do we have numbers on those we lost?"

Her complexion paled; Slim caught the slightest

quiver in her upper lip and sighed. "Too many," he concluded. "I want all surviving clan and family leaders to regroup and report to Morgen's headquarters. There is a plot to remove the elves from existence and I am going to need all the help I can get to prevent it. That includes you, Viviana."

She nodded and motioned for him to follow her, an unreadable look twisting her features.

Curious as to what she wanted to say to him, he walked alongside her as they headed back to the auditorium. The dwarfs, armed for war and scowling, fell in step behind her.

"Baron where is the queen?" she asked once they were away from the bustle of activity.

"Safe," he replied. *For now.* "Start pulling in your security detail and stop sharing intelligence with our DESA friends unless I clear it. Am I understood?"

"Yes," she replied.

Viviana stormed off, a woman on a mission.

Let to his devices, Visilias weaved through the cleanup crews and clumps of men and women conversing. Few looked up. He heard them muttering as they made notes on any details of the assault they came across. He was at least happy the consensus of everyone here right now was to unravel the Invisible Hand's motivations and potential next moves.

He paused, watching one man sitting in a chair and chatting on the phone. His eyes narrowed. *A spy?* He watched a little longer before picking up the words "beer" and "I'll be home soon, honey" and scoffed. Humans, he had no love for most of them. They seldom laid their cards on the table, and he'd learned long ago how devious they were. The ones he trusted fully were already deep in the North Carolina mountains.

He headed for the stage to take in the blade marks, noticing bloodstains still on the crimson seats; he imagined they were going to be hard to remove. His eyes fell back onto the main stage, and he ascended the steps. *How had the Hand penetrated our defenses so thoroughly?* The obvious answer haunted him. He had learned of the defensive system Max Schneider had set up before arriving in Raleigh: entire squads of undercover guards were to be warding each entry point. Every accessway was fitted with scanners and cameras. Security had been as tight as possible...

Our security forces had been infiltrated by Hand agents. Knowing no elf or dwarf would turn traitor, that left DESA who brought in agents. *Unknowingly or on purpose?* A cold chill spread through him. Slim needed proof. He needed Constantin. Dour as the old elf may be, the Old Guard was the premier military force among the clans and one of the first responders on scene last night.

Slim turned to head out when a glittering object caught his eye. Jumping off the stage and into the first row of seats, he reached down between a stained seat's armrests and produced a small foldable cell phone; nondescript and silver. He considered calling one of the investigators over before slipping the device into his jacket pocket. *I can't trust anyone.*

Hands in his pockets he left with a clue that could unravel the mysteries of the night.

Away from the constraints of leadership and government overwatch, Constantin Andros felt his energy return the moment he stepped back into the Old Guard barracks. Guards sharpened weapons and banged dents from their armor. He noticed the low morale among them until the whispers started. Many stopped to give him an appreciative nod or word of encouragement. One injured guard told him that seeing him march through the barracks inspired him to get up and prepare to fight the enemy.

He spoke little before he found his locker where he shed his battered uniform, depositing the blouse and trousers in a large trash can nearby before stepping back to his locker. No time to clean up, Constantin slipped into a new set of fatigues and grabbed his Kevlar body armor and helmet. It felt good being in his own gear again. He knew the others watched, taking note on what he was doing. Concealing his pride when some headed for their own gear, Constantin slammed his combat knife into its hilt and strapped on his army style utility belt. Grabbing the assault pack taking up most of his locker space, he turned to face his people.

"The queen lives. She is being secluded in a DESA safehouse in the mountains," he announced without delay. He gave them a moment to cheer before continuing. "That is not good enough for me. I want ten—Sergeant Bettis, you lead."

"Sir," Bettis called out in confirmation. He dominated the barracks with his presence. Gruff and professional, he served the Old Guard for several hundred years and had a distinguished career second only to Constantin. "When do we leave?"

"Immediately. You have air clearance to depart. Move in, secure the queen, and destroy any enemy forces."

"Any friendlies in the AO?"

Constantin paused. He considered listing the humans as opponents. True, they comported themselves honorably in battle, but Blackmere was DESA and that alone reached the limit of his trust.

"Three. Daniel and Sara Thomas continue protecting the queen along with Agent Blackmere," he said after some deliberation. "Max Schneider is there as well. I want all of them protected."

Murmurs rippled through the normally taciturn Guards.

"Ah, sir, scuttlebutt says the Hand infiltrated DESA. They could all be compromised," Bettis said.

"That is a possibility but one I am not willing to entertain in this instance. Blackmere lost two men and assisted in eliminating several assassins," Constantin replied. "Take your team and bring our queen home, Bettis. The rest of you I want outfitted and ready for battle within the hour."

"What's the target?"

"That is for Baron Visilias to determine. We are his sword. We strike where and when he says. Prepare yourselves. This will be the fight of our lives. Expect casualties. Unleash havoc. Tonight, we fight for the honor of the kingdom and glory everlasting!"

"Glory everlasting!" the remaining Guards chanted.

Satisfied his people were ready, Constantin strapped his power sword to his back and followed Bettis and his team to the waiting van that would take them to the private heliport. After struggling to keep up for the better part of a day, it felt good taking the fight to their enemies.

Long live the queen.

THIRTY-FOUR

"My name is Keth Murdis," the Hermit announced.

The two humans exchanged confused looks, as if they were supposed to know what that name meant. He doubted they would and their blank stares did little to impress Keth, leaving them weaknesses in his opinion.

Only the dwarf showed any sign of recognition when he flinched. The barrel of his machinegun rose, slightly. "You're dead," he said through clenched jaws.

An owl's hoot broke the still of the night. With the sounds of battle drifting away, a certain measure of calm attempted to reassert itself through the mountain valleys. Sirens could be heard far away and drawing nearer. *We don't have much time.* A light mist began crawling up from the streams and mountain lakes, spreading across the land without regard.

Keth stared at the dwarf with a blank expression. "Am I? I do not feel dead. Perhaps you are mistaken."

"Max, who is this guy?" Daniel asked quietly. He felt the moment slipping away and, judging on how poorly events turned out for them so far after losing control of the situation at the safehouse, saw their bodies adding to the circle... an impressive circle. *Well at least we know who our mystery killer from the woods is.*

"A relic," Max replied.

"A hero," Keth defended.

Max waggled a thick finger. "You abandoned the king when he needed you the most. Not very heroic I say."

"I did what was best for the high families at the time. Would you not have abandoned all you knew and loved for the sake of preserving our society? Or have dwarves returned to their petty greed and mistrust? I do not claim to repent my decisions, for they are a thing of the past."

"Uh huh," Max said without taking his hand of his weapon. "Say what you want, but you left as soon as things turned bad. Do you have any idea how hard it was to keep pushing forward during the war?"

"War is the reason I left," Keth admitted. His voice dropped to a whisper. "I had hoped by leaving Alvin and Morgen might settle their differences and reunite the clans."

"How long have you been missing?" Blackmere asked now looking uneasy himself. The last thing they needed was internal strife.

Keth cocked his head, strands of grey hair swishing over his shoulder. "A long, long time." He resumed his conversation with Max. "Where are the king and queen?"

Daniel gritted his teeth, recognizing the dismissal. They didn't have time for this.

"Yeah, about that," Max started. He tugged on a great chunk of his beard. "Alvin's been dead for a few years now."

"Dead?" Keth gasped.

Max ran a finger across his throat. "Ashes in the wind. His own kid wound up doing it. Morgen is out here somewhere, running from these same bastards."

"Assassins," Keth replied. "They are not very good."

Daniel held back at groan at that. *Of course this elf thinks they aren't good.* The sirens grew louder.

"Look, we can play catch up once we're clear of this mess, but there's work left to do," Max stated. "We don't know how many more of these assassins are roaming the woods between us and our exit vehicles. Either you can help us or go back to your caves or swamps or wherever you have been. One way or another, we're going home tonight."

Keth Murdis returned Max's impassioned glare with disinterest. Daniel could clearly see the bad blood between them and wasn't sure how he should intervene, if at all. "So…"

Stiffening, Keth announced, "Very well. I shall continue assisting you. This is already a red night. I would not have your senseless brand of violence spill over into a new day. The sooner I know she is safe, and these vermin scoured from my realm the better. Come, let us hunt." He took off without waiting, his mighty sword strapped to his back.

"Max, can we trust this guy?" Daniel asked before taking a step forward. *The elf was fast.*

"Probably, but who knows. I'm thinking he's been sniffing a little too much moss," the dwarf replied with a shrug. "He was one of the best, before the split. Xander only got the job of Champion of the Light because Keth disappeared." He suddenly grinned. "Wait until Morgen sees his face! Won't that be fun."

Daniel rubbed his eyes before following behind dwarf and now returned high elf champion. Behind him he heard Blackmere hastened to catch up.

Hundreds of meters might as well have been a mile. Surrounded by darkness and strange sounds suddenly cutting off the moment they approached, Sara felt like walls were closing in. She was never one to enjoy camping or being in nature. That arena fell under Daniel's purvey. Instead, she preferred a good book and a glass of wine by their very comfortable bedroom fireplace. Yet here she was. Covered in grime and playing host to countless insects, worms, and God knew what else crawling over.

The roar of ATV engines sounded far behind them, but she knew the night played tricks on her hearing. It took little imagination to envision a horde of bloodthirsty assassins slipping quietly through the gravel and underbrush, knives barred and eager to finish their assignment. Only having Xander at her back prevented total panic from setting in.

The promise of escape lay just ahead, somewhere in the mist and fog. She shivered, more from the thought of an ambush than any drop in temperature. Heart racing, an old nursery rhyme filled her head. Sara forced herself not to hum, lest she give away their position. She then had to stop herself from laughing, confronted by the ridiculousness of it all. She focused on staying a step behind Morgen and not twisting an ankle on one of the thousands of rocks determined to make her life miserable.

They were far enough away from the cabin that the flames were barely visible. An orange glow clung to that part of the valley. The promise of a harsh reality they had barely escaped. Winds carried the stench of burning timbers down through the trees. Sara clamped down on a cough. Ash from those trees too close to the cabin drifted in their path, falling in her hair. Knowing she looked worse than she felt, and that was a close pairing, she ignored the obvious.

The sounds of gunfire had long since faded: Night reclaimed its due. She thought she saw the bobbing figures of homeowners peeking out from lighted windows in homes scattered up and down the mountainside as they passed. Were they watching her right now? Worried for her safety or concerned she and her companions were criminals determined to rob them for all they were worth? How would she react if their roles were reversed? *I wouldn't invite them in for coffee, that's for sure.*

The crack of a pistol firing behind her head had her flinching, reflexively ducking lower to escape the line of fire as Xander rose up from the ditch they still travelled along just enough to take aim and rapid fire six more quick shots. She thought she heard a man grunting but with the ringing in her ears it was impossible to tell.

"Run!" Xander shouted. "They've found us!"

An arrow whistled through the night, striking the bole of the nearest tree. Sara screamed despite herself. Another followed the first. Then a third. Her mind screamed back at her, demanding she step in and help Xander. They were outnumbered and in hostile territory, it was all Sara could do to keep pace with Gwen and Morgen who bolted in front of her.

She plunged forward with reckless abandon, eager to get to get as far away from the cabin as possible. Bullets and arrows dug into the lip of the ditch around Sara as she ran. Puffs of dust blew rocks and grime in her face, peppering her exposed flesh with tiny slivers.

Sara stumbled and looked back: Xander, ever resolute, held his ground while they escaped. Stalwart and fierce, he unleashed his fury on the surrounding assassins, but he would not be enough to stop them all. *Daniel, where are you?*

"Where did that come from?" Daniel hissed as echoes of gunfire rippled up and down the valley.

"This way!" Keth picked up his pace.

Biting back a curse at the already grueling pace, Daniel was jealous of the elf's familiarity of the terrain that he had no hope of matching. Determined not to fall behind, or stumble into an ambush, he began a measured pace keeping the Keth's back just in view. Flanking him, Max and Blackmere shared his sentiment and proceeded with caution.

They were beaten down. Exhausted. Muscles screamed. Daniel's body and mind begged to shut down and recover. That would have to wait until the Invisible Hand threat was removed, or at least they linked up with Sara and the others and fled back to the false security of Raleigh. He wanted to break into a run at the thought of Sara. Anything to close the distance and prevent the assassins from getting to his wife.

"There. Muzzle flashes!" Blackmere announced.

Daniel turned to follow the agent's arm and ran headlong into a body. They collapsed in a tangle of flailing limbs and grunts. He lost his grip on his rifle and, once he rolled to a stop and got up on one knee, drew his blade out of instinct. The other body, a man, landed a short distance away and crouched glaring at him behind his veil. *Assassin!*

Other figures swarmed them. Daniel figured two full Hand groups had laid in wait knowing going downhill was the only logical exit point. Deciding not to wait for them to attack first, he lunched himself forward and clipped the downed assassin with the toe of his boot to the chin. He was rewarded by the crunch of bone and an agonizing cry. A leg swept knocked his feet out from under him and Daniel found himself back on the ground.

Face wreathed in blood and spitting curses, the assassin landed an elbow to Daniel's sternum. He followed with two quick strikes to the chest and shoulder, producing lancing pain as they aggravated an old shoulder injury. Tears filled Daniel's eyes. He swiped blindly but his blade caught only air. Desperate now, he continued lashing out just to keep the assassin from finishing him.

Daniel grunted when the man's full weight collapsed on his chest, pinning him to the bed of leaves and broken branches. He felt the tickle of a point of steel scraping against his body armor before the weight was wrenched away. Clearing his vision, Daniel saw Keth looming over him, sword running through the assassin. There was no emotion in his eyes. An elf like that killed out of necessity and nothing more. *Well at least he is on our side.*

Keth whipped his sword free and moved off before Daniel had the chance to get to his feet. The bark of machinegun fire announced Max had entered the fray, but it was immediately cut off. With enemies swarming in from all sides, it didn't take a tactical genius to envision a mistaken shot to one of their group. Max couldn't risk it. Daniel took heart in having the sword wielding Keth on their side, but how much was too much before even he became overwhelmed?

He caught the report of returned pistol fire coming

from the night. Sara and the others were out there, and in trouble no doubt, and there was nothing he could do about it. Not allowing himself to spiral, he took a deep breath. *Steady.* He snatched his pistol from the ground and fired into the back of the assassin stepping up on Blackmere's exposed back. *I'm coming, Sara.*

THIRTY-FIVE

Keth Murdis clove a path of destruction through their foes with the certainty of an elf born of singular purpose. He had been trained for this. His blade, that he kept sharp, sliced and hacked into arms, chests, and legs with a ruthlessness the world had not seen in generations. He had to wonder at the faces of those around him, their surprise and horror. He had truly been out of touch for a long time. Keth slashed through the wrist of an attacker and used his momentum to whip around and take the man's head in the same motion.

The assassins nearest him paused, suddenly unsure of their chances. As one, the assassins stepped back to give him space and, they hoped, an opening to slip in and dispatch him. With a smile, Keth advanced: each stroke a masterclass of swordsmanship no human could emulate. The skirmish lasted mere moments. He stood, alone and uninjured, in the center of the fallen assassins. All ten of them. Blood dripped from the tip of his sword.

He watched, bemused, as those assassins still nearby melted back into the darkness. His message was sent. They would go off in search of easier prey, for the cruel ever took vengeance upon those they deemed weak. Keth cocked his head with a sigh. It had been a long time since he last tested himself in battle, but he had not lost a step. Shaking the blood from his blade, the high elf listened as pistol shots rent the air.

Blackmere caught the new elf's martial display from the corner of his eye. His stomach threatened to empty as the violence and intensity increased. He heard rumors of beings capable of such feats but never thought to see one. Now that he had, he wished he hadn't. Some things deserved to be kept from the masses, tucked away from the public eye, and hushed lest the fool speaking invoked them. Ultimately, it was the smell of death, that iron tang of blood in the air, that made him bend over and vomit down the side of a tree.

"Blackmere, keep moving," Daniel called as he pinched a pair of rounds off at a running assassin. One pitched forward and lay still.

The agent wiped his mouth with the back of his sleeve and hobbled closer. "I think we're being herded."

"I know. They are pushing us where they want us to go." Daniel reloaded a fresh magazine, tapping the forward assist to ensure the chambered round seated properly. "We need to slip the ambush and turn the tide."

"How are we supposed to do that?" Blackmere spat, the acidic taste of bile still clinging to his tongue.

Daniel gestured toward Keth. "Him. Max. Between them we stand a good chance at breaking free and linking up with the others."

"They could be anywhere out there." Blackmere knew better than to jinx himself on a mission. There were certain phrases one just didn't say but he couldn't help himself.

"I don't have a choice. My wife is out here in the middle of this shitstorm, Blackmere," Daniel replied. "I need to find her."

Blackmere nodded, no words felt comforting enough for the situation. They needed to find Morgen and the others.

Daniel started forward and Blackmere moved to follow.

"Hey! Where do you think you're going?" Max barked and hurried to catch up. "Don't you know it's bad luck to make a dwarf run in the dark?"

"I thought your people lived in caves," Daniel quipped.

Blackmere saw Max's smile before he glowered and pushed by him. "Funny. Remind me to knock some of your teeth out when this is finished. Come on. I have a good idea where these bastards are leading us."

Daniel eyed him then looked back at Blackmere who shrugged. He had no idea how the dwarf would know that, only just realizing a few minutes ago they were being herded.

"You lead. We follow."

At their backs, Keth's low grunt went almost unheard.

Xander cried out after being punched in his wound. He felt his flesh tearing open, undoing all of Gwen's work. Blinded with agony, he shoved the assassin off. It took all the strength he could muster not to double over. Xander scampered out from under a powerful roundhouse. He felt the whistle of clothing and flesh passing a fraction from his face. Bracing for the follow up blow, he loosened his muscles.

The blow never fell. Blinking his vision clear as the pain subsided enough for him to think straight, Xander watched the assassin, a man easily twice his body mass, gesture downhill.

"Run along, little elf. Your friends are waiting for you," he said and disappeared back into the night.

Confused, Xander expected a trap. Why else would the assassin back off when holding the advantage? Still, he scrambled clear and hurried to find Gwen and the others. Whatever games the Invisible Hand chose to play this night, he wasn't about to let a potential opportunity for temporary escape to slip through his fingers.

It took longer than he anticipated to catch up with them, thanks to the agonizing sensation spreading through his abdomen but he soon found the women within eyesight of a parked vehicle on a small cut off to the side of the road. Xander figured it belonged to the assassins.

He heard the click of a gun and shouted, "It's me!"

"I thought you were dead!" Gwen called back. He saw she still had her pistol drawn.

"I'm working on it," he replied, gesturing to the wound now seeping blood. "Is it clear?"

Morgen answered, "From what we can tell, though I would not put it past our hosts to have a surprise in store for us."

He chose not to tell them what had just happened in the woods since he too suspected they were planning something. "I agree." At their silence, he took a moment to study them for any injuries, first Sara then Gwen then the queen, who held herself in a defeated way despite still attempting to project strength. Xander knew they were all at the end of their ropes. How much of a shove would it take to push them over the edge and seal their fates?

"Look!" Sara blurted out just as a twig snapped from behind him.

Xander's head snapped around. Relief washed over him as he caught their first glimpse of the others heading for them. His relief was short as on their trail came a host of black clad assassins with blood in their eyes and a measured, leisurely pace. *Trap indeed.*

"Collapse on that vehicle," Xander ordered. "We might get out of this yet." *Doubtful, but there's always a chance.*

He did a double take when he caught the features of the slender figure leading the way toward them. *Keth Murdis.* The very high elf he assumed his position of champion from. *But he was dead.* Hope rekindled in Xander, for he knew there were few who could withstand the impassioned fury of a former champion.

Keth gave him no regard to him as he passed. Joining him, they moved side by side, leading the others to the waiting escape vehicle. Xander doubted the Invisible

Hand meant to give them a fair shot: Headlights raced down from the burning cabin in a winding column of ATVs. Figures moved in the darkness, surrounding them on three sides in concentric circles.

A preliminary count suggested close to thirty of the assassins. Xander knew they lacked the strength or firepower to fend the Hand off for long. Not even bolstered by Keth's presence could they hope to defeat so many. Not without a miracle. Car keys mocking him from his trouser pocket, Xander had but one play.

He hefted his sword, now heavy and cumbersome, to his shoulder and stepped away from the others. Morgen renamed him champion and that was a title he aimed to live up. Even if it killed him. Anything to protect his wife and child.

"Come no closer," he said at the top of his lungs. "Come no closer, I warn you. This night shall not end the way you envision."

The assassins mocked him with silence.

His cheeks flushed crimson. Xander raised his sword higher, daring them to break ranks. "This is your final warning. All who come within range will know the fury of my sword."

This was their final hour. A last stand of epic proportions none would ever learn of should they fall. Xander found it oddly comforting. He had struggled to uphold an image for so long, often losing sight of himself along the way. The man he once was resurfaced. A shining paladin returned to exact justice at the tip of his sword. He felt…whole.

Xander dug a line in the dirt with his sword. "Very well. You bring your destruction upon you. Come, let us finish this dance and discover our destinies together!"

The assassins stepped closer. Inch by inch they drew their trap tighter.

Xander swallowed his rising nerves, for he had bitten off far more than his wounded self could handle with the act he had just down. The Invisible Hand recognized this. He saw it in their eyes.

"That was foolish," Keth told him after moving to stand beside him. "Most foolish, indeed."

"It seemed prudent in the moment," Xander replied without taking his eyes off the killers. "Do you still know how to use that thing?"

Keth snorted, amused. "Keep to the left. I will ward your right. Let us dance blades as we once did, Champion of Light."

"What about the queen?"

"Fate will do as it deems best. Who are we to stand in the way?"

Xander frowned. He had forgotten the ease with which his predecessor managed to confuse the situation through simple words. A gifted tongue notwithstanding, there wasn't another soul on the planet Xander would rather fight beside. He rolled the soreness from his shoulders, twisting his neck to stretch away the kinks.

The assassins gave them no quarter. Each step reducing their ability to maneuver, Xander and the others were forced into a tighter group. Pain lanced through his torso, threatening to drop him to his knees. He summoned what little strength he had remaining in the face of multiple arrows nocked and ready to fire. Should they get a clear shot not even his body armor would protect him. Xander made the only move he had left—

He attacked.

Bodies littered the area. Several assassins were too disabled to fight and had withdrawn from the battle to nurse their wounds or die alone in the trees. The others pressed the attack despite their dwindling numbers.

Cuts, slashes, broken bones.

Finding himself but a step away from the obstruction the vehicle now provided, Xander struggled to regain his breath. His muscles ached. His arms were heavy.

Sweat coated every inch of him, and he still fought, refusing to fall without spending his last.

Then the unexpected happened. The assassins paused. Several glanced skyward, gesturing with their knives or pointing. Xander followed their gazes and found himself staring at a pair of blinking red and green lights. Raising an arm to shield his face from clouds of now swirling debris, he felt the chill of forced air blowing down.

"What is going on?" Daniel called.

Xander saw that only Morgen stood strong. Her clothing was torn in several places. Her face filthy and bloodied. He saw the spread across her face and the shine of tears. He returned his gaze to the sky. Less than twenty feet above hovered a lone helicopter. He saw the flash of an emblem and sucked in a breath.

Troops.

The queen's troops.

Morgen raised her arm and several figures leapt from the chopper.

THIRTY-SIX

They dropped from the night. Massive figures resplendent in armor and bristling with weapons. Faces hidden behind ornate battle masks harkening back to a more regal time, they were emissaries of death. Each a behemoth of destruction, they were the best of the best. Men and women sworn to the crown.

The moment their boots struck the ground, the Old Guard worked to form a perimeter around the stricken survivors. Bettis identified the queen and, to his surprise, the heir to the throne, in the middle of a desperate situation. Above, the thump of rotor blades was barely detectible.

"To the queen!" Bettis roared, power sword raised high.

The battle cry was taken up by the others and they launched into a flurry of destruction. This night there would be no prisoners. No mercy for the destroyers of elfkind.

Bettis took pleasure in every slash of his blade.

The assassins were broken and discarded where they fell. It was over in minutes. They wilted under the pressure and sudden reversal of roles. Soon only the panting of the Old Guard was the only sound.

Satisfied the battle was finished, Bettis knelt before Morgen and bowed his head. "Your Majesty, I am Sergeant Bettis. Commander Andros dispatched us to find you. It appears we arrived just in time."

"So it does, Sergeant," she said. "My thanks to you and your team."

He rose, deactivating his power sword. "If it pleases you, we are to escort you back to Raleigh. Though he did not say, I fear there is a greater plot against us in play. I would be there to stand at Andros' side."

"You have certainly earned that much," Morgen agreed, a glitter in her eyes. "Come, let us gather the others.

How much room is there in your helicopter?"

Bettis stared at the odd assortment of humans and elves, gaze lingering on Xander. "I can safely take three, your Majesty. The rest would overburden the bird's capabilities."

"Now hold on. We've come too far to break up now," Daniel protested as soon as the words left the Old Guard's mouth.

Morgen whirled on him. "Indeed, but one cannot argue with machinery, Daniel Thomas." At her reprimand, he stepped back in surprise. She nodded then continued. "Agent Blackmere, will you do the honor of accompanying myself and Xander back to Raleigh?"

Shifting uncomfortably, the DESA agent glanced at Daniel. "I, ah, don't know if that is wise."

"Why not? I need you there when I confront your deputy director."

"Your Majesty, what if I'm wrong? What if Corman isn't playing both sides? I don't want to be the man who plunges us into a war," he replied.

"Look around, pal. We're already at war," Max added without malice.

"Oh, for fuck's sake," Daniel muttered.

Blackmere fumed as exhaustion and adrenalin crashed. "DESA is not your enemy, Max. If I'm not mistaken, the queen wishes to show a unified front to her enemies in Raleigh. By the three of us arriving together she is sending a strong message."

"This is not an argument for the moment, gentlemen." Morgen stepped between. "We must collect ourselves and see to the future. I fear this assault was but the first salvo in a campaign designed to topple the clans. We must return to Raleigh so I may reassert control. Have them land, Sergeant Bettis."

"Yes, Your Majesty."

The helicopter overhead veered off in search of an

adequate landing zone.

Daniel watched, shielding his face and Sara's from debris kicked up by rotor wash. His thoughts raced, threatening to get the best of him. Part of him had no problem being left behind, safe and out of harm's way. The other part, that little sliver of having to be in the know, whispered otherwise.

"If it's all the same, Sara and I want to go with you," Daniel stepped up. "We've been through too much to not see this through."

"I should think you ready for the comforts of your home, eager to forget this night ever happened."

"Sure, but there's no way this is forgettable," Daniel admitted. "Besides, we have scores to settle with the Hand. I'd rather not be forced to look over my shoulder for an assassin blade for the rest of my life."

She turned to Sara. "You agree with this?"

"Yes."

The first crack of dawn slit the veil of night with assurity. Shadows surrendered to the light. The wail of advancing sirens drew nearer.

"There's no way I'm going to sit this one out. Not after tonight," Gwen added on. Her normally placid face was twisted with fury.

"I suppose you have earned that much," Morgen agreed and pursed her lips. She turned to face the waiting Old Guard. "Sergeant Bettis, detail some of your men. They will take the assassin's escape vehicle and return to Raleigh on the ground with all possible haste."

"Your Majesty are you sure that's wise?" the Old Guard asked.

Daniel winced at the elf's wording and waited.

Morgen surprised them all by laughing. "Sergeant, I'm not sure what is wise or not anymore. All I know is the time has come to end this farce and restore my proper place at the head of the table. Now, detail those men if you please. Time is of the essence and it's a four-hour drive back to

Raleigh."

Bowing respectfully, Bettis went to break his team down. He passed a curious glance to the human made famous by his comedic novels, questioning why he was deemed important enough to join the queen.

Satisfied at least one aspect of the night was going her way, Morgen took in the chaos surrounding her. There was a time when she was considered among the fiercest on the battlefield, a fury unlike any other. While those days were long behind her, Morgen found value in the efforts of those at her side. She scanned her group of survivors, stiffening at seeing the face of a man she never thought to see again.

Morgen stepped over and around bodies to join Keth who leaned beside a young sweet gum tree. "Keth Murdis. It has been a long time."

He nodded, eyes reflecting the slightest hint of flames roaring high above. "It has. I never intended on coming back."

"I never asked you to," she replied. "How have you been?"

"At peace for the first time since I can remember."

She smiled at the relief in his voice and grew envious. "You have more than earned your break. Thank you."

"It was only through chance I stumbled upon your hunters. Clumsy. Arrogant. I have no doubt Xander could have handled them were I not in the vicinity."

"Perhaps," Morgen agreed.

"I made these mountains my home not long after relinquishing my title," Keth explained without provocation. "It is peaceful here. Pristine in many ways and so unlike the trappings of the throne. The clarity does wonders for my soul, Morgen."

"I am happy for you, truly, but I must ask a boon," she said. "There is still a place for you at my side. I have need of allies now more than ever."

His head hung, hair dangling over his face. "I had hoped you would not ask such of me. My heart goes out to you with Alvin's loss, but I no longer have a reason to be part of society. Civilization offers only wicked torment and baseless temptation. These are not what I need. Here among the animals and trees, I have rediscovered purpose. My quality of being soars beneath the mountain waterfalls and endless forests. This is how all elfkind is meant to live, not locked away in a human skyscraper of glass and metal."

"There was a time I might have agreed, Keth, but needs must," she lamented. "I must look to securing our future if the clans have any hope of surviving this strange new world."

"It is indeed strange." He cast a glance back at the others. "I never thought to find you fighting side by side with humans."

"They are good people with better qualities than I," she admitted. "Do not be so rash as to judge them all by the deeds of a few."

"I must go, before the human authorities arrive," Keth announced abruptly. He reached out to take her hand in his. "I am not hard to find, Morgen. Should you truly need me. Call my name on a stiff morning breeze and I will return."

"Thank you, Keth. You have ever been an example I strove to emulate." Morgen gave his hand a gentle squeeze and turned back to where the whine of a turbine announced the helicopter had touched down.

She saw electricity dancing with each turn of the blades, creating a circle of ethereal lights over the dark body. Straightening her shirt, Morgen proceeded with as much regal bluster as she had remaining.

"It is time, Your Majesty," Sergeant Bettis said.

Four of his team stood off to the side, each wearing mixed emotions. She knew none wished to leave her, yet all were honor bound to uphold her decrees. The stood at attention, weapons across their chest in salute. She made to speak with them when in the distance, the first sign of flashing red and blue lights could be seen.

Time was up.

"Lead the way, Sergeant," she said and gestured toward the waiting helicopter.

"What about the bodies?" Bettis asked.

Morgen's face hardened. "Leave them. This is a human affair."

Unable to argue a valid point, Daniel saw the value in doing as Morgen suggested. Local authorities would find a bloodbath and, if matters were allowed to play out, further investigation would rip the lid off the Invisible Hand and bring the organization to justice. He just wished it didn't come at human expense, for people like Daniel would be dragged into this.

Thankful he wasn't going to be the first on the scene, Daniel let out a low whistle that went unheard under the noise the helicopter made when he got a better view of the area in the light. This was the stuff of nightmares. Who knew how many bodies were strewn up and down the hillside. Certainly more than enough to keep every therapist in the county in business for decades.

He could see the headlines now: The battle of Valle Cruces would go down as a slaughter, perhaps even the work of a serial killer. No one would ever know the truth. That a handful of reluctant heroes banded together to hold off a killing wave and keep a monarch alive at all costs. That, he deemed, was the true injustice.

He caught up to Sara and led her into the waiting helicopter. After helping her strap in with the safety harness, Daniel took a seat beside her and reached for her hand. The others filed on with military precision. Sergeant Bettis went last, choosing to strap himself to the deck with his feet dangling out the door rather than be constrained in a seat. His remaining Old Guard team copied him. Daniel found himself grinning, for there had been a time when he did the same, though with a pack and a parachute strapped to his back.

The Blackhawk helicopter lifted off and began the trek back to Raleigh.

Keth Murdis watched through the trees as the remaining Old Guard shed their body armor and weapons in the back of the SUV and follow the queen home. Minutes later convoys of fire trucks, police cruisers, and news vans entered the area.

He turned away, happy to remain a relic of older days. He had done his part, reluctant as he had been in showing himself after of so long. He'd helped save the queen and, in doing, reclaimed a measure of honor his character had been missing. But he no longer felt the need to be with his kind. Time alone reminded him of a better way of life, lacking the hassle and torment of political manipulations and constant strife. No, men like himself were better alone.

Humming an old Rolling Stones tune, Keth gave the sky a final look before slipping back into the trees and becoming the Hermit once again.

THIRTY-SEVEN

The walls were closing in. There was no better way to describe it. Slim stared at the gathering of what he deemed hopeless royals and family heads. Now mired on the verge of infighting, Morgen's dreams of unification threatened to unravel under his unskilled hands. The absurdity of it mocked him. Taking over from his late father was one thing but attempting to bring all the clans together proved damned near impossible.

The weight of the cult of personality in the room threatened to subsume his common sense. Petty demands intermingled with the ridiculous as leaders jockeyed for hierarchy in the proposed new order. Though he had spoken to them the night before, given them the ultimatum, of which they accepted, this time they fought without listening to him. Slim was qualified to proctor none of it. His head pounded from the stress piling on his shoulders, leaving him miserable in every regard. Making matters worse was the potential DESA and Invisible Hand coalition. Yet he couldn't unleash Constantin without proof, and that was short in coming.

At the raising of voices, Slim punched his fist into the cool glass overlooking downtown Raleigh. His thoughts swirled around the endless possibilities facing elfkind. None of them proved enheartening. He was backed into a corner, fighting for his life. He just didn't know what form the threat was coming in. The answer came much sooner than he was prepared for as Constantin burst into the room.

"They're coming," the Old Guard commander announced.

The room fell silent. Old worries and fears threatened to rob those assembled of what little courage remained.

Slim stiffened. "So soon? You are certain?"

"Why are you acting surprised? Corman and ten others are heading for the elevators now. They are all armed and in body armor."

"I hoped there was more time. That maybe we were wrong," he lamented. "How many men do you have on this floor?"

"A dozen or so. But do you want to provoke a fight in the middle of the day with all these civilians around?"

"You're asking like the choice is mine," Slim countered. "Get them in strategic positions but no one acts unless you or I give the command."

"Roger that." Constantin turned to leave before stopping and fixing a wild grin at him. "There hasn't been this much excitement since the Wars of Schism."

"Right, excitement," Slim intoned dryly. "Get your people in place and hurry back. We might be able to talk Corman down from whatever he has planned."

Constantin nodded and strode out. Slim looked over the assembled. His mouth went dry. "Listen to me, I want everyone one up in the ballroom on the top floor. Close the doors and bar them. Do not come out unless myself or Andros comes to get you. Go!"

The elf nobility fled. All sense of order was gone.

Deputy Director Corman exited the elevator first. His cocksure attitude permeated through his hand selected squad. Each loyal to him before the agency, they were the hammer to his anvil. Dressed in identical black suits concealing their weapons and armor, the agents reflected his attitude perfectly.

Storming into the City Club Raleigh with the authority of the federal government, Corman ignored the receptionist. He knew Morgen's lair well and refused to be waylaid by any menial or ignorant civilian.

Word of the disaster in the mountains reached him early in the morning. Decades of planning ruined in the span of mere hours.

"Sir you can't just—"

One of the agents secured the receptionist, preventing her from saying more or alerting anyone on either floor.

The others filed past, intent on bringing the age of elves to an inglorious end as he commanded. He allowed a grin. Corman was a high-ranking Invisible Hand operative. He had infiltrated DESA and risen through the ranks under the guise of a man determined to see peace between the species. It was all a lie. His hatred of the elves stretched back far. He held them responsible for the death of his mother when he was but a child. The Hand took him in, promising vengeance when the moment arrived. It was with thoughts of the past burning in his gaze he stepped into Morgen's unofficial throne room.

"Baron Visilias, I order you to desist all actions and submit to DESA for immediate questioning," he announced. His eyes lingered on the hilt of Constantin's power sword poking from behind his back.

"Under what authority?" the dark elf demanded.

"Mine. You and your queen have been found in breach of standing treaties and accords. Your actions resulted in the breaking of many laws without regard for human safety," Corman replied, and drew himself up. "As of this moment, regency of the elf clans falls under my purvey."

Constantin's hand went up for his sword.

"Do that and you both die," Corman warned.

On cue, the men at his back drew their weapons and took aim. He loved watching the hatred enter the Old Guard's eyes as the elf lowered his hand.

"Tell me something, Deputy Director," Visilias started. "How long have you worked for the Invisible Hand?"

Corman broke into a wide grin. He had wondered if they'd figure it out. "Since your kind killed my mother. I was a little boy when a gang of elves assaulted her, leaving her dead in the streets. Since that day I have been consumed with revenge. Now, I finally have it. I am the instrument of your demise, *elf*. By my hand will your legacy be brought to ruin."

"Or how about we just forget the whole thing?"

Corman tensed at the unfamiliar voice.

He and his agents spun to find themselves staring down the barrel of a pistol. There, in the middle of the hallway, stood the very creatures Corman hoped to kill in the mountains. His teeth ground in muted rage.

"And you are?" he asked.

"Viviana Cal," the elf replied, wrath dripped from her tongue. She stood, shoulders square, fists clenched, ready for a fight.

"Ah yes, the queen's right hand. You'll make a welcome addition to the Grinder," Corman snapped. "Arrest her."

Two of his agents moved, only to be jerked away from behind. The others spun, pistols rising. Before them stood a pair of dwarves in full body armor with axes in hand. The agents faltered. This was meant to be an easy assignment, not one risking dismemberment, or worse.

"Yeah, that's not going to happen," Angus snarled and tapped the axe head against one of the men's chest. "See, you take her, you take us all. Me and Fritz here, we don't much plan on sitting in a cell while your fuck of a boss takes out the queen. Ain't that right, Fritz?"

"Been a while since we got to crack a few human skulls," Fritz grinned. "I admit I missed it. Who dies first?"

Corman clapped, slow, arrogant. "Bravo, gentlemen. A lovely show. But it will do you no avail. As we speak your queen is dead and the elf clans are finished. You sad remnants are all that stands in my way and completing my purpose. Never again will one of filth stain this world. Your time ends here."

Angus made a show of looking around Corman. "Hey Slim, who is this dickhead?"

"The man responsible for killing so many of us last night," Slim replied.

The dwarf nodded. "Got it. Ok, here's how this goes. You good people drop your weapons and leave now before your blood paints the carpets. Oh, not you, big man. You and I are going to finish this one on one."

"I said arrest these *creatures*," Corman spat.

Angus didn't wait. He shoved the man in front of him, knocking him off his feet. Fritz added a backhanded swing with the flat of axe and dropped two more. The remaining agents milled together, guns wavering. The schraak of a blade being drawn, followed by an ancient elven war cry announced Constantin Andros wading into the middle of it all. His power sword glowed in the artificial lights.

Her eyes never left Corman's. The slender blade in her hand appeared no larger than a letter opener but it was the bringing of so much pain over the years. Viviana gave her sweetest smile. "Stand down, *human*. We don't have much reason to keep you alive, all things considered, but I want to take my time with this. Revenge is a luxury we all must indulge in from time to time."

"Kill me and you seal your doom," Corman replied. An edge of fear landed in his voice. "Every agency in the federal government will be after you. Hunting you down one by one."

She glided forward and jabbed the blade under his chin. A single drop of blood trickled down the steel. "I've been hunted before. It can be quite exhilarating."

"You're dead," Corman's eyes narrowed. "All of you."

"Is that anyway to talk to my aid? Hello James," Morgen said as she swept into the room. "Happy to see me?"

"You should be dead," he spat.

She stepped forward, pistol in hand. "You should have sent more men."

Knowing his fate was sealed, he reached inside his jacket for his weapon.

"That would be a mistake," Max growled. He swung the machinegun barrel on Corman. "Touch that gun and your brains go splat."

"You dare!" Corman hissed.

"Yup. See, thanks to you I'm in a killing mood," the dwarf replied. "Now be a good boy and tell your men to lower their weapons. No need to mess up the paint scheme."

Desperation flared. Corman scanned the group of newcomers before settling on the one man he should have known better than to trust. "Agent Blackmere. I order you to arrest this gang of miscreants. You are a DESA employee."

"I'm afraid I can't do that," Blackmere said. "I learned a few things these last couple days. The most important part is you are an enemy agent and responsible for all that has occurred to the elf clans this past week. It is my federal duty to place you under arrest and relieve you of your position."

"Drop the fucking guns," Max emphasized when no one reacted.

"Hey, Pop," Angus beamed. "Took your time getting here."

Max glared but held his tongue. Damn, it was good to see his boys here. Now.

"You should do as he says," the Old Guard warned. "My friend there isn't known for his restraint."

Max blew them a kiss and slipped his finger onto the trigger.

"Do it," Corman relented.

Daniel stepped in to collect the weapons from the floor while Max forced the agents to line up against the wall with their hands behind their backs. The click of handcuffs locking in place was the most satisfying sound he heard in years.

"I should have known you were trouble," Corman snapped at him.

Daniel shrugged. "Buddy, I've been trouble for a long time."

"Let's go, Deputy Director," Blackmere said, grabbing Corman by the wrists after handcuffing him. "I wonder how well they're going to treat you in the Grinder."

Corman's face paled as he was led from the room.

"So long, asshole," Daniel called after them.

Tension gone, Slim stepped out from behind Morgen's desk and gestured for the queen to take her rightful place.

"Thank you, Baron," Morgen said as she settled into the well-worn chair. "Now that this bit of unpleasantry is concluded, I trust you have good news to report."

He explained all that had happened since they parted company at the rest stop; Morgen listened with mild interest. She expected problems among the surviving nobles and already formed plans to mitigate any potential resistance. Slim's report concluded and she felt the weight of all she strove to accomplish settle in. With some in agreement, the rest she could manage.

"How did you get here in time?" he asked, arms folding across his chest.

"With a little help," she said. "None of this would be possible without all your efforts. I sit here in your debt. Truly. Elfkind will continue, perhaps even flourish given the opportunity. We stand upon the precipice of a new era, and I couldn't have done it without you."

"I think I might have had enough of leadership for a while," Slim blew out the breath he'd been holding since Corman arrived. "This is for the birds."

"Does that mean we can go home now?" Daniel asked.

Morgen stifled a smile. "Daniel Thomas, it is to you I owe the largest debt. We may not have always seen eye to eye, but I have come to respect you in ways I will never be able to voice. Of course you may go home."

"So this means you'll take care of our mortgage?" he said. She enjoyed that she had caught him off guard. "We should stop making this a habit."

"Goodbye, for now, Daniel," Morgen's eyes twinkled and waved Daniel and Sara out.

She swiveled her chair back to face Slim, Constantin, Gwen, and Xander. "Now that that is done, we have much to discuss before convening the others. Let us speak of the future and where we all fit."

They passed Blackmere and the prisoners in the lobby awaiting transport. Daniel doubted any of them were going to like their new accommodations. Not that he cared. They were all traitors in his eyes. Wicked men willing to abandon principle for violence. If he never saw another assassin, he wouldn't complain. He and Blackmere shared a nod before he opened the door and held it for Sara to pass through first.

Once outside, Daniel stretched and breathed in the afternoon air before realizing it was a mistake. Nothing like a little pollution clinging to the tight corridors of the inner city to remind you how nice being in the country was. He coughed a little, his mouth filled with exhaust fumes.

Sara laughed and he looked to her with a smile. "I'm beat."

She nodded, leaning on him. "I could sleep for a week."

"Too bad the kids are due home tomorrow. We could use a vacation."

Snorting, she started for the parking garage. "You do still have the keys, right?"

He patted his jacket and felt the fob shift. "Yep. Can you believe Morgen is willing to take back Xander and Gwen after all they've done?"

"She is about to be a grandmother. It seems only

right," Sara said.

Daniel froze midstride. "Wait, you mean?"

Sara nodded. "Gwen's pregnant. There's about to be another little elf baby in the world."

He gave a low whistle. Of all the news, that was the least expected. Perhaps family always found a way to reconcile.

"Do you think I have a shot at being godmother?" Sara asked as they crossed the street.

He didn't have an answer. Didn't want to think on it. They had enough to worry about without being drawn further into the royal elf family. Instead, he wanted just to bask in the satisfaction of what they accomplished over the last two days.

He and Sara got in their car and headed home. It was the one place where things made sense, even amidst the chaos of raising children, having dogs, and trying to balance life.

Halfway home, Daniel said, "Hey, I've been thinking a lot lately."

"About what?" Sara kept looking out the windshield, though she already knew where he was going with the conversation. Sometimes it paid to make him sweat a little.

He ran his tongue over his lower lip, suddenly unsure of the wisdom in what he was about to say. "Well, remember when I went to New York to help capture Xander?"

"Yes."

"Blackmere cornered me that night and offered me a job." He started tapping his fingers on the dashboard.

"You told me that already. Daniel, please say what's on your mind. Save the suspense for your books," she chided.

"He wants me to join DESA and I've been thinking a lot about that."

She placed her hand on his thigh. "Silly man,

you've been thinking about it since that first night we learned elves were real. The real question is, have you decided?"

"Yeah, I think I have," he admitted.

EPILOGUE

Three weeks had passed since the night at the mountain cabin. Three weeks filled with meetings, deals, and compromises. The elf world changed in a whirlwind. Centuries of established guidelines shattered in the blink of an eye. The past faded, echoing into the annals of eternity while a new tomorrow was forged. For many, it was the beginning of the end. For others, the dawn of a new promise. Gone were the clans of light and dark. They became whole and if that was the only culmination of her legacy, Morgen could die a happy woman.

Morgen oversaw the endless string of negotiations with her usual poise. A woman of vast intelligence, she watched her world crumble. No longer would the throne dictate daily affairs. The obsolete form of rule transitioned into a formal parliament governed by elected members. She retained the throne, though in more of a ceremonial role as a figurehead. The age of monarchs was ended. Now came the time for the people to have a voice in their futures.

Any hesitations of giving up her power washed away the moment she learned Gwen was pregnant. The thought of becoming a grandmother offered Morgen the only opportunity of redemption she would ever have. She vowed to do all within her power to ensure their family remained strong. No more clan wars or squabbling. She didn't expect a smooth or easy transition. Going from one voice to several presented unique challenges, but if the humans could do it the elves would meet the challenge.

For Morgen, it began with returning Xander's title and position. As Champion of Light, it fell on his shoulders to serve the new government with unbiased judgment. He vowed to uphold the new order and that was enough for her. Others were appointed to new positions: Against his protests, Slim accepted a role as Prime Minister with direct report to her. The Old Guard remained, expanding their role to protect all members of parliament. Constantin considered stepping down, pleased as he was with the outcome, but Morgen would have none of it.

Her last official act as ruling queen was to vacate her offices at the Wells Fargo building. It served its purpose during the rift between Alvin and herself but now she found herself needing a change of pace. The time had come to return to her home. The home she once thought to share with her husband again. Now it would contain the laughter of children and, she hoped, the promise of a better world.

Morgen stood in the doorway of her office, taking in her desk and view. Emotions warred within. A tear in her eye, she clicked the lights off.

The doorbell rang, causing the dogs to go crazy. Scrambling over the hardwood floors, and each other, they stormed toward the front door in a flurry of barks, snarls, and saliva only true dog owners understood. Sara and Daniel followed the clouds of settling fur.

Reaching the door and, after kneeing one of the giant dogs aside to get the handle, Sara looked at Daniel with raised eyebrows. "Ready?"

"No, but that's not going to change anything." Her mind teased what came next. That hidden mix of known and unknown.

She pulled the door open, watching both dogs blast past their guest. While they barked up a storm on a good day, neither had much interest in the comings and goings of guests. Otto headed straight for the rose bushes on an island in the middle of the lawn and lifted a leg. Baloo sat down and stared up at the crepe myrtle trees, searching for his most hated foe, the squirrel.

Thaddeus Blackmere watched them, mouth open in confusion since he had been clearly expecting them to come at him. Sara's laugh had him smiling and loosening his stiff stance. "Sara, good to see you again."

She gave him a hug. "Good to see you too, Deputy Director."

Blackmere blushed. His promotion came at the cost of almost losing his life to the Invisible Hand and the admissions of guilt taken from Corman and his traitor agents. While he took no pride in having to arrest fellow agents, Blackmere showed his value and loyalty in unprecedented ways. Rumor had it he was due for an award from the President. That didn't interest him. What he wanted was the ability to reform the Department of Extra Species Affairs to match the new direction of the elves and, through that, reforge their relationship with the elves for the betterment of all.

But that wasn't why he had returned to Raleigh. Not today at least.

"Thank you," he replied. He extended his hand. "Daniel, I hear you've got something to tell me."

Shaking his, Daniel bobbed his head. "I suppose I do—I'm in."

Just like that. No hesitation. Daniel knew if he paused, he'd retreat inside and close the door, missing his opportunity to be part of something bigger than himself again. Joining DESA was the missing piece to his life and the chance to prove himself on a grand scale without the oversight or fanfare associated with the military.

"Are you sure?" Blackmere asked. "This is a big deal, Daniel."

"Yeah," he said after a moment. "I'm sure. As long as I can pick and choose missions. My family comes first."

Blackmere smiled. "I'm sure we can work that out to satisfaction."

"Good, because there's one other criteria," Daniel added with a wince.

"Oh?"

Seeing his hesitation, Sara slipped between them.

"I want in too."

Blackmere's eyes widened as his mouth fell open. "You?"

Daniel coughed to hide his laugh as she crossed her arms and spread her legs defensively. "Yes, me. I've already proven myself several times. We're a package deal. He doesn't go without me."

"I hope you know what you're asking for," Blackmere said after wilting from the fire in her gaze. "Very well. If this is the way it is, I will be in touch."

He turned away, stuffing his hands in his pockets and turned around. "Oh, I almost forgot. This was in your mailbox." Waving, he whistled his way back to his government issued sedan.

Daniel opened the envelope, eyes wide. "Well, I'll be damned."

Inching up to see the paper for herself, Sara asked, "What?"

"Looks like Morgen took me seriously. Babe, the house is paid off!"

He kissed her on the forehead. Sara started inside when Daniel turned toward the lone car parked under a sweet gum tree halfway down the block and waved. He followed her in with a smile on his face. *DESA can wait at least one more day. Tonight, we have celebrating to do.*

There, a few houses down, sat a brand-new purple Challenger. Watching. Waiting. Just in case.

END

Thank you all for taking this ride with me. I didn't know what to expect when the idea first came to mind. I will say the whole idea came as my middle finger to Twilight and sparkly vampires. The popularity of that series shifted the market for fantasy, forcing me out of my comfort zone. Looking back, I can honestly say that was a good thing. It forced me to expand my concepts and storylines. I still don't care for sparkly vampires but have to thank Twilight for helping me grow and providing you with these stories.

Hopefully you enjoyed Daniel's journey with the elves. I put a lot of me into Daniel's character, from the time in service, to his combat deployments and then becoming an author. A lot of what is mentioned in this series happened, like me flipping off my neighbor every day for months after he called the police on me. This series is over, but I have a feeling Daniel and DESA will return soon enough… who knows what mischief they'll get into next time.

THE FRACTURED UNIVERSE I
DREAMS
OF WINTER
CHRISTIAN
WARREN FREED

It is a troubled time, for the old gods are returning and they want the universe back…

Under the rigid guidance of the Conclave, the seven hundred known worlds carve out a new empire with the compassion and wisdom the gods once offered. But a terrible secret, known only to the most powerful, threatens to undo three millennia of progress. The gods are not dead at all. They merely sleep. And they are being hunted.

Senior Inquisitor Tolde Breed is sent to the planet Crimeat to investigate the escape of one of the deadliest beings in the history of the universe: Amongeratix, one of the fabled THREE, sons of the god-king. Tolde arrives on a world where heresy breeds insurrection and war is only a matter of time. Aided by Sister Abigail of the Order of Blood Witches, and a company of Prekhauten Guards, Tolde hurries to find Amongeratix and return him to Conclave custody before he can restart his reign of terror.

What he doesn't know is that the Three are already operating on Crimeat.

Christian Warren Freed
Coward's Truth
A Novel of the Heart Eternal

Welcome to Ghendis Ghadanisban.
City of god-kings. City in turmoil.

The god-king is dead! Whispers of murder spread through the city known as the Heart Eternal. His death allows an ancient evil Razazel to return and resume its quest to dominate all life. As if that isn't enough, warring factions threaten the jewel of the desert. The only way to prevent this is by a group of reluctant heroes to escort a young boy filled with the dying god's essence to the ancient mountain of Rhorremere so the god-king can be reborn. It is a quest bound to claim lives, for evil never stops.

Far off in the mountains, a squad of stranded space marines sells their services in the hopes of being rescued. Their search brings them in conflict with too many enemies. Forced to join the quest, it is a decision that may prove their ultimate doom.

Fate and destiny clash as agents of good and evil set forth to stake their claim.

Welcome, friends, to the Heart Eternal.

Buy Coward's Truth: A Novel of the Heart Eternal now!

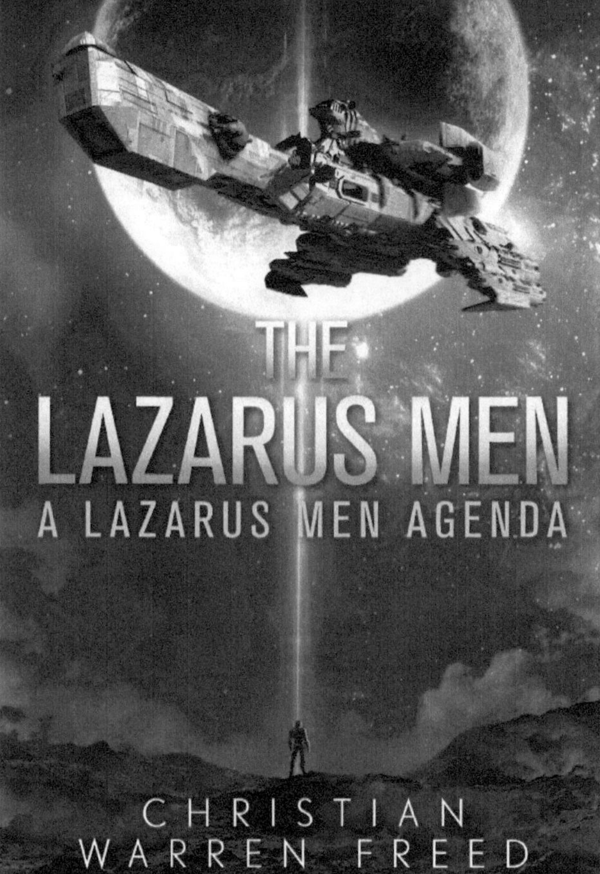

THE
LAZARUS MEN
A LAZARUS MEN AGENDA
CHRISTIAN
WARREN FREED

Welcome to the world of the Lazarus Men.

A thrilling sci-fi noir adventure combining the best mystery of the Maltese Falcon with the adventure of Total Recall and suspense of James Bond.

It is the 23rd century. Humankind has spread across the galaxy. The Earth Alliance rules weakly and is desperate for power. Hidden in the shadows are the Lazarus Men: a secret organization ruled with an iron fist by the enigmatic Mr. Shine. His agents are the worst humanity has to offer and they are everywhere.

Gerald LaPlant's life changes forever the day he accidentally witnesses a murder and discovers an alien artifact in his pocket. Forced to flee, he is chased across the stars by desperate men who want what he has and are willing to stop at nothing to get it. Along the way Gerald meets a host of villains and heroes, each with hidden agendas. If Gerald has any hope of surviving, he must rely on his wits and avoiding the one thing that could get him killed more than the rest: trust.

For he has the key to the galaxy's greatest treasure. Half want him dead. Half need him alive.

It's a race against time to see which wins.

THE CHILDREN OF NEVER

A WAR PRIESTS OF ANDRAK SAGA

CHRISTIAN WARREN FREED

The war priests of Andrak have protected the world from the encroaching darkness for generations. Stewards of the Purifying Flame, the priests stand upon their castle walls each year for 100 days. Along with the best fighters, soldiers, and adventurers from across the lands, they repulse the Omegri invasions.

But their strength wanes and evil spreads.

Lizette awakens to a nightmare, for her daughter has been stolen during the night. When she goes to the Baron to petition aid, she learns that similar incidents are occurring across the duchy. Her daughter was just the beginning. Baron Einos of Fent is left with no choice but to summon the war priests.

Brother Quinlan is a haunted man. Last survivor of Castle Bendris, he now serves Andrak. Despite his flaws, the Lord General recognizes Quinlan as one of the best he has. Sending him to Fent is his best chance for finding the missing children and restoring order. Quinlan begins a quest that will tax his strength and threaten the foundations of his soul.

The Grey Wanderer stalks the lands, and where he goes, bad things follow. The dead rise and the Omegri launch a plan to stop time and overrun the world. The duchy of Fent is just the beginning.

The follow up to the L Ron Hubbard Writers of the Future award winning short: The Purifying Flame, the Children of Never is an all-new novel set in a world of raw imagination.

Evil never rests and neither can we.

Pick up a sword and join the team!

Warfighter Books

Sign up for our newsletter today and follow us on social media for updates, new releases and more!

Newsletter:
https://www.subscribepage.com/warfighterbooks

BIO

Christian W. Freed was born in Buffalo, N.Y. more years ago than he would like to remember. After spending more than 20 years in the active-duty US Army he has turned his talents to writing. Since retiring, he has gone on to publish more than 20 science fiction and fantasy novels as well as his combat memoirs from his time in Iraq and Afghanistan. His first book, Hammers in the Wind, has been the #1 free book on Kindle 4 times and he holds a fancy certificate from the L Ron Hubbard Writers of the Future Contest.

Passionate about history, he combines his knowledge of the past with modern military tactics to create an engaging, quasi-realistic world for the readers. He graduated from Campbell University with a degree in history and a Masters of Arts degree in Digital Communications from the University of North Carolina at Chapel Hill. He currently lives outside of Raleigh, N.C. and devotes his time to writing, his family, and their two Bernese Mountain Dogs. If you drive by you might just find him on the porch with a cigar in one hand and a pen in the other.